Tip of the
Needle

Tip of the Needle

Ashraf
Elghandour

ARCHWAY
PUBLISHING

Archway Publishing books may be ordered through booksellers or by contacting:

Archway Publishing
1663 Liberty Drive
Bloomington, IN 47403
www.archwaypublishing.com
844-669-3957

ISBN: 978-1-4808-9831-8 (sc)
ISBN: 978-1-4808-9829-5 (hc)
ISBN: 978-1-4808-9830-1 (e)

Library of Congress Control Number: 2020920974

Print information available on the last page.

Archway Publishing rev. date: 11/30/2020

This book is dedicated to Cristina Jacks the mother of my two children. She passed away too soon on April, 3rd, 2020 at the age of 56 from cancer. She was a rough diamond, not a diamond in the rough, that I failed to make shine during our marriage of 21 years-with regrets. I'm sorry, I never let you know how much I loved you. May you rest in peace in our creator's beautiful gardens with rivers that run under, among the beautiful souls, for eternity, with your beloved German shepherds, Zeus and Indie, drinking and eating your favorite dark roast coffee and dark chocolate.

Contents

1

The Sermon

Moshe Ackerman stood before his congregation of devout followers. He had been a controversial figure in his community, a community of Orthodox Jews in the heart of West Jerusalem who had partitioned several militant settlements with the help of the Israeli government. The settlements were established in the old Palestinian town of Hebron with a deep and rich history dating back to 3000 BC. Rabbi Ackerman had been no stranger to controversy, a man of deep belief and the son of Holocaust survivors. He saw the pain and suffering inflicted on his parents during their internment in the concentration camp of Auschwitz and vowed never to inflict such pain on another human being in his lifetime. As a young child in the camps of Auschwitz, in the face of the most inhuman acts committed by one human being against another, he saw the purest of love and humanity as his parents and other prisoners protected him and shielded him from the evil that permeated through every aspect of their daily existence. He was read to, sung to, cuddled, and loved as if the horror that existed outside were a nightmare to be awakened from.

Moshe cultivated a community of like-minded individuals who engaged Palestinians who were seeking peace and coexistence, who saw each other as human beings first and as Jews, Muslims, or Christians second. He created the first interfaith group in the community that consisted of himself, an imam, and a priest that saw the three most dominant world religions as the progression of faith based on the tenets of Abrahamic teaching. He would often say, "We are all the sons and daughters of Abraham. What separates us is not nearly as great as what unites us as God's children." One of his favorite quotes was "An abused child should never grow up to be a child abuser. The cycle of pain should never be allowed to continue. As Jews, we have experienced the atrocities inflicted on a group just because of their ethnicity and their religious identity, and we of all people should never inflict such pain on others just because they are different from us."

As Rabbi Ackerman stood before his congregation, he could not help but focus on one face in the crowd, the face of a young man who was no older than fifteen. A face with piercing blue eyes that exuded such sharp intellect, he had an angelic face with such a profound aura of inner peace and tranquility that clearly was not acquired but was innate to him. The synagogue was modestly decorated and housed in an inconspicuous building that did not attempt to promote any of the traditional religious ornamentations. Inside the synagogue stood a small congregation of attentive listeners, but at the fringes of the crowd were those who were clearly not there to heed the rabbi's words of wisdom, but as agitators. They were settlers hell-bent on shutting down this heresy and silencing the rabbi and his followers.

Moshe began his sermon by declaring, "As Jews, we are the chosen ones." As he uttered those words, he looked at the expression on the face of the young man in the front row. It was a face that he was very familiar with, a face that he had adored from the first day he first laid his eyes on the boy. That was the day his beloved wife Robbin had given birth to their son, Addis. Addis's face had the slightest frown as this topic of God's favoritism of one group over his other creations didn't comport well with Addis's sense of fairness. He had been a curious boy since he opened his eyes to this world, and Moshe loved him for it. He had an insatiable appetite for knowledge, and his thirst was never quenched.

Moshe proceeded: "God has bestowed on us the gift of intellect, the gift of creativity, music, art, and science, and some of us choose to use it for material gain and worldly riches, and even to do the devil's bidding. With this gift, God has shown that he loves us enough to make us his agents on this earth, and yet we have betrayed his love. We took his gift and said, 'Thank you very much, but we have other plans.' My brothers and sisters, we owe it to him to make sure that we use this gift to serve him by serving all of humanity, black, white, Jewish, Christian, or Muslim—it makes no difference. And let me say it without any equivocation: it does not even matter if you are an Israeli, a Jew, or an Arab."

As he uttered those words, the settlers standing in the back of the room began shouting, "Traitor! Heretic! Arab lover!" Their voices were getting louder, and their anger was beginning to manifest itself in their body language. They began pointing and shaking their accusatory hands and fingers at the rabbi. The bulges under their coats were clearly visible; everyone knew that they were armed to the teeth. The parishioners began to cower in the face of the intimidating gestures of the disrupters. They became smaller and smaller in their pews as the agitators became louder and more animated, except for one individual who showed no fear. With deliberation, the blond, blue-eyed child of fifteen stood up in silence for what seemed to be a long pause, but it was only for a few seconds. His action had a shocking and yet calming effect on the unruly crowd. The agitators turned and looked at him as if Moses himself were about to speak. The silence in the synagogue was so absolute that one could almost hear the air rush in and out of one's neighbor's nostrils with every breath.

Then the boy spoke. The voice was so angelic, and the tone was so pure and rhythmic, that the crowd seemed to be transformed into a hypnotic state, totally under his spell. He could have asked them all to stand on one leg, and they would all have obediently complied. Addis lifted his head, stared into empty space, and uttered the words:

Love is patient, love is kind. It does not envy, it does not boast, it is not proud. It does not dishonor others, it is not self-seeking, it is not easily angered, it keeps no record of wrongs. Love does not delight

3

in evil but rejoices with the truth. It always protects, always trusts, always hopes, always perseveres. Love never fails. But where there are prophecies, they will cease; where there are tongues, they will be stilled; where there is knowledge, it will pass away. (1 Corinthians 13:4–8)

If anyone kills a person it would be as if he killed all mankind. (Koran, Sura 5:32)

I am the Lord thy God, who brought thee out of the land of Egypt, out of the house of bondage. … Honor thy father and thy mother, that thy days may be long upon the land which the Lord thy God giveth thee. Thou shalt not murder. Thou shalt not commit adultery. Thou shalt not steal. Thou shalt not bear false witness against thy neighbor. Thou shalt not covet thy neighbor's house; thou shalt not covet thy neighbor's wife, nor his man-servant, nor his maid-servant, nor his ox, nor his ass, nor any thing that is thy neighbor's. (Torah 7664)

"As a wise man and Holocaust survivor said once, 'The purest definition of evil is the absence of empathy for the pain and suffering of others.' That man was my father."

Addis paused for a second, looked down in humility as if he suddenly had been awakened from a dream, looked at the congregation with an expression of confusion, and began to walk out gingerly. Every eye in the room followed him until he exited the building. The congregation was stunned, and so was Rabbi Ackerman. When the rabbi finally spoke, he said, "Well, I couldn't have said it any better. From the mouths of babes." The congregation began to file out of the synagogue peacefully and without the slightest display of the aggression, intimidation, or fear that had filled this house of worship a few minutes earlier.

Moshe placed the Torah in its designated place, cleaned up after his flock, locked the building, and proceeded to his car. As he approached the vehicle, he noticed that Addis was waiting patiently in the passenger seat, totally consumed by his own thoughts. Moshe sat down in the driver's seat, turned his head, and looked toward Addis, but Addis did not acknowledge his gaze; he seemed to be having an out-of-body experience, transported to a place not of this world. The rabbi drove home in total silence—not a single word exchanged between him and his son.

As they approached the driveway of their modest home, Addis turned around, looked at his father, and said, "How did the sermon go?"

The rabbi, taken aback by the question, replied, "You were there. What do you think?" almost surprised by the intonation and indifference of Addis's question.

"Well, Father, I am so sorry, but I think I fell asleep toward the end of it."

The rabbi was confounded but thought it would be best to leave the subject alone since this was not the first time that Addis seemed to have been totally disconnected from reality. As they exited the car, the rabbi made one of his quotes, which he was known to do from time to time to make a point. "You know, Addis, you should never judge people by their words. Instead you should judge them by their actions. The most powerful tool of both the devil and the prophet is their words; however, their deeds couldn't be more different."

Addis, knowing exactly what his father meant, replied, "I know, Father. I hope I'm the latter rather than the former."

2 Interfaith

That evening Rabbi Ackerman and his family were invited to an interfaith meeting and dinner at Imam Mohdi el-Shafique's house. The rabbi was excited to spend time with two of his closest friends—the imam and Father Yousef Baraka—and to get some good Middle Eastern home cooking. The rabbi's daughter, Sarah, seemed to be especially excited. She had spent an inordinate amount of time trying to pick the right outfit. Sarah had hijacked the only bathroom in the rabbi's house for what seemed to be a few hours. When she finally emerged, she looked so beautiful that both Addis and Moshe stood there with their mouths open, in total disbelief, as if they were two deer frozen by the headlights of an approaching vehicle.

"Honey, you look so beautiful."

"Yeah, Sis, you look great."

With a bashful look, Sarah replied, "Thanks, guys." Sarah had always been a tomboy and preferred jeans and T-shirts over dresses and skirts, but this evening was different. She exuded femininity and grace as if she were Cinderella and was about to attend the most important evening of her life. Moshe didn't make too of much it; he just thought that she was simply reaching that age where she was becoming more self-aware. He wished that his beloved wife Robbin were

alive to see their beautiful daughter, but Addis suspected something
else altogether.

After waiting patiently for Sarah, they all piled into their ten-year-
old Hyundai Sonata for the short ride to the imam's house. Addis
chose to sit in the back seat, intent on watching his sister's body language. He always had been a people-watcher and took pride in profil-
ing people and figuring out their personalities as if it were a mystery
being solved by his favorite fictional character, Sherlock Holmes.

The trip to the imam's house required that they go through several
checkpoints, which the rabbi always disliked, but he accepted it as a
way of life for a resident of the West Bank. The Israeli army soldier at
the gate crudely asked the rabbi for his identification. Moshe handed
him his ID as the soldier inspected him, the occupants, and the car.

"It says here that you are a rabbi. What is your reason for going to
the Palestinian section?"

"To visit a friend."

"A friend? Who is that?"

"Imam el-Shafique."

"Really? You know you are totally on your own in there?"

"Yes, I know."

The soldier gave him a look of disapproval and waved him through.

As the Ackermans drove through town, the streets were abuzz
with activity, with shoppers rushing to get the traditional delicacies
for breaking fast at sunset. The mood was cheerful,; the streets were
illuminated with the most colorful and festive lights; and the shops
were all decorated with the most ostentatious decorations, vying for
shoppers' attention. This was Ramadan, one of the holiest months for
Muslims. It was the month when Muslims all over the world fasted
from sunrise to sunset, abstaining from consuming any food, drinks,
or tobacco. Usually during the fast, people tried to conserve their
energy during the day, but once sunset was near, the streets became
alive with shoppers trying to get their chores done before el-*adhan* call
to prayer, which signaled the time to break the fast. This was a festive
month, when family and friends made a point of getting together and

enjoying each other's company, breaking bread, and celebrating this holy month.

As the Ackermans were driving through the local streets, they couldn't help but notice the occasional looks that they received from pedestrians and occupants of other vehicles, but they tried to blend in as much as they could. The rabbi did not mind. He was honored to have been invited to his friend Imam Mohdi's house during this holy month, which was usually reserved for close family and friends. He wanted to make sure that they timed their arrival exactly before the breaking of the fast. He didn't want to add to his friend's burden while he and his family were trying to prepare for breaking their fast. As the rabbi approached their house, the call for prayer was being announced from every mosque minaret in town. The rabbi always found the Muslim call to prayer to be haunting and beautiful. At times it moved him to tear up, in spite of his reluctance to do so.

After the second ringing of the house bell, Nader el-Shafique, the youngest of the imam's two sons, opened the door. The rabbi greeted Nader with the traditional Muslim greeting: "Assalamu alaikum, Nader."

Nader replied with the traditional Jewish greeting: "Shalom, Rabbi Ackerman." Nader immediately locked eyes on Addis; after all, they were classmates at the International School for the Gifted. Although they acknowledged each other in school and when in the different classes they shared, they weren't the best of friends. They both knew that they had cultural and religious boundaries, so they maintained their relationship at arm's length.

Nader led the Ackermans to a small and modest living area that was adorned in Muslim religious symbols with the name of Allah and that of his prophet Muhammad prominently displayed on the walls. A large framed quote of the most recited sura from the Koran, al-F tihah, was also on full display. The rabbi greeted his close friend Father Yousef, who had arrived a few minutes earlier, in a hushed voice so as to not disturb the imam and his eldest son, who were begin-ning the Maghrib prayer. Nader had been invited to join in the prayer, but his body language showed less of an enthusiastic desire to comply. The imam began the prayer by raising both hands to the sides of his head with his palms facing forward and firmly proclaiming, "Allah akbar." The boys followed with the same proclamation. Then, the imam began to recite a verse from the Koran. As he was leading his children in prayer, he could not help but notice on the wall in front of him, adorned in reflective tiles, the image of his guests in the adjacent room, especially the image of Addis, who was quietly moving his lips as if he were reciting the same suras the imam was reciting.

After completing their prayers, the imam rose to greet his guests with a beaming smile and open hands. He embraced Rabbi Ackerman and Father Yousef in an affectionate hug with a kiss on both cheeks, a traditional Arab greeting, but only reserved for family and very close friends. He extended his hand and shook Addis's hand and bowed his head in a respectful gesture to Sarah.

"Thank you for coming. It has been awhile since we have seen each other. You remember my sons, Mustafa and Nader?"

"Of course," Father Yousef replied. "They have grown since the last time we saw each other."

"My friends, you must be very hungry. Please excuse me while I get everything ready." Then the imam gently addressed his sons. "Mustafa, please get some drinks for our guests. Nader, please set the table." Mustafa seemed to be oblivious to his father's voice and appeared awkward, attempting to redirect his gaze in any direction other than Sarah's.

The imam proceeded to the kitchen; it was his favorite place in the house, the place where he shared so many fond memories of his beloved wife, Ahab, preparing meals for their two sons, friends, and family. Although customarily in the Arab marital hierarchy the kitchen was a domain reserved for the women of the house, he loved spending time with Ahab, sharing their passion for cooking. Their kitchen was a place where they shared the burdens of the day that seemed to be a permanent fixture in every Palestinians' life. This was their place of respite where they could laugh, be flirtatious, and shun the outside world. The imam missed his wife very much. It was one thing among many that he shared with Rabbi Ackerman: they both had lost their wives to cancer at about the same time.

The guests were invited to the dinner table. The imam sat at the head of the table and invited the rabbi to sit at the opposite end. It was not out of disrespect for Father Yousef, but out of respect for the age difference. Father Yousef was a considerably younger man, closer in age to the children than he was to the imam and the rabbi. As they all enjoyed the delicious cuisine of lamb, couscous, and seasonal vegetables, the guests would often comment between bites on how wonderful the food was. The conversation at the table was as palatable and stimulating as the cuisine, and it seemed to be more engaging for some, but not all. While the imam, the rabbi, and the priest discussed the current state of affairs and the social, political, and religious divide that was inflaming the country, Nader looked on and listened to the conversation of the elders with great interest. However, Addis was more interested in watching the exchange of looks between Sarah and Mustafa. He suspected this was not a casual acquaintance but something a lot deeper than that. Tonight was the night that he was going to prove his suspicions.

After the meal was voraciously consumed by all, the imam invited his guests to the living area for the sweet tea and desserts that are commonly served during the month of Ramadan. Mustafa began to clear the table, and immediately Sarah volunteered to help. As they proceeded to the kitchen with the dirty dishes, Addis was in tow, which elicited an annoyed look from Sarah. Nader was quickly dismissed by his brother, who said, "I've got this. Just take the dessert to the living room." Nader was more than happy to comply since he would rather have listened to the grown-ups' conversation than clean dishes. Nader immediately joined the adults in the living area, but Addis chose to hover in close proximity to the kitchen. After a few minutes, he stopped hearing the rattling of the dishes and heard a careful and muted attempt to open the back door. He quickly tiptoed into the kitchen, only to see Sarah and Mustafa embracing from an open kitchen window. She held his face in the palm of her hand and gently pulled him in for a kiss, and he embraced her with the tenderness and passion of one who had been longing for this moment and could no longer exercise any self-control. Addis smiled, thinking, *Suspicion confirmed.* But at the same time, he wondered to himself, *Will I ever experience that kind of love?*

The conversation in the living room was lively. The three men of faith were trying to solve a problem that had eluded the most powerful men in the world for over fifty years. However, their sheer faith and conviction was not going to make this minor fact an impediment. They were determined to do whatever it took to change the status quo and finally bring peace to this region that had seen so much hate, bloodshed, and turmoil for so long.

The imam declared to his guests that the Israeli leaders were engaging in a war of attrition. "They are not interested in a fair negotiated settlement with the Palestinian people. They are interested in waiting us out, in making our lives so miserable that the younger generations will have no reason to stay. The solution is to demand a one-state solution, where we all, Jew, Christin, Muslim, Arab, and non-Arab, are citizens of one country with equal rights under the law and with the right to pursue happiness and have a dignified and peaceful coexistence."

Father Yousef nodded in agreement, adding, "But you know the current government will never agree to this. This is totally contrary to their master plan. And frankly, as Palestinians, we have not helped our cause very well by insisting on a two-state solution."

"That is right. The strategies, demands, and protests of old have to change. We must try something new, something that will awaken the world to the plight of the Palestinian people, their pain and suffering, and not continue to fight about a piece of land and who has claim over it," added the rabbi. "We have to create a movement of civil disobedience modeled after the reverend Martin Luther King. No violence, no stone throwing, no burning tires—a nonviolent and a peaceful uprising that will have Jews, Muslims, and Christians standing side by side and demanding change."

It took the imam and Father Yousef a few seconds to see the optics of such a movement, but slowly a smile began to simultaneously break out on both their faces. The imam said, "Let's do it. But where do we start?"

The rabbi quickly replied, "You start with your flock, and you start with yours, and I will start with mine. And with a little help from social media, we should at least make a start of it, God willing."

"Inshallah," responded the imam.

Nader sat quietly and listened to the exchange between his father and his guests, but he was angry and he had no interest in peaceful anything; he wanted to fight and inflict the same pain he'd seen being inflicted on his people under the Israeli occupation. He hadn't always been an angry young man, but after the death of his mother, his mood had turned dark and rebellious. He had worshipped his mother, and she had worshipped him. She had always referred to him as her gift from God. Just before she'd found out that she was pregnant with him, she'd had a dream. In her dream she was resting under a palm tree in an oasis surrounded by olive trees and a reflective pool of water. A woman dressed all in white appeared to her and handed her a bundle covered in white cloth, along with a pitcher of water. She received both offerings willingly and began to drink from the pitcher of water. Immediately she went into the most beautiful trance. She believed she saw heaven. She never shared her dream with anyone except for her husband, and she was convinced that the bundle she had received in her dream was Nader. After she had contracted cancer, Nader began to pray very hard, hoping that through the strength of his prayer, God would spare his mother. It was not to be. When his mother passed away, he lost his religion, and his spirituality turned into anger: anger with God, anger about the unfairness of the plight of his people, and anger about the occupation. The only thing he loved was the certainty of science and mathematics. For him, that was where everything was fair, balanced, and predictable.

It was getting late in the evening. The guests excused themselves and thanked their host for a wonderful evening and for his hospitality. As the rabbi and priest stood up to exit, they agreed to set a date for the protest and promised to immediately begin the campaign to rally their parishioners in their respective communities and through social media. The children exchanged their goodbyes politely, However, Sarah and Mustafa were experiencing gaiety and were doing everything in their power to keep their emotions in check. Addis had a smirk on his face, having confirmed what he had long suspected, but Nader had a frown on his face and wore his anger with pride.

The front door opened. The rabbi exited the imam's house first. He instantaneously recognized the inconspicuous van parked across the street with its darkened windows, the same van that he had noticed while trying to find a parking spot earlier. This time the passenger's-side window was rolling down as the occupant was discarding his cigarette. The man exchanged looks with the rabbi and immediately rolled his window up, realizing his timing was a big mistake. The rabbi noticed the man's awkward behavior and made sure to commit his image to memory. This was not difficult since the man was in his midtwenties with very distinct Middle Eastern features and a thick head of hair.

3 The School for the Gifted

Two weeks later, the headmaster of the International School for the Gifted was in his office late into the evening, reviewing several letters from the most prestigious institutions of higher education in the world. It was late in the academic semester, and this was usually when the offer letters for the most gifted students in his academy started pouring in. He always found the occasion of introducing the news to the students and their parents somewhat unpredictable. Some rejoiced at the opportunity, and others rejected it. He had given up on predicting which direction each of the recipients would take. On his list of five recipients were the names of Addis Ackerman and Nader el-Shafique, two of the brightest students he had encountered in his thirty-year career as an educator. They were both off-the-charts smart; however, their personalities could not be more different. The headmaster picked up his phone and started to call the home numbers of the individual recipients in alphabetical order. His first call was to the Ackermans. On the second ring, Addis picked up the phone.

"Hello?"

"Hello, this is Master Joshua Levine from the International School. Is this Addis?"

"Yes. Hello, Master Levine."

"Addis, can I please speak to your father?"

"Sure, let me get him."

Joshua Levine could hear the boy's voice in the background saying, "Abba, you've got a call."

"Who is it?"

"Master Levine from school."

"Is everything okay?"

"I think so."

"Hello. This is Rabbi Ackerman," the rabbi said into the handset.

"Shalom, Rabbi. Thank you for taking my call. There is an urgent matter that I want to discuss with you and Addis in person. Are you available this Thursday at 2:00 p.m.?" the headmaster said.

"Yes, I will make myself available. Is everything okay?"

"Yes, everything is fine, no need for concern. I will elaborate further when I see you. Good night."

The headmaster's third call was to Imam el-Shafique's house. The conversation went very much the same way as had the two previous phone calls.

It was Thursday, late afternoon, and Master Levine had timed his meetings to introduce the scholarship offers to the students and their parents half an hour apart. Both Addis and the rabbi were sitting anxiously in the receptionist's area, not knowing what to expect. It was 2:00 p.m. As the rabbi looked at his watch, the phone on the receptionist's desk rang. She replied to the caller, "Sure," then hung up the phone and immediately stood up. She approached the Ackermans and said, "Mr. Levine will see you now."

The headmaster greeted them with a warm smile. After shaking hands with both of them, he invited them to take a seat. Neither Addis nor the rabbi was in any mood for cordialities; they just wanted to find out why they had been summoned.

The headmaster began, "I'm sorry for being so tight-lipped about the reason for our meeting today, but I found it best not to preannounce what I'm about to tell you, for several reasons. Addis, you have been offered a full scholarship to attend the prestigious Oxford University in England. You will be one of a select number of very bright students from around the world who will be attending the Oxford Academy for the Gifted. Alumni of this program have their PhDs completed by their early twenties, and ultimately some have gone on to become the most renowned scholars in the world. All your expenses will be paid for by the academy for the seven-year program. You will be able to visit your parents on holidays and summer breaks, and all travel expenses will be covered by the academy. In addition to your room, board, and educational expenses being covered, you will also receive two thousand pounds a month for any additional expenses. This amount will be deposited monthly in a bank account in your name, and your parents will be designated as custodians until you are eighteen years of age. This amount will increase annually in order to be commensurate with your need as you get older. I realize that this is a very important decision for you and your family to consider, so I suggest that you take a few weeks to consider it. And please don't hesitate to call with any questions that might arise."

Both Addis and the rabbi were stunned by the news. They turned around and looked at each other with a confused expression, giving the information that they had just received a few minutes to sink in. The rabbi eventually turned back around and addressed the headmaster. "You are right; this a lot to digest. Thank you for the time to discuss this opportunity with my son. We will definitely take you up on your offer to follow up with any questions. I anticipate we will have an answer for you in the next week or so."

"Thank you. I look forward to your answer."

With that, the headmaster stood up and walked from behind his desk with an extended hand to bid the Ackermans farewell and to wish them both the best of luck with their decision. Before opening the door, he turned around and addressed them with a very stoic face. "I would really appreciate it if we could keep this matter private and not mention it to anyone other than those who have a need to know. This is an extremely competitive student body with extremely competitive parents, and this kind of news can set off a whole set of dynamics that, frankly, can be ugly at times. Thank you again, and good luck."

As they exited the office, the rabbi immediately noticed that Imam el-Shafique and his son Nader were sitting patiently in the reception area.

"Assalamu alaikum, brother," bellowed the rabbi.

"Walaikum salaam, brother," the imam said as they embraced.

The headmaster was taken aback by the display of affection as he invited the imam and his son into his office and firmly asked Addis to go back to his classroom.

A few hours later, the students were dismissed for the day. Nader was exiting the building toward the designated bus reserved for Arab students. He was in a very jovial and excited mood. He couldn't stop thinking about his future at the Massachusetts Institute of Technology (MIT) and the interesting fields of studies he would be pursuing. The prospect of leaving home, the West Bank, and living in the United States really appealed to him. He had grown tired of everything that reminded him of his mother's death, and his relationship with his father had grown cooler and more distant ever since.

As soon as he exited the building, there were three other students from the settlements who were waiting for him. The leader of the group approached Nader in a very hostile manner, pushed him against the wall, and yelled, "We hear the sand nigger got accepted to MIT." As those words were being uttered, Addis seemed to appear from nowhere, and swiftly stepped in between the boy and Nader. Addis was an early bloomer and already had the physique of an athletic seventeen-year-old, in contrast to Nader, who still had a baby face and the awkward body of a teenager.

Addis looked directly at the confrontational boy and said, "I know your name. It is David, is it not? You competed against Nader in the science fair. You did not beat him using your brains, so now you are trying to beat him with your brawn?"

The boy barked back at him, "Get out of the way, you fucking Arab lover, or we will kick your ass as well."

17

Addis responded calmly and without any display of emotion, "Do you know that it takes one-millionth of second for the mind to translate a thought into physical action? I bet I can predict what you will do before a thought can go through that small brain of yours."

With a look of confusion that quickly turned to anger, the boy threw the first punch. Addis's eyes went blank a second before the punch was launched, and instantaneously he put his open hand up to block the punch as it was about to connect with his jaw. The boy immediately released the second punch with his left hand. That one met the same fate as the first punch. Addis quickly twisted one of the hands of his attacker behind his back and, with a swift kick to his legs, swept his feet from under him. The boy fell hard face-first on the concrete as his friends stood awestruck. The boy's face was all bloodied; he was dazed from the head-on collision. Addis gently bent down, lifted him up, wiped the blood off his face with his handkerchief, brushed him off, straightened back up, turned around to face the others, and said, "I think we are done here," as he handed the boy to his friends. Addis grabbed Nader, who was speechless, by the hand and led him to the parking lot, where his sister, Sarah, was waiting as she did every school day.

Sarah was surprised to see the sense of urgency on Addis's face and the new passenger he had in tow. "What is going on?" she asked.

"Nothing. We are taking Nader to his house."

The drive to Nader's house was quiet, except for the words of gratitude that Nader finally uttered to Addis with a follow-up question. "Is it really true what you said to David, that it takes one-millionth of second for a thought to be translated into physical action?"

Addis said, "I made that shit up."

Nader laughed.

Sarah watched the interaction between her two passengers quietly and decided to let the matter be until she was in the car alone with Addis. Her thoughts were elsewhere. The only thing she was focused on was whether Mustafa would be home when they reached the imam's house.

Soon they found themselves knocking on the door of el-Shafique's house. The imam opened the door, surprised to see Addis and Sarah standing next to Nader. "What a surprise! Come on in." He showed them to the living area, where they'd last seen each other a few weeks ago. From the look of them, the imam suspected that something had transpired and that he was about to hear about it. He braced himself and asked, "Is everything okay?" Nader took the lead and described to his father the whole scene at school in detail.

The imam looked at Addis with an expression of admiration and gratitude. He said, "Thank you, Addis, for helping my son."

"It was no problem. Those guys were envious of Nader, and that is the only way they know how to express their feelings."

"Addis, you never cease to impress me. You are wise beyond your years."

"Thank you, sir. You are very kind."

"Tell me, Addis. The last time you were here, I could not help but notice that you were reciting the Koran while I was praying with Mustafa and Nader. Are you familiar with the Koran?"

"Yes, sir. I like the way it sounds when it's being recited, so I listened to the whole book on my computer."

"How did you come to memorize the Koran?"

"I have a photographic memory; I only need to hear or see something once to remember it."

"Amazing. Listen, your father must be worried about you by now, Addis. I will follow you in my car to the checkpoint. Thank you again for helping my son. And thank you, Sarah, for bringing Nader here." Sarah was disappointed that Mustafa was not there, but she knew she would be seeing him later.

On their way back from the checkpoint, Nader broached the subject of their discussion with the headmaster earlier in the afternoon. "Baba, I am so excited about going to MIT. It's considered to be the one of the top schools in the world for science and technology."

"About that, Nader, I don't think it is a good idea for you to leave your home and your country at such a young age."

"What do you mean? I want to leave. There is nothing here for me. I hate it here."

"I know it has been tough for you since your mother passed away, but you're only fifteen years old. You have a lot of growing up to do and a lot to learn before you can go to a foreign country that has different ways than ours."

"You mean religion. Well, I do not believe in religion. And I have been wanting to tell you that for a long time."

"Astaghfirullah" (God forgive us), uttered the imam, with a look of deep disappointment. He was disappointed in his youngest son, but he was more profoundly disappointed at himself as a father and as an imam for having failed to teach his son to be a person of faith.

"I'm sorry, Son, but I have been giving this a lot of thought. My decision is final."

Nader never prayed, never fasted during Ramadan, and never attended the mosque with his father after that. Their relationship became even more distant. Nader could not wait for the day when he could finally get out of that house and that country.

That evening, Rabbi Ackerman was having a similar conversation with Addis. Addis, unlike Nader, rejected the idea of leaving and confessed his deep desire to become a man of God and to follow in his father's footsteps and become a rabbi.

4 Intifada

It was the birthday of the prime minister of Israel. He decided to leave his office early and spend a quiet evening with his family, celebrating his birthday. After dinner, he retired to his veranda overlooking the Mediterranean Sea to smoke a Cuban cigar and drink a glass of a hundred-year-old cognac reserved for special occasions. He had given his assistant clear instructions that he didn't want to be disturbed this evening, except for absolute emergencies. His phone rang as he was about to take a puff of his Cuban cigar, which brought a frown to his face, except when he looked at his two cell phones sitting on the table, it wasn't his secured government phone that was ringing, but his personal one. When he looked at the caller ID, he realized that this was a call he must take. Reluctantly, he picked up the phone and answered as he usually did: "Hank here."

"Happy birthday, Hank. I hope I'm not disturbing you."

"Just about to indulge in a Cuban cigar and a glass of cognac. How can I help?"

"I will make it quick. It just came to my attention that Rabbi Ackerman, a priest, and an imam are planning a protest in the next few weeks. It is all over social media, and it appears that their cause is gaining momentum. You know that this movement should not be allowed to become grassroots or to grow."

"I know."

"Well, what are you doing about it?"

"This is an internal matter. Frankly, I cannot discuss it. And you don't want to know."

"What I know is that I am having a hell of a time keeping the troops in line. Israel's relevance and support over here is waning. The Cold War is over; demographics in this country are changing; and the other side is getting a political foothold. We can't continue to preach the moral high ground and say that we are the only democracy in the region if we are perceived as an apartheid state. The optics of a rabbi, a priest, and an imam advocating for the same cause will have an irreparable effect on world opinion, especially here in the States. We can't call them anti-Semites and Jew haters if our own people are standing side by side with Christians and Muslims. We will lose the war of public opinion."

"I understand."

"I need you to do more than understand. I need you to kill it before it takes root."

"Thank you, Zack. I will be in touch soon. And keep up the good work over there. We need you. Good night."

The prime minster hung up the phone, resenting the tone of the conversation and the interference in his internal affairs, but he knew how much power this man wielded. It would be political suicide to cross him. The cigar and cognac did not have the same appeal they had had a moment ago. Instead he picked up his secure phone and called his top intelligence officer, setting up a meeting for the following morning.

A few weeks later, it was a beautiful sunny day in late May as the crowds began to congregate after the Muslim afternoon prayer outside al-Aqsa Mosque in Jerusalem. The three holy men, Rabbi Ackerman, Imam el-Shafique, and Father Yousef, had mounted a concerted campaign to drive the attendance of their respective followers. Social media and the national media were abuzz with news of the upcoming event. The protest had been debated purposefully by pundits on both sides of the issue on television, in the internet cafés, and between family members. Proponents and detractors were emotionally charged and geared up for making their presence and opinions known. The Israeli police and intelligence community were also on high alert. This movement had gained momentum beyond their expectations, and their focus had turned form containment to damage control. The last thing they wanted was for this thing to go from a local movement, to a national movement, to an international movement.

The three holy men were arm in arm in front of the crowd. They were intent on making this a peaceful protest. Behind them were droves of followers hundreds deep. There were Christians, Jews, Muslims, and atheists of all ages with beautiful colorful banners. And both the Israeli and Palestinian flags were flapping in the wind side by side. One of the banners read, "One nation under God, indivisible, with liberty for all"; another, "A house divided will not stand"; another, "We are all Abraham's children"; and yet another, "Peace for all or peace for none." In front of the banners, there was an angry mob of settlers, Orthodox Jews, and conservatives who found the idea of anything other than a Jewish state offensive and treasonous. Separating the two crowds were armed soldiers and policemen in full riot gear. In a not so distant command center stood several high-ranking intelligence officers in a small situation room with several video monitors, some telecommunications equipment, and a network of computers. On the center screen, mounted on the wall, was a live shot of the rabbi, the imam, and the priest arm in arm. The other screens showed a 360-degree video feed of the whole area. One screen had a live feed of a sharpshooter positioned on the roof of a building, overlooking the protest. The commander of the operation had a headset and was directly communicating with the sharpshooter and the field commander at the scene.

The commander asked, "Do you have him in your sights?"

The shooter replied, "Affirmative."

The commander told him, "As we rehearsed, take no action unless it is a direct order from me."

"Yes, Commander," the shooter replied.

The protest was receiving tremendous media coverage. There were reporters from local and international news outlets ready to capture the action in real time, and none expected the scene to be peaceful for long. The police and army soldiers had been instructed to be on their best behavior and had been told that there would be zero tolerance of any individual action or fuck-ups. This was to be a textbook operation of crowd control, well choreographed and well rehearsed. Any variation was to be executed only as a result of a direct order from the field commander.

The protest was going better than expected. The crowd was peaceful and festive. It was starting to look more and more like a Vietnam peace march from the sixties. Jews were holding hands with Arabs, and the crowd was chanting and spontaneously breaking into a John Lennon song. "All we are saying is give peace a chance."

The three holy men were beaming with pride and adulation at how well the protest was going. It was everything they had hoped for and more. This mood of euphoria was not to last for long, however. As the three men were standing shoulder to shoulder, the rabbi noticed in his peripheral vision a young man in his midtwenties pushing his way through the crowd. He had a look of purpose and a determined manner about him. His eyes were laser focused on the imam. It took but a few seconds for the rabbi to recognize the man. It was the same individual he'd seen while exiting the imam's house, the same person who had discarded his cigarette from the inconspicuous van. The man's hand was in his coat pocket, and he seemed to be concealing something. He quickly approached the imam from his right side, pulled a handgun, pointed it at the imam's head, and pulled the trigger. The gun jammed, causing the imam to remain oblivious to his assailant's action a few feet from him. However, the rabbi quickly pulled his friend from harm's way as he injected himself between the assailant and the imam. At that very second, two orders were given by the intelligence officer in charge at the command center. The first was to the field commander, and the second was to the sharpshooter: "Execute.

"Execute."

As those words were uttered, the field commander gave the order to his soldiers to fire in the air above the heads of the people in the crowd as rehearsed. The sharpshooter used the cover of gunfire to conceal his shot. The shot missed its intended target and pierced through the rabbi's neck just as he stepped in front of the imam.

The mood quickly turned from festive to panicked as the front row of protesters saw the active shooter and the encroaching soldiers with their guns blasting. There was a stampede that resembled a wave hitting a rocky shore, but this was a wave of humanity; people were climbing over each other to get to safety. The imam was on his knees, cradling the rabbi with both his hands on his neck, trying to stop the gushing blood that seemed to explode with every remaining heartbeat. With tears in his eyes, he looked as his friend and said, "Stay with me. Stay strong."

With his last breath, and in barely an audible voice, the rabbi whispered, "Look after my children."

"I will, my friend, but you are not going anywhere." Then the imam began to pray to Allah for the life of his friend. His prayers went unanswered. The rabbi took his last breath and closed his eyes as his body went limp. Tears began streaming down the imam's face as he brought his friend's lifeless body closer to his chest and kissed his forehead.

The assailant quickly shed his coat and the traditional Palestinian headscarf and blended in with the crowd, not to be seen again. The sharpshooter, with the precision of a well-trained special operations soldier, dismantled his power rifle and packed it in its designated case, quickly descending the stairs and blending into the fleeing crowd as well.

The assailant and the sharpshooter quickly made their way to a safe house not far from the scene of the crime, where the intelligence officer was waiting. He was enraged at their incompetency.

"Everything we practiced went to shit. What the fuck happened?"

The assailant said, "My gun jammed."

The sharpshooter explained, "The rabbi stepped in front of the imam as I took the shot. It was unavoidable."

The commander said, "I will take care of this." Then he impatiently informed the assailant that he had been assigned to the Mossad station in South Africa and that he must immediately proceed to the military plane waiting for him at a secret airport. The sharpshooter was ordered to go back to his unit at base.

That evening, a cover-up story was concocted by the director of intelligence and was submitted to the minister of defense.

The following morning, the minister of defense held a news conference in front of hordes of reporters and cameras. He read from the official statement provided to him by his staff: "We have identified the assailant as a Hamas operative, and our security forces have launched a nationwide manhunt for his capture. Our investigation has also yielded the following facts: As the assailant fired his gun, our security officers on the ground attempted to bring him down, but unfortunately our efforts were unsuccessful and he was able to slip through the crowd during the confusion. We believe this was a targeted assassination attempt against Rabbi Ackerman by Hamas. This was mainly a peaceful event except for the action of an organization that is only interested in fomenting violence and division among us. We regret this turn of events and hold Hamas ultimately responsible for the death of Rabbi Ackerman. We will do everything in our power to bring the perpetrator and those responsible for this heinous crime to justice. With that, I will take a few questions."

The minister had a list of questions and answers that his staff had prepared for him, anticipating reporters' questions. He stuck to the script and ended the news conference after a few minutes.

The rabbi's burial and funeral was scheduled a few days later as mandated by Jewish custom. In attendance were the rabbi's children, the imam and his children, Father Yousef, and a sea of mourners paying their respects to this man of peace. The crowd was somber, the euphoria that had prevailed a few days earlier now having been replaced with sorrow and tears. Sarah had asked the imam to give the eulogy as she knew that it would be her father's wish. After several speeches by the rabbi's closest friends, singing his praises as a man of peace with deep love for his children and for humanity, the imam stood up and walked slowly to the podium, where the rabbi had stood so many times before in his beloved synagogue. The imam stood silently for a few moments as he tried to ingest the enormity of everything that had transpired in the last few days. He still couldn't fathom that his dear friend was gone forever and that he would never have the chance to tell him how much he loved him as a brother.

The imam took a moment to recite the F tihah in silence to himself as every Muslim does upon the remembrance of a deceased one. He slowly lifted his head and spoke: "Under the least expected circumstances, in the least expected place, and at the least expected time, I developed a friendship with the best that humanity had to offer, a man who epitomized everything that is good and decent about humanity, a man who sacrificed his life for me as he would have sacrificed it for any other human being in a time of need. I thank Allah every day for the blessing of his friendship and for the time I had to know him and learn from him. He made everything that he touched blossom, and everyone he ministered to became that much closer to God, including me. Whether it was the God of Abraham, Jesus, or Muhammad, it didn't matter to him; it was the same God, Allah, or Yahweh. In his presence, I felt cleansed from the burdens and ugliness that is so common in our daily lives. In him, I saw a ray of hope, a better day to come, a more loving union. He would often say to me, 'The universe is balanced on the tip of a needle. Every action requires a simultaneous reaction of equal force to maintain the balance. Everything we do matters.' I'm proud to have called Rabbi Ackerman my friend, and I'm ever so grateful for the profound light he brought to my heart. I know he will always be with me in spirit, and if I'm one-tenth the man he was, I know Allah will be merciful on my soul and allow me to be in his company for eternity in jannah inshallah. May Moshe Ackerman dwell in peace in God's beautiful garden, where rivers run for eternity, and may God bless his children." The pain of this profound loss was evidenced on the imam's face as he stepped down, proceeded to his chair, and bowed gracefully to the children as he took his seat.

The next day, the imam got a surprise visit from Sarah Ackerman and his son Mustafa. Mustafa and Sarah wasted no time in getting to the point. "Baba, Sarah and I have been seeing each other for over a year, and we are very much in love. We have decided to get married and move to Germany. I have accepted the scholarship to Ludwig Maximilian University of Munich, and Sarah will be attending there as well. And Addis decided to accept his scholarship to Oxford. Sarah will become his legal guardian until he reaches the age of eighteen."

Sarah spoke, "Imam Shafique, I know this is all too sudden, but after what happened, Mustafa, Addis, and I have no desire to be here. Although Mustafa and I have been wanting to tell you and Abba of our plans for a long time, we wanted to wait until our final year of high school and before we both left for college before we asked you both for your permission. I hope and pray that you will give us your blessing." They both looked at the imam with anticipation, fearing the typical response to any interfaith union between a Muslim and a Jew.

To their surprise, the imam, with a beaming face, said, "It would be my honor for the daughter of my dear friend to be wed to my son. I would consider it an honor and a blessing. May you both have a blessed life together, and may Allah protect you."

Two weeks later, Sarah and Mustafa were married in a civil wedding attended by their immediate family. Within a few weeks they departed for Germany, and Addis went to England.

Once Nader reached the age of eighteen, he also left, departing to the US to attend MIT against his father's wishes, leaving the imam heartbroken. The imam was never the same after that. After the loss of his best friend and the departure of his children, he had lost his interest in changing the world. His passion for the cause and for life had waned, as did the Israeli intelligence's interest in him.

5 College Life

The cell phone chimed on the nightstand, waking Nader at 7:00 a.m. He sat on his bed in a state of confusion. His head was pounding, and his vision was blurry. This had been a common occurrence; he was accustomed to feeling this way almost every morning. He gingerly turned his head and noticed the silhouette of a body lying next to him, naked. His memory foggy, he could not remember who this person was or what had happened the night before. It took a few minutes for him to gather his wits as flashes of the night before slowly began to stream into his consciousness. He remembered bits of the flirtatious conversation he'd been having with one of his patrons at the local watering hole where he worked as a bartender. Nader supplemented his income by working as a bartender at Joe's, a college hangout where the drinks were cheap and the staff was friendly. This was not just a job for Nader; it was where he trolled for chicks and for easy one-night stands. He was a master at it. He always went after the easy mark, the new patron drinking alone with no prior knowledge of his reputation. With his good looks, a few free drinks, and a little charm, his chances of closing the deal were almost certain. Looks and brains were not a prerequisite; it was all about adding another notch to his belt. This morning, he was less disappointed with his choice as he more closely inspected his latest bedmate. "Not bad," he murmured to himself as he stood up to relieve himself and splash some cold water on his face. He grabbed two aspirins and a glass of orange juice, as he normally did, while attempting to put his sweatpants and T-shirt on. It was getting late, and he had a class in half an hour at the other end of campus. He carefully sat on the bed and inspected his companion's naked body again, wishing he had a few more hours to spend. This conquest was a considerable improvement over his usual choices. He gently shook her arm as he delivered his standard wake-up call: "Good morning, sunshine."

She slowly opened her eyes and looked at him, saying, "Hi."

"Hi. I am sorry, but I've got a class to go to at the other end of campus. Can I get you a glass of orange juice or something?"

"No, that is all right. I have to go too. I had fun last night."

"Yeah, me too."

She quickly got dressed as he was busy fixing his backpack. They met at the door. He reached in and gave her a kiss. He opened the door. As she was stepping out, she turned and said, "Give me a call later?"

"Sure will."

"But you do not have my number. Do you even remember my name?"

"Sorry. I am a little groggy this morning."

She reached in her pocketbook, pulled out a pen and paper, and wrote her number and name—Meghan. He reached over again and gave her another kiss. "I will call you later." He never did. He put his flip-flops on and ran to his 8:00 a.m. class at the far end of campus.

Nader needed one more class to get his undergraduate degree in physics. He had chosen an easy elective that he could sleep through with a pass or fail grade. It was one of the few summer courses that he could take to get himself over the hump. The subject matter was not of great interest to him, but he figured he could bullshit his way through it without too much effort. Nader had a 4.0 grade point average and was able to complete his degree in three years with minimal effort. This was a demanding degree and a demanding university, and while most of his classmates found it a challenge to maintain a passing grade, he had no problem managing his studies and a highly active nightlife. Since he'd come to MIT, he embraced his newfound freedom, having found the American way of life intoxicating. He was not about to put any limitation on himself or say no to himself.

He grabbed the most inconspicuous seat at the back of the auditorium and got himself ready for a much-needed nap. He made sure to check his phone to see what messages he had gotten from his string of female admirers. The first text message was from his father the imam. "The only antidote to man's insatiable appetite for worldly pleasures is the quest for spiritual relevance." Nader always found these texts eerie, as if his father somehow had a telepathic connection with him and was watching his every move. He ignored the message as he always did and began to ease himself into a comfortable position for his well-deserved nap. The professor began by introducing himself.

"My name is Professor Anderson. You all can refer to me as Professor Anderson. The title of this course is the Anthropology of Religion, so if anyone here took a wrong turn and ended up in my classroom by mistake, this is the time for you to stand up and exit right." As he completed his sentence, the door opened and an impeccably dressed young woman walked in. She was a head turner; even the professor paused for a second to take in the sight. She was tall with long blonde hair and piercing blue eyes. She had a figure that was akin to that of a model and an athlete combined. She was wearing gabardine dress pants and a cashmere sweater that was tight-fitted, showing every contour of her voluptuous figure. She stepped into the room as if she were on a catwalk modeling the latest European fashion. With an incredibly soft but confident voice, she apologized for her tardiness as she proceeded to a seat in the front row. The professor and the rest of class were still gawking, until he finally broke the silence by addressing the class.

"This class is about the anthropology of religion, the concept of creationism versus evolution and whether they are reconcilable. I will demand and expect the participation of everyone in this class. As a matter of fact, your grades will depend on it. With that, let me begin at

the beginning. Who can describe to me the story of Adam and Eve?"
The first hand to go up was that of the blonde woman in the front row.

"Your name please, miss?"

"Sacha Zimmerman."

"The same Zimmerman as the famous tech mogul Zack
Zimmerman?"

"We are related."

Sacha was always uncomfortable with any name-dropping or the
association with her famous father. She wanted to keep that fact secret
and be judged on her own merit.

"Sorry for the interruption. Please continue."

"It is the story of God's first creation, discontentment with the
status quo. Although that status was the best God has to offer, man's/
woman's curiosity and insatiable appetite for more made them susceptible to temptation."

"Very interesting. Please go on."

"Well, I think this story is used by the three most dominant
religions as a parable intended for the consumption of its audience at
the time."

"But what do you think it is?"

"I think it is the story about the birth of the universe. It is about
the yin and yang, positive and negative energy, good and evil. The
survivability of one depends on the survivability of the other. The
existence of only one means darkness, but when you combine them,
there is light, energy, creation."

"Anyone else care to debate that point?"

Nader's antenna was now up. His desire for a well-deserved nap
had dissipated. He was intrigued by the woman and the subject matter. Nader put his hand up.

"Go ahead, sir. And please introduce yourself."

"Nader el-Shafique. Am I correct in assuming that the premise of
your statement is that humanity wouldn't have survived without the
existence of both good and evil—the yin and yang as you call it? And
if so, is there any way you can prove your hypothesis?"

"Ms. Zimmerman, care to respond to his challenge?"

"Well, sure. Just go back to the beginning of humankind's history as we know it and assume that the early human was devoid of either good or evil. Would the caveman have survived and, thus, humanity? Being good and sharing your limited resources with your neighbor would have meant that both of you would perish. Or the opposite: killing your neighbor for his resources would have meant that you cut the probability of humankind's survivability by half. The survivability of humankind is only ensured when there is a balance between these two forces."

Nader could not help but find her smart and exciting, but he thought she was probably too much work.

That evening, Nader was standing behind the bar at Joe's, entertaining the patrons with his quick wit, with his friendly disposition, and with generous servings of alcohol. His employer didn't mind his frequent indiscretions; after all, he was their biggest draw. Nader knew many of his patrons by name and had converted many of them into regulars.

It was eleven o'clock on a Thursday night, and the place was packed. She walked into the place, and it was like a gust of wind blew in. Every male in the joint and many of the women pushed the pause button in midsentence and gawked at the newcomer. She had that effect on people, and she exercised it with absolute precision. Sacha grabbed an empty seat at the bar, maintaining a very erect posture as if she were onstage readying herself for the next act of a well-rehearsed play. Nader was watching attentively, as was every male in close proximity to Sacha. They were preparing their plans of attack and the opening lines that would earn them audience with this highly coveted prize. They came in one after another with the alcohol-induced confidence that was quickly deflated with the precision of an assassin. Nader was entertained by the whole scene; he knew the type and had no interest in being one of her victims.

He finally addressed her. "What's your poison?"

"That's original. Hey, I know you. Aren't you in my class?"

"Yes."

"Is this your day job?"

"Well, it pays the bills."

"I will have Absolut vodka on the rocks."

"Sorry, we do not carry the fancy stuff here."

"Just the best vodka you have."

"This one is on me," he said, handing her the drink.

"That's okay, you need to pay your bills," she replied, dropping a hundred-dollar bill on the bar and disappearing into the crowd.

Nader, feeling like a charity case, murmured to himself, "Bitch."

It was 3:00 a.m. Nader had just announced last call a few minutes before. He started to clean up the bar and could not wait to go home and go to bed. He had decided not to drink tonight; his head was still throbbing, and his legs were a little wobbly. He closed the bar and proceeded to the empty parking lot, where his car was parked at the far end. This was his pride and joy, a 1977 Camaro SS 396 muscle car. He had been in love with American muscle cars since he was a kid watching iconic American movies like *American Graffiti* and *Vanishing Point*. On many nights he would go to his friend George's garage, where the old man would teach him all about working on cars in exchange for tutoring his kids in math. Nader stepped into his car, put his key in the ignition, and was about to fire up the engine, when a black Porsche Carrera 4S pulled next to the driver's side. Sacha rolled down her window. As she was fixing herself a hand-rolled cigarette, she looked at Nader with a very subtle smile and asked, "Is this your piece of shit?"

"Piece of shit?! It will kick the ass of that Eurotrash tin can you are driving."

"Well, maybe you want to try your luck at kicking the ass of this Eurotrash tin can as you call it."

"Anytime, sweetheart."

"How about now?"

"Now?"

"Unless, of course, you are all talk and no action."

"Where?"

"Follow me."

Sacha put the cigarette in her mouth, lit it, and proceeded toward the outskirts of town. Nader followed her obediently, wondering if this was really happening. She came to a long and straight strip of road, where she pulled up to the red light and waved to Nader to pull up next to her. It was almost 4:00 a.m. and the road was totally deserted. She rolled her window down and calmly asked if he was ready.

"Whenever you are."

"Okay, it's a go when the light turns green. I will wait for you at the next light."

"Dream on, baby."

They were both revving their engines when the light turned green. Both cars launched at the same time. The screeching sound from their tires was deafening. In a few seconds, Nader was looking at Sacha's taillights in absolute frustration. She was waiting for him when he pulled up alongside her at the next light. Rolling her window down, she asked with a coy smile, "You want to try your luck again?"

"Go for it."

Nader was determined not to let the same outcome happen again. The light turned green, and he found himself having the same view of her car's rear end as before. This time she pulled into an empty parking lot and waited for him to pull in. She exited her car as he pulled in and approached his window. Nader was visibly angry as Sacha stood in front of him, taking her time to savor the moment. When she finally spoke, her words were less than consoling.

"You suck at this."

"Oh, go fuck yourself."

He put his transmission into first gear and was about to leave, when she put her hands on the window and asked, "Do you want to go swimming?"

"Swimming? Where?"

"Just follow me."

Again, Sacha took the lead and Nader followed obediently, feeling totally emasculated. She took him on several back roads before they reached a wire fence that was eight feet tall with no end to be seen on either side. She quickly exited the car and climbed the fence and was on the other side before Nader knew what was happening. In pursuit like a dog following his master, he climbed the fence right after her. She quickly shed all her clothes and stood at the shore of the man-made reservoir as the glow from the full moon reflected off her porcelain skin. She had the body of a goddess, an artist's perception of perfection. Nader was frozen by the sight; he had never seen anything so beautiful or that perfect before.

Sacha dove into the water and swam to a small barge a few hundred feet from the shore. Nader was clumsily trying to take his shoes, pants, and shirt off and managed to fall face-first in the sand several times. He swam to the barge and climbed up to find her standing in the glow of the moonlight, waiting for him. Naked, she embraced him with a strong hug and kissed him passionately. He immediately became aroused. They made love for the next few hours. It was tender, passionate, and at times aggressive. It felt to him more like a spiritual experience than a mere act of copulation.

They were lying naked on the barge when the sun came up and the morning traffic began to stream in on the distant highway. They quickly swam back, got dressed, and climbed over the fence before they could be noticed. Before getting in the car, Sacha asked Nader if he wanted to have breakfast with her. "I'm buying."

"Sure."

He followed her again, this time to a local diner not too far from the reservoir. Nader was still in shock, trying to take in everything that had happened to him in the last twelve hours.

After the waitress took their order, Nader sat quietly, listening to the voice of Sacha. She was doing all the talking, but he did not mind; he just wanted to look at her and take in everything about her. Her voice, the contour of her lips when she spoke, how one eyebrow went up when she was making a point—everything about her turned him on. As they were eating their plates of eggs and hash browns, Sacha took her right shoe off, used her toes to climb the side of Nader's leg up to his inner thigh, and placed her foot on his groin. As he looked at her perfectly shaped foot, which was impeccably manicured, he became aroused again. She looked at him with a *Mona Lisa* smile and proceeded to stimulate him. He was helpless in her hands and completely under her spell. A few minutes later he was untucking his shirt to conceal the spot on the front of his pants as they proceeded to the cashier. Sacha pulled the cash from her pocket, paid the bill, left a generous tip for the waitress, grabbed Nader's hand, and led him to his car. She reached in, kissed him on the lips, turned around, and headed toward her car. Nader expected the typical departing statement, "Call me later," but he did not get it.

When he arrived at his apartment, he could not remember the trip there. He was in a dream state, and his mind was consumed with the flood of images from his encounter with Sacha. He sat on his bed for a while, trying to determine whether the last four hours were real. Or were they a figment of his imagination? What had happened to him did not feel real; it was like watching a Hollywood movie.

At that moment, his cell phone chimed, indicating that he had received a text message. His heart began to beat faster, thinking that the message could be from Sacha, but he realized that they had never exchanged phone numbers. He opened the message; it was from his father: "Those with a compass lead, and those without follow, but worst of all is following those who don't have a compass at all." Nader loved his father regardless of their history, but he wished he would stop sending him these messages. They made him question himself, and he didn't like it.

After some much-needed sleep, Nader got up, showered, and got dressed. He went to Joe's at 6:00 p.m. to start his shift. He could not get Sacha out of his head; the scenes from the previous night were being replayed in his head on a continuous loop. He was still in a state of disbelief and wanted to relive every moment with her over and over again. He hoped that he would get to see her again tonight, but that strong urge, and his loss of self-control, scared him.

He was setting up the bar as he always did before the influx patrons in a few hours, when he noticed a young man in his early twenties enter the empty bar. He was tall and well-built, and his eyes were laser focused on Nader. He approached the bar and, without saying anything, grabbed Nader from behind the bar. Then he lifted him up and crashed him into the glass window. Nader was stunned. When he finally gathered his wits, he saw the man break a leg off one of the barstools with the intention of using it on Nader. Nader quickly stood up, deflected the blow, and pushed the man to the ground. At that moment the bouncers, who were outside smoking a cigarette, noticed the commotion and stepped in through the front door. The man, realizing that the odds were against him, stood up and ran toward to the back emergency exit with tears streaming down his face.

One of the bouncers asked, "What the fuck happened?"

"I have no fucking idea," Nader replied. "I do not even know the dude. Did you guys ever see him before?"

"Yeah, I saw him come in a few times with the chick who gave you the hundred-dollar tip."

Nader shook his head in disbelief.

A few minutes later, Sacha walked into the bar with the poise and gracefulness of royalty, Nader approached her languidly. He was still shaken up by his encounter, and his clothes were covered with shattered glass.

"Was that your boyfriend who attacked me a few minutes ago?"

"Ex-boyfriend!"

"Did you tell him about last night?"

"Yes."

"What the fuck? Are you crazy?"

"Don't get mad. I will explain after you're done with work. I will meet you in the parking lot." She turned around and exited as quickly as she had come in.

That night Sacha and Nader were making love on a swing set at Clement Morgan Park at four o'clock in the morning.

 **The Birthday Party**

Over the next three months, the relationship between Sacha and Nader became more or less exclusive. They had been seeing each other almost every night. This was not your typical relationship— no quiet evenings at home watching movies and eating popcorn, no lazy Sundays sleeping in. It was a whirlwind of new and exciting adventures. The sex, the conversation, and the experiences were all unpredictable, unconventional, and supercharged. Sex was rarely in the same place or in the typical setting. It was in an elevator, in the back of a car, and often in a public place a few feet from the prying eyes of the general public. Sacha and Nader's conversations were intense and vigorously debated. They covered a myriad of subjects: politics, religion, and most often science. She was his intellectual equal and no pushover when it came to mounting a persuasive and factually grounded argument. There was rarely small talk or awkward silent moments between them. The conversations flowed freely as if it were a Ping-Pong match between two master players.

The more time Nader spent with Sacha, the more difficult it became for him not to fall in love with her. It took every ounce of self-control to keep his emotions in check. This bird would never be caged, and he knew it. He embraced every moment with her as if it were his last. He was in for the ride of his life and was resigned to the fact that this was a fleeting moment to be savored and not preserved.

It was a sunny Sunday afternoon in early September. Sacha and Nader were taking a leisurely stroll along Newbury Street in downtown Boston, when Nader swiveled his head for a split second to look at a storefront. The beautiful leather jacket in the window of a very trendy and expensive store caught his eye. His mathematical mind quickly calculating how many nights he would have to work at the bar in order to collect enough tips to pay for this overpriced jacket, he decided it was not worth the sacrifice. Sacha noted his attraction as they proceeded to their favorite café a few blocks away for a latte and the café's famous pumpkin pie. The conversation began innocently enough about a recent campaign by a well-known atheist group to remove all religious symbols from schools and public buildings. The movement had argued that this was a form of state-sponsored indoctrination, something that chose winners and losers and pit one religion against another. Their argument was grounded in the Establishment Clause and the Separation Clause in the First Amendment and the intended outcome of separation of church and state. Sacha argued that people should have the absolute freedom to believe and practice any religion, including the right to believe in no religion at all, and that putting religious symbols in any public place was tantamount to an endorsement. At the end of her statement, Sacha poignantly asked Nader, "I am surprised I never asked you this before, but as a man of science, do you believe in God?"

Nader was taken aback by the question, but he had given this subject matter a considerable amount of thought since the death of his mother and the falling-out with his father. With that question, Sacha seemed to have opened the floodgate of emotion, causing his emotions to begin gushing out, slowly at first, then progressively more freely and unrestrained. He spoke of his most intimate and personal feelings, which he had never shared with anyone before, as he broached the subject of his mother's passing when he was twelve, his subsequent loss of faith, and his relationship with his father the imam and how disappointed his father had been with him when he left Palestine. Nader shared his recollection of Rabbi Ackerman and his son Addis, telling Sacha how much he admired them both, the rabbi for his wisdom, his wholesomeness, and how he had sacrificed his life for Nader's father. When it came to Addis, Nader's description was more akin to describing a superhero with special powers. He wondered what had become of Addis after leaving the West Bank.

Sacha listened with great interest. She was finally able to peel the layers of the onion and see the raw and soft underbelly of this man whom she had been dating for the last three months. No longer feeling guarded or vulnerable, she began to share her own personal story with him. The only child of a technology mogul who had started his company as a freshman in college and built it to be one of the largest tech companies in the world, she described her father as driven, single-minded, and often ruthless. He had no tolerance for weakness or failure, and she often found herself being chastised for not being the best at whatever task she was performing or for the smallest infraction. She was never good enough for him, and as hard as she tried, she could never meet his standards. She described her mother, on the other hand, as having a nonconfrontational demeanor, a person more interested in the social scene and enjoying the wealth that had been bestowed upon her than her husband was. "Growing up," Sacha said, "my self-confidence was shit. I could not wait to get out of my father's house."

Nader replied, "At least we both have that in common. Maybe we are kindred souls?"

Sacha said, "Now you are going too far." Both chuckled. "But seriously, you never answered my original question."

"What was that?"

"Do you believe in God?"

"Wow, we are getting deep now. What happened to the spontaneous sex, a few laughs, and a few drinks and then calling it a day?"

"Seriously, I want to know more about what you believe in."

"Well, I look at my body and I see God's work. Let me change that and give a better example. I look at your body and I really see God's work."

"Well, thank you. But be serious."

"Well, think about it: Every cell, every atom, and every molecule in my body has a singular purpose in keeping me alive. They all work together in perfect harmony, perfect synchronicity, and they are all interconnected and interdependent. However, I operate this perfect machine without even being conscious of the fact that I am pushing all these levers. As if there is an intermediary between me and this machine, I give the order, and the intermediary receives it and begins to pull all the levers upon my command. I often wonder, what if there is no intermediary and I am both the commander and operator, where I am consciously connected with every atom, every cell, and every molecule in my body, and what would that feel like? I think that would feel like I am the god of my own body. So, to me, it is not inconceivable that the universe is a celestial body and there is a God who is connected to every atom, cell, and molecule. As a matter of fact, I believe that the whole universe is our celestial body and we are that body. Everything in the universe is there to support our existence like every atom, cell, and molecule in our body."

"Let me get this clear. You think this vast universe is here just for us?"

"I think we are a part of one ecosystem, where everything is interconnected and interdependent. As a very wise man once said to me, 'The universe is balanced on the tip of a needle. Every action requires a simultaneous reaction of equal force to maintain the balance. Everything we do matters.'"

"Who said that?"

"Rabbi Ackerman, the family friend I told you about."

"Why does that name sound so familiar? Anyway, go on."

"Well, there is perfection and order in this universe, where everything operates like a fine-tuned Swiss watch. The whole thing is balanced on the tip of a needle. How can this be a random occurrence? The laws of physics and mathematics are not random; they are a matter of fact. How can all of this not be a creation? And if it is, who created it and why, is the better question."

Sacha said, "I guess that is what humanity has been asking since the beginning of time and what religions have been trying to answer for them."

"How about you? Do you believe?"

"I believe the forces of evil and good exist and they are in a constant struggle for dominance. There is a fine balance between them, and when that balance is disrupted, things go bad. I always wondered if these forces can be measured both on an individual and a societal level. As a matter of fact, I would like to make that the focus of my PhD in psychology."

"It sounds like you believe in the 'the universe is balanced on the tip of a needle' theory?"

"I guess. Maybe I do. I will make that the title of my PhD thesis."

Sacha and Nader left the café after several hours of seamless conversation that seemed like a few minutes rather than a few hours. Their time together seemed to fly by and was never labored. As they were walking toward their cars, Sacha draped her arm around Nader's shoulders in a display of affection that was new to their relationship. She said, "I must go home this weekend for my father's fiftieth birthday. My mother is throwing a big party for him in their summer home in the Hamptons. I would love it if you could come with me."

"Do you think your family would like me, you being Jewish and me a Palestinian? Plus, from what you have told me of your father, I don't think he and I would get along."

"Don't worry, it will be only for a few days. And I will block and tackle for you if he gives you a hard time."

"Okay. If you want me to. Plus, I have always been curious about the gene pool that created this goddess standing in front of me."

She reached out and gave him a long and affectionate kiss. "Thank you."

The next morning Nader woke up to a knock on the door of his apartment. He had only gotten in a few hours ago from Joe's and was tired and groggy. He opened the door and was met by a UPS deliveryman with a large package.

"Sorry to disturb you, sir, but I have a package that I need you to sign for."

"A package? Are you sure you've got the right address?"

"The name is Nader el-Shafique, right?"

"Yes."

"Yes, sir, the package is for you. Sign here."

Nader took the package inside and immediately opened it, curious as to what the contents might be and who had sent it. It was the leather jacket he had admired the day before, with a note. The note was from Sacha, with the caption "Every time you wear it, think of me." He put the jacket on, and it was a perfect fit. It had her subtle scent on the inside of it. He immediately became aroused.

Saturday morning, they woke up early, packed the Porsche, and started their drive to the Hamptons on a beautiful, warm, sunny day. Sacha put the top down and used the Bluetooth for her playlist of indie music. Nader loved her taste in music. Both were singing along and enjoying the ride and each other's company. Nader randomly asked, "Did you ever tell your parents about me?"

"No. I like to keep my private life private. It is none of their business who I date."

"Do you think they would mind that you are dating a Palestinian Arab?"

"Frankly, if they do, that is their problem."

"I never told you, but my brother, Mustafa, married the daughter of Rabbi Ackerman."

"Really? How did that go over with your father and the rabbi?"

"Well, that was after the rabbi was murdered, and surprisingly, my father did not object. As a matter of fact, he was honored that the daughter of his best friend and the man who had given up his life for him would wed his oldest son. He gave them his blessing and attended their civil wedding. Of course, as you might imagine, it created a lot of controversy in both communities. I have a feeling that your parents will not be that generous."

"I am afraid you might be right. My father pretends to be liberal on the outside, but in private he is all about preserving the Jewish race. His parents were Holocaust survivors who ingrained in him the necessity of maintaining the Jewish identity. He is also a strong supporter of Israel."

"So why I am here again?"

"You are my boyfriend, and whether they like it or not, it is my choice, not theirs. Plus, they will be so distracted by all the commotion and their fancy guests, they will not have the time to focus on anything else."

"I'm sorry I did not pack my flak jacket. I think I'm going to need it."

"Don't worry, I've got your back. And I really love you for doing this for me."

"Love me? That is a first."

"Get over yourself; it is a figure of speech. But you are very lovable; I will give you that."

"Baby, I will take whatever you can give me." He reached out and kissed her.

They got off the main road and turned onto a private road. A few minutes later they were standing in front of a large gate with a shrubbery fence on both sides that went as far as the eye could see. There were several security cameras that instantaneously swiveled and pointed their lenses toward the Porsche. A deep voice on the intercom assertively commanded, "Please announce yourself."

"This is Sacha Zimmerman."

"Welcome home, Ms. Zimmerman."

A few seconds later the gate opened, and they proceeded down a beautifully manicured driveway with the most exotic and unique plants. The driveway came to a dramatic finish in front of a water fountain that rivaled anything in existence at the heart of Rome. There were several limousines parked on the side with their chauffeurs waiting patiently for their employers. Sacha and Nader exited the car and proceeded to the front door.

Nader, taken aback by all the formalities, commented, "How rich is your father?"

"Filthy!"

The door opened, and Nader and Sacha were greeted by an impeccably dressed and well-mannered butler. "Welcome home, Ms. Zimmerman."

"Thank you, John. It is nice to see you."

Before Sacha was able to introduce Nader, Mrs. Zimmerman came charging in with a drink in her hand. She looked like she was already a few drinks into her daily ritual.

"Hi, baby. I missed you!"

"Hi, Mom."

"Who is this?"

"This is Nader."

"Nader, what a wonderful name. What kind of name is that?"

"It is Middle Eastern, Mrs. Zimmerman. It is wonderful to meet you," Nader answered.

"It is wonderful to meet you as well. I noticed your wonderful accent. Were you born here?" Mrs. Zimmerman asked.

"No, I was born In Palestine and came to the US at the age of eighteen."

"Palestine?" She turned to Sacha, asking, "Honey, have you introduced Nader to your father yet?""

"No, Mother, we just got here."

Mrs. Zimmerman murmured to herself, "That should be interesting." To Sacha and Nader, she said, "Come on in and make yourself comfortable."

"Where is Dad?"

"He is in the study meeting with a few very important people."

"About what?" Sacha wanted to know.

"Between you and me, I think he is thinking about running for office."

"What office?"

Mrs. Zimmerman replied, "The presidency of the United States, of course."

Nader followed Sacha and her mother into a magnificent sitting room overlooking the spacious grounds and the Atlantic Ocean. Taken by the ostentatious display of wealth, he couldn't help but wonder how many people in the world who went hungry every night could be fed from the proceeds of one of the multiple paintings inauspiciously hung on the walls. The three of them each took a seat.

The French doors to the study opened, and several well-dressed men ranging in age from early fifties to late sixties came streaming out. Zack Zimmerman was escorting them to the patio for afternoon cocktails. Zack noticed his daughter and quickly called to her, "Honey, come on over. I would like to introduce you to some good friends of mine."

As Sacha stood up, so did Nader, at which point Zack took notice of his daughter's guest with a querying look. Zack began introducing the impressive list of senators, corporate chieftains, and dignitaries. After the formalities, he excused himself for a moment and summoned his butler to escort his guests to the patio. He quickly turned to Sacha.

"Honey, it is so nice to see you. And I see you brought a friend."

"Yes, Daddy. This is Nader."

Nader straightened up and approached Zack, also taking notice of Sacha's demeanor and the intonation of her voice and how it changed dramatically in the presence of her dad. She sounded more like a teenage girl looking for her daddy's approval than the strong woman he knew.

"Hello, sir. It is nice to meet you."

"Nice to meet you as well, Nader. I am sorry, but I didn't get your last name."

"El-Shafique."

"That is a Middle Eastern name, no?"

"Yes, sir. I was born in Palestine."

"You mean Israel."

"Where I come from, we call it Palestine."

"Fair enough. We must chat more after I am done entertaining our guests. You are staying overnight, I hope?" he said to Nader.

"Yes, sir. I look forward to it."

"Great. And, ladies," Zack said, turning toward his wife and Sacha, "I look forward to a dance with each of you this evening."

Zack proceeded to the patio to continue his conversation with his very powerful guests. They were laying the groundwork for launching an exploratory committee to elect Zack as the next president of the United States. Timing was key. They debated vigorously whether this was the right time to launch their campaign or if they should wait until the current president completed his second term. The current president had been in office for only two years, and although his popularity was in the low fortieth percentile, they feared that unseating an incumbent president would be too difficult a task. However, they felt the time was right for Zack to increase his public persona given the policies and the divisive nature of the sitting president. They wanted Zack to begin to formulate his agenda and his public policies, and take to the airwaves to counterargue the nationalist agenda being advocated by the current administration. There was a wave of nationalism that had swept the country in the last election that had polarized the country and the world and had caused the political discourse to become extremely ugly. These gentlemen were globalists, and they felt the time was right to change the course of not just this country but also the world. After a few cocktails and many ideas on how to proceed, they agreed to meet monthly in secret to put their plan into action.

The guests retired to their individual guest rooms to join their wives and get some rest before their private dinner with the Zimmermans and then the follow-up birthday gala. The wives were being entertained by Mrs. Zimmerman and Sacha. Nader was the third wheel. The women took great interest in him and his story; however, he was extremely uncomfortable in the limelight and couldn't wait to get some private time with Sacha. After everyone had retired to their respective rooms, Sacha and Nader took a walk on the beach. She thanked him again for coming with her and acknowledged how uncomfortable it must have been for him.

There were forty people sitting at the dinner table, with Zack sitting at the head of the table on one end and his wife sitting at the other end. Sacha and Nader were sitting next to each other toward the middle of the table. The guests were all formally dressed. Sacha had had to borrow a jacket from her father for Nader, which added to her guest's discomfort. The butlers were busy serving the guests. There were multiple conversations going on at the same time, punctuated with hearty laughter from now and again. After dinner was completed, the servants began to clear the dishes in preparation for after-dinner drinks and dessert. Zack interrupted the multiple conversations taking place and thanked his guests for coming. He also thanked his wife and introduced his daughter and her guest to the attentive audience.

"I'm very proud of my daughter, Sacha, although she doesn't come and visit as often as I would like her to. She always reminds me that she is busy completing her PhD program in psychology. Although I tried to convince her to go into computer science, she chose psychology. Well, God knows we can always use another psychologist in this household." The audience laughed. "She also brought a friend, Nader el-Shafique. I hope I'm pronouncing that correctly." Nader nodded. "He is another brainiac, starting his PhD this fall in physics. He has just completed his master's in physics with an undergraduate degree in microbiology." The audience nodded in approval. "Sacha tells me that Nader was born in Palestine and he is the son of an imam." Zack directed his look at Nader and said, "I just hope he is not going to demand my daughter wear a hijab." The audience laughed.

Nader immediately responded, "As long as she doesn't ask me to wear a yarmulke." There was awkward silence in the room except for the quiet chuckle that Sacha was trying to conceal.

Zack replied, "Touché." He raised his glass and thanked his audience again.

The birthday party that followed would not be rivaled by any grand ball held by a king or a queen. No expense was spared with all the trappings of boundless wealth. The latest hit band was performing with the full accompaniment of a symphony orchestra, the music varying from old to new and the genre ranging from classic rock to disco. The drinks and food were flowing freely, and the guests were having a grand time. The guests were the who's who: well-known celebrities, corporate titans, politicians, and some of the wealthiest individuals in the world. The guest list could have doubled for a Forbes list of the hundred wealthiest individuals. They all sported the latest fashion, and every woman was in competition with every other woman for wearing the most expensive dress and jewelry.

After a short speech from Zack, thanking his guests for taking the time to celebrate his fiftieth birthday with him, he began to work the room with the savvy and charm of a seasoned politician. Nader tried to mingle and blend in as much as possible, but he felt like a fish out of water. As much as Sacha tried to include him in every conversation, it seemed contrived, and he found the same questions over and over again about his heritage and the conflict in the Middle East exhausting. Closer to the end of the evening, he excused himself and decided to take a walk on the beach and grab a smoke. On his way back, as he stepped onto the patio leading to the study, he heard the voices of Zack and Sacha speaking. Zack's voice was terse and direct.

"Of all the men who would bow and kiss your feet, this is the guy you bring home? You couldn't find someone of your own kind?"

"And what kind is that, Dad?"

"The kind who will respect who you are and where you come from."

"Jewish, and come from a lot of money? Is that what you mean?"

"Honey, you always had a penchant for picking up stray dogs. It is time for you to grow up."

"Well, Dad, I've never been able to please you. It did not matter how high my grades were or how many goals I scored on the soccer field; I could always do better. Happy birthday." She walked out. Nader had caught the conversation from outside and decided to take the long way back to the party.

That night Sacha snuck into Nader's room, and they made love. As she lay next him, he asked very gently, "Do you mind very much if I go back to the city tomorrow morning? I can take the train back. You stay and spend some time with your parents."

"You're uncomfortable here?"

"Just a bit."

"I understand. We will both leave tomorrow, early in the morning."

"You don't mind?"

"Not at all. We did our obligatory duty; now it is time to go back to the real world."

They both smiled at each other and exchanged a good-night kiss. The next morning, they arose before dawn while the household was still asleep. After they had packed their bags, Sacha left a short note on her father's favorite chair: "Happy birthday. Had to leave early. Jammed with work. Call you both soon. Love, Sacha." Then she left Dodge in a hurry.

7   **The Dream**

It was December. Nader and Sacha had been seeing each other for almost six months. Within the last three months, their relationship had become purely exclusive. They had become very fond of each other and had no interest in seeing other people. Their relationship had evolved from lovers to also being the best of friends. They had shared their most intimate feelings, their weaknesses, and their fears with each other without being judgmental. It was an unconditional type of love that was based on total and complete acceptance. However, Sacha had noticed lately that Nader had been growing more restless and was struggling with his spiritual identity. The topic of religion and spirituality, and the "What does it all mean?" question, kept on creeping up more and more into their conversations. His hyperactive mind was seeking answers to questions that had eluded many before him and were not easily answerable. Sacha suspected that all these feelings that had been bubbling up as of late had to do with Nader's need to reconcile with his past, deal with his conflict with his father, come to accept the death of his mother, and come to terms with the subsequent loss of his faith. Sacha had always been a keen observer of others' emotional states and subtle psychological clues. However, she was helpless in quelling Nader's need for answers.

It was December 22, late in the evening, and Nader had just

arrived at his apartment after a growling night at Joe's. The continuous holiday parties being hosted at the bar, combined with the excessive drinking, had taken a toll on him. Tonight was no different from the last twenty nights, except tonight, Sacha had left town to see her parents for the holidays, and Nader was home alone. He was hardly able to stand but decided to take a shower before going to bed. Unable to stand the smell of the bar and the odor of the alcohol on his clothes and body any longer, he wanted to cleanse himself of the smell. He took a quick shower, put on pajama pants and a T-shirt, and immediately went to bed.

Nader suddenly woke up a few hours later in a pool of sweat and immediately sat up in his bed. His heart was racing so fast, he could almost hear the pounding of every beat, as if it were someone pounding on his chest. The dream he had just had was so vivid that it felt as if it were real. A few minutes later, he was still shaking as his mind was repeatedly going over the dream scene by scene. He knew that this was not the kind of dream that would be forgotten a few minutes later; this one would be permanently emblazoned in his mind and soul. In his dream, Nader had seen himself driving an expensive SUV resembling a Range Rover. In the back of the vehicle sat his mother and father. Out of nowhere appeared a stretch limousine, followed by a procession of other vehicles that cut him off, causing him to veer sharply in order to avoid a direct collision. He was angered by the careless disregard for the safety and lives of his mother and father and was determined to confront the passengers of the limousine.

In the dream, Nader continued to follow the limousine until it came to stop. A man exited the limo and was immediately surrounded by a huge crowd. Nader attempted to break through the crowd, but they were too densely packed; he couldn't muscle his way through no matter how hard he tried. He was able to get a closer glimpse of the man and was struck by how handsome he was. Nader persistently followed the entourage, determined to address the man and reprimand him for his behavior. The man walked into a building and disappeared behind a set of French doors with a large-sized waiting area just outside. A large group of Orthodox Jews dressed all in black, in their traditional garments, were waiting patiently to meet with the man behind the French doors. Upon Nader's entering the waiting room, it appeared that the group in waiting all smelled him first before they saw him. Their facial expressions turned to frowns as if they had smelled the foulest of odor. Their frowns quickly turned into anger once they became aware of Nader's presence. Their anger was primordial, the type that can only be satisfied when the recipient of the anger is utterly annihilated.

The group of Orthodox Jews collectively began to charge Nader as if they wanted to tear him limb from limb. Terrified, he ran out, closing the doors behind him and using all his strength to keep them closed. But the men's hands began to slither from every crack in the door, trying desperately to reach him. He was mortified and in fear for his life, when suddenly his dream transitioned into a scene where he was sitting in a train, traveling through the most scenic landscape. His seat was facing the side of the train, which was made of glass. He was so taken by the beautiful scenery that he did not notice the two individuals on either side of him. On his left stood a woman covered from head to toe in white. On his right, there was a man dressed in a suit that resembled the Swiss flag, which caused Nader to wonder why this man was wearing the Swiss flag. The woman in white approached Nader and handed him a crystal pitcher to drink from. Without question, he began to drink. As he tilted the pitcher upward, trying to get the last drop, he looked at the bottom of the pitcher. It was as if he were looking at a kaleidoscope. He was immediately awash with the most genuinely beautiful feeling, a feeling that he never had experienced before. It felt to him like what heaven ought to feel like. He was so immersed in the feeling that he didn't want to leave, but something snapped him out of it. He woke up in a cold sweat. His body was drenched, and his heart was beating so fast, every heartbeat felt like a drumbeat. He was visibly shaken, and his hands were trembling. He sat in his bed, trying to make sense of what had just happened. *Was this a dream or a nightmare that I just experienced?* After a few minutes, he was finally able to slow his heart, but he could not help but feel that something very profound had just happened to him.

It was not as if Nader knew what the dream meant, but what he did know was that something spiritual, not of this world, had just touched him. The feeling was so overwhelming, he wanted answers. *What did I experience? What does it mean?* He stood up, went to his closet, and pulled out the suitcase he'd arrived with when he first came to the States. Opening the suitcase, he pulled out a book that was covered in a Palestinian shawl. The wrapping was as pristine as when his father had handed it to him as a departing gift before leaving home five years ago. Nader knew that the gift was a statement from his father (*Don't forget your faith or your heritage*). He unwrapped the Koran and randomly chose a page in the middle of the book. It was Sura Yousef, which read as follows:

And he raised his parents upon the throne and they (the brothers) fell down in prostration before him, and he said: O my father! (yaa abati) this is the significance (tawil) of my vision of old; my Lord has indeed made it to be true; and He was indeed kind to me when He brought me forth from the prison and brought you from the desert after the Shaitan (Satan) had sown dissensions between me and my brothers, surely my Lord is benignant to whom He pleases; surely He is the Knowing, the Wise.

My Lord! Thou hast given me of the kingdom and taught me of the interpretation of sayings: Originator/Splitter of the heavens and the earth! Thou art my guardian in this world and the hereafter; make me die (ta-waffa) a Muslim and join me with the good. (Koran 12:100–101)

The verse spoke to Nader as if it were a direct message from God. He began to cry. He reached for his phone on the nightstand, turned it on, and went to the text messages he had been receiving from his father for the last five years and never had had the heart to erase. He opened one of the messages. It read, "No man can serve two masters. Let the voice inside your heart and mind be your master, not the voice outside." Nader had the strong urge to speak to his father. It felt like when he was a child and he'd run to his father to be consoled after scraping his knee playing soccer in the street or being bullied at school. He dialed the number and desperately hoped that his father would answer the phone. After the third ring, a voice he had missed very much spoke on the other side: "Aloh?"

"Assalamu alaikum, Baba."

"Nader? Walaikum salaam, habibie [my love]. It is so nice to hear your voice."

"Baba, I am sorry I haven't called in a while. I have not been a good son. Please forgive me."

"There is nothing to forgive. You are my son, and my love for you is never wavering. I have prayed to Allah every day to hold you in the palm of his hand and let his angels protect you and guard you from harm and evildoers."

"Baba, I had a dream last night, and I am frightened by it."

"What was it?"

Nader began to tell his father about the dream, knowing that his father was the one to whom everyone went in the village to decipher their dreams. The imam had an uncanny talent for explaining the meaning of their dreams. After telling his father the dream in detail, Nader waited for him to respond, but there was silence on the other end. When the imam finally spoke, there was an appreciable sadness in his tone, and his voice was clearly quivering. He began by reciting the F tihah from the Koran.

"Nader, I believe you have been touched by the hand of Allah. Your dream is a prophecy of something that will have a profound effect on the future."

"But what is it, Baba?"

"The man in the limousine is the Antichrist. The woman in white is the Virgin Mary. The man wearing the Swiss flag suit is the prophet Isa [Christ]. Your mother and I represent your homeland. The rabbis represent Israel's interests. The expensive car represents a time of prosperity. The train is a voyage you will take, and the pitcher you will drink from will be your absolution."

"But what does that mean?"

"There will come a time when you will intervene to work against an immensely powerful man who is in unholy alliance with Israel. Their actions will cause harm to the Middle East. It will happen during a time when the world is experiencing great prosperity."

"Is that it?"

"That is what I think your dream means."

"Baba, why me?"

"I do not know, Son. But do you remember how your mother used to call you her gift from Allah?"

"Yes."

"Well, I never told you this, but before your mother knew she was pregnant with you, she had a dream. In her dream she was visited by the woman dressed in white. The woman handed her a pitcher to drink from and a bundle. Your mother believed the bundle was you."

"Baba, I miss you and I want to come to see you soon. As soon as I am done with my academic year, in the summer, I will come and visit you and stay for a while."

"Please do, habibie. It has been too long."

As soon as they hung up the phone, the imam began to cry. There was a lot more to the dream than the imam cared to share with his beloved son. He believed that his son had seen his death in his dream.

After hanging up the phone with his father, Nader got up, took a shower, got dressed, and left his apartment. It was five o'clock in the morning. The local mosque had just opened for the Fajr prayer. The mosque was still empty except for the imam. Nader approached the imam and declared his wish to renew his vows as a Muslim. The imam asked his name and, without further questioning him, asked him to proclaim three times "Ash-hadu alla ilaha illallah, wa ash-hadu anna Muhammadar rasulullah" (There is only one God, and the Prophet Muhammad is his messenger). Nader enthusiastically made the proclamation and then asked the imam to teach him how to pray again, which the imam did. After the Fajr prayer was completed and all the worshippers had left the mosque, Nader stayed behind and began to read the Koran from the beginning.

Later, as he was exiting the mosque, Nader received a text from his father: "Your destiny is a dance where you never get to lead but always have to follow. The trick is not to resist and to follow with grace and poise."

Nader thought back on his life and realized how true his father's text was. He was never in control. Everything that happened to him somehow felt predetermined, and he was just in for the ride.

Later in the morning, Nader received a call from Sacha. "Hi, honey. How are you?"

"I am fine."

"Is everything okay? You sound different."

"I've got a lot tell you, but I don't want to do it over the phone. When are you coming back?"

"In a few days. You are kind of scaring me," she said.

"No, everything is fine. I will tell you more when I see you. Are you enjoying your visit with your parents?"

"You know how it is; you gotta do what you gotta do."

"I understand. See you when you get back," Nader concluded.

Sacha replied, "Okay, bye."

That afternoon, Nader called the bar and asked for the manager. He resigned his position as bartender. He never drank again.

Sacha was back in Boston a few days later. Her first stop was at Nader's apartment. She used her key and entered unannounced. She had suspected the worst, but she found Nader sitting on the couch reading. She quickly jumped in his lap, straddled him, and gave him a deep and affectionate kiss on the lips. Nader did not reciprocate the affectionate embrace. He pushed her back and stood up.

"What is going on?" asked Sacha.

"I have a lot to tell you."

Sacha looked at the book Nader was reading. "Are you reading the Bible?"

"Yes."

She looked at the coffee table and saw that the Koran was also on the table, with multiple page markers with copious notes. "What is going on?" she asked.

"I had a dream a few days ago."

"What dream?"

Nader told her about his dream in detail. He also discussed his conversation with his father and his visit with the imam at the local mosque, not failing to mention the fact that he had quit his job and had not had a drink since then.

"You are freaking me out."

"I'm sorry, but I have this strong feeling that the dream was a wake-up call, as if God has shown me a glimpse of the future and somehow it is my calling. I still don't totally understand what it means, but what I know is that I must make some changes to my life."

"What does that mean for us?"

"I don't know. But what I do know is that I care for you very much and I don't want to lose you. But our relationship can't be the same. Otherwise, I will be violating every covenant I must make."

"Does that mean we can't have sex?"

"That is a part of it."

"What are you asking me? Are you asking me to convert to Islam, wear a hijab, and be an obedient wife? Because that is not happening."

"I don't want you to do or be anything you do not want to do or be, but I also know I don't want to lose our friendship either. This is about me. I am not on a mission to convert the world or change anybody's mind. This is an individual journey that I must take. I will always love you and accept you for who you are."

"You know I have no problem competing against another woman, but religion? That is a battle I don't think I can win. This is a lot to digest, and right now I am overwhelmed. I must give this a lot of thought."

Sacha stood up, grabbed her bag, and exited the apartment without saying goodbye.

The Professor

Three years later, Nader had completed his PhD program in physics. He was one of the youngest PhD recipients ever to have received an assistant professor position at MIT. He very much enjoyed the experience of teaching and the interaction with young and inquisitive minds. He was teaching an introductory class in physics and another for which he had constructed the subject matter based on his dissertation: *Evidence of Science in Scripture*. The MIT faculty heads were reluctant at first to mix religion and science, but later, because of Nader's power of persuasion and the substantial body of work he was able to provide, they acquiesced and allowed him to teach one class on a trial basis. The class size reflected the nuanced nature of the subject matter, and the students in attendance were mainly looking for a filler course to complete their electives requirement. Nader did not mind. As a matter of fact, he preferred the small-sized classrooms over the lecture halls. He enjoyed the intellectual give-and-take with his students that was more attainable in a small classroom environment.

It was 11:00 a.m. He had just finished his 8:00 a.m. class in physics and was catching up on paperwork in his small office, which he shared with another young assistant professor. He had a lot to do today—another class at 5:00 p.m., several exams to grade, and preparation for his presentation to the United Nations General Council in a few weeks. In addition to his teaching position, and as a result of a strong recommendation by a tenured and well-respected MIT professor, Nader had been recruited by the United Nations as the science advisor to the General Council. He'd been tasked with the responsibility of (1) reporting to the council on any material technological or scientific changes that promised to have a worldwide impact and (2) helping the council formulate policies. The council, having been blindsided many times in the past by technological and scientific changes that had had impactful public policy ramifications, wanted to be less reactive and more proactive. The distributive nature of some of the technological changes had, at times, created substantial economic disparities between member nations and had sown political unrest. The councilmembers were also troubled by the covert actions of rogue nations using technologies to subvert democratic processes and undermine different sovereign governments. Nader loved the challenge of being a technology and science detective, but also a futurist with the power to predict what the world would look like five, ten, and twenty years from now.

His side of the office was packed with MIT press reports and papers, technology publications, and the latest books related to anything dealing with technology. The office was getting so cluttered that his office mate was beginning to protest the encroachment upon his work space.

Nader's three o'clock appointment was on time and was waiting patiently outside his office. Nader invited her in. She looked around the office for a space to sit, but every available space was packed with papers, books, and scientific publications. His designated space in the office looked like a disorganized mess, while his office mate's desk was clean and organized with only a few family pictures to give any indication that the space was occupied. Nader stood up, cleared the papers off a chair that was adjacent to his desk, and invited the student to sit down. This was one of his brighter students in his Science in Scripture class who showed a great interest in the subject matter and wanted to be on his research team. Nader could use the extra help, especially with the project he was working on for the UN General Council.

"Good afternoon, Professor."

"Good afternoon, Ms. Kramer."

"Please call me Donna."

"Hello, Donna. How can I help you today?"

"Well, as I mentioned to you after class, I am looking to join a research team to earn some extra credit, but also I think it will look good on my résumé."

"Do you have a specific area of interest?"

"Well, I've always been interested in public policy issues related to technology and science. That is why I find your class remarkably interesting; it addresses more of the philosophical, rather than the technical, aspects of technology and science."

"I see. Well, I am currently working on a project for the UN that I could use some help with."

"What is the project?"

"It addresses the disruptive nature of technological changes, the unintended consequences seen and unseen, and the necessity for creating worldwide protocols."

"That sounds very interesting. I'm in, if you think that I'm a good candidate."

"Well, you have shown a lot of initiative both inside and outside the classroom. Yes, I think you will be a great candidate."

"Great. When do I start? And what do you call this project?"

"You can start now. It is called 'the Spike.' The spike is the theory that every technology creates a whole new set of unintended consequences. As the rate of new technological changes increases, the unintended consequences increase too, but at a faster rate. However, there is a lag effect, and there will come a time when we as a race are unable to innovate quickly enough to remedy the onslaught of unintended consequences."

"Now that is very interesting. Where do you want me to start?"

Nader pointed the student to a large folder placed on the floor on the corner of his office titled "Unintended Consequences." "You can start by reading the contents of this folder. Then let's talk again in a few weeks."

As the student was standing up to say goodbye, Nader's cell phone rang. He looked at the caller ID; it was Sacha. Nader said his goodbyes to the student and apologized for needing to take the call.

Once Donna was gone, Nader answered his phone. "Hey, stranger. I have not heard from you in a while. How have you been?" he said.

"Hi, Nader. I have been well. We have a lot to catch up on. Are you free for dinner? I'm buying."

"I never say no to a free dinner. And knowing you, it will probably be an awfully expensive place."

"Don't get your hopes up. Plus, I thought you'd be more interested in my company than in the food."

"That is true. I guess good conversation with a pretty lady and a Big Mac is good enough for me."

"You are such a flatterer. I think we could do something slightly better than a Big Mac. How about 7:30? I will text you the name of the place," Sacha said.

"Sounds great. I am looking forward to it."

"Me too. I'll see you later." She hung up.

Nader had just finished teaching his five o'clock class and was walking back to his office when he received a message from Sacha: "Let's meet at Del Frisco's for a steak. I made reservations for 7:30."

He replied, "I was so looking forward to a Big Mac and fries. See you there."

He rushed home, took a quick shower, changed, and decided to get some fresh air by walking to the restaurant. He arrived a few minutes late. Sacha was already seated, nursing a glass of red wine. On his side of the table, his usual drink was already waiting for him—half cranberry juice, half seltzer. Sacha gave him a kiss on the cheek, and they embraced for longer than customary. She immediately asked, "Where have you been? It has been awhile."

"I know. I'm sorry. I've been busy with teaching and with my new position with the UN."

"You must tell me all about that."

"No, not this time. You always get me talking about myself, but tonight I want to hear all about you and what is going on in your life."

"What is going on with me? Well, a lot. You know the book I was telling you I was writing?"

"The book based on your dissertation?"

"Yes. Well, I finished it, and a publisher picked it up."

"Wow, that's great. When is it coming out?"

"Sometime in the next few weeks. And they scheduled me for a lecture and book tour on both coasts for the next couple of months. I am giving you a formal invitation right now for the first lecture and book signing in three weeks, right here in Boston."

"Are you kidding? I wouldn't miss it for the world. I will even wear my wing-tip shoes, my tweeds, and my tortoiseshell glasses for the occasion. I am so excited for you."

"I also accepted a full-time position. With my dad," Sacha said.

"What?!"

At that moment, the waiter interrupted their conversation and asked if they were ready to order. Nader had a stunned look on his face, and Sacha decided to break the awkward moment by placing her order. Afterward, the waiter directed his attention to Nader and asked, "And for you, sir?"

He quickly replied, "I will have the same," and redirected his attention back to Sacha. "That is so unlike you. I thought you wanted to free yourself from his overpowering take-control-of-everything nature."

"I know, but the offer was too good to refuse. He offered me full access to the company's software, engineers, and technology to develop my thesis into a functioning algorithm. So far, it's all been theories and hypotheses; I want to test-drive it and see if it works. Plus, if I am right about all this stuff, there may be a lot of social and economic applications that I wouldn't be able to develop without the capabilities of a company like my father's. His company is the largest tech company in the world. I will never have this opportunity anywhere else. Again, it was an offer I couldn't refuse."

"Are you sure about this?"

"No, but I know I want to see the fruits of my labor."

"You know, my father once said to me, 'Both angels and demons walk side by side with us; their proximity depends on whom you offend and whom you please with your actions.'"

"What are you saying?"

"I am just saying be careful."

"Don't worry, I've got it under control. I've been around him for so long, I know how to manage the manager. But enough about me. I want to know all about the stuff you're working on. But first let's devour this steak. I'm famished."

Nader began to tell Sacha about some of his students and how much he loved teaching. He also described the project he was working on for the UN. "That technology is like the Wild, Wild West, and the international community wants to put this genie back into the bottle by creating a worldwide protocol. They want to create privacy mandates and protective mechanisms to stop bad individual and state actors from gaming the system, something similar to the World Trade Organization."

After dinner, Nader walked Sacha to her apartment. She invited him in for a cup of tea, but he politely declined. He kissed her on the cheek and said, "You know I still have feelings for you. I can't reconcile being true to myself and true to you at the same time. I wish things were different, but they're not. I keep hearing the voice of my father saying to me, 'At an early age, we master saying no to others, but never to ourselves. The former never serves us as well as the latter.'"

"What does that mean?"

"Every time I see you, I have to say no to myself, and it is extremely hard."

"Does that mean that you don't want to see me anymore?"

"No, it means that I am a recovering addict and I must avoid the temptation."

"You know I will always love you, but I also accept you and respect who you are as you unconditionally accept me. And if I cannot have you as a lover, I am okay having you as a friend rather than not having you at all."

He kissed her on the forehead and proceeded to walk to his apartment. She stood still for a few seconds, looking at his silhouette disappear in the dark with an aching heart.

A week later, Nader woke up to another text message from his father. The text message, delivered at 2:10 a.m., read, "Life is a journey of self-discovery. What you learn about yourself will enlighten you more than what you learn about others." Nader promised himself to give his father a call after he was done with his eight o'clock class.

Nader was standing in front of his class, engaging a student in a philosophical debate about whether a certain scripture that spoke of a scientific fact, which was later validated by modern science, was a coincidence, when he was interrupted by the dean's assistant.

"Dr. el-Shafique, I am sorry to interrupt, but you have an urgent call in the office." Nader excused himself and followed the assistant to the dean's office.

"Hello?"

"Nader, it is your brother, Mustafa. I have some bad news. Baba passed away last night in his sleep. I am taking the first flight back to Palestine to make arrangements. Are you able to come?"

Nader was overwhelmed with grief and had to hold the tears back. He somberly replied, "I will be there."

He proceeded to the dean's office and asked for permission to leave for a few days to attend his father's funeral. Permission was granted. He was on the first flight the next morning to Palestine.

9 The Funeral

The flight to Palestine was thirteen hours. Nader could not bring himself to sleep. The memories of his father were flooding his brain: the tender love of his father as he was growing up, his boundless patience even when Nader was impertinent and rebellious, his intelligence and quiet wisdom. Nader missed him already and longed for his voice and embrace. He felt emptiness in his heart and regret for the time he had lost not being in his father's presence. He wanted to feel his father again, when he remembered all the texts he had received from his father that were saved on his phone. He opened his phone and began to read all of them from the beginning, remembering his state of mind when he received them. It struck him that, although the two of them were not always physically together, his father was always with him in spirit. That thought brought Nader comfort as he knew that his connection with his father was not of the physical world and that he would always be with him, even in death.

Although the flight had taken thirteen hours, it seemed to Nader as if it took only a few hours. He was so lost in his thoughts that he had lost track of time. The seat belt sign was turned on as the flight attendant announced, "We will be landing in fifteen minutes." It took awhile to disembark the plane and proceed to the security line.

The Israeli officer at the security desk was devoid of any expression.

He asked Nader for his passport and entry documentation. He looked at his computer screen and back at Nader a few times. On the screen, Nader's picture, profile, family affiliation, and history of entry and departure from Israel was listed in full detail. The officer looked back at Nader again, this time with a long and intimidating stare, and asked, "What is the purpose of your visit?"

"To attend my father's funeral."

"How long are you staying?"

"A few days. A week at the most."

"Do you have anything in your bags to declare?"

"No."

"Okay, Mr. el-Shafique, please step to the side."

Nader complied, and within a few seconds, two armed officers had surrounded him and escorted him to a private room. He was strip-searched, and his bags were relieved of all their contents, dumped on a table unceremoniously. After being interrogated for a few hours, Nader was allowed to leave. He spent a few minutes repacking his bag and left the airport feeling violated.

Nader hailed a cab and directed the driver to take him to his father's house. He sat quietly during the ride, not exchanging conversation with the driver, just taking in the view. As he approached his town, he saw that the streets looked the same as the last time he had visited, except there was that feeling of hopelessness that permeated the air. He had the same feeling every time he came back, like a dark cloud that never dissipates. But people were going on with their lives, just trying to survive for another day. There were the coffee shops packed with young and old unemployed men playing backgammon and cards and smoking hookahs. There were the shops peddling their sparse inventory. Somehow these people found joy in the simplest of things, if only to find a reason to go on for another day.

When Nader arrived at his father's house, he saw droves of people waiting to pay their respects. He exited the cab and proceeded to the house, where he was welcomed by his community with hugs, kisses, consoling words for his loss, and declarations of their love for his father. He politely thanked them as he moved his way into house, but he couldn't help but think, *That is a life well lived. To have touched so many people's lives, and to have left a legacy of love and kindness, must be the greatest wealth a person can ever hope for.*

Upon entering the house, Nader saw his brother, Mustafa, sitting in the living room, engaged in conversation with some of the community leaders from the village. Next to Mustafa sat his wife Sarah and their two children, whom Nader had not seen in a few years. Next to them sat a blond man wearing his hair long with piercing blue eyes and sharply defined features. He looked like an oddity among the mostly brown eyes, dark hair, and olive complexions that described every other person in the room. Nader recognized those features right away, the same angelic face that he remembered so well from his childhood. It was Addis.

Mustafa stood up, grabbed his brother in a tight embrace, and kissed him on both cheeks. Nader turned to Sarah and kissed her on both cheeks as well. He immediately bent down to hug the children, asking, "Do you guys remember me?"

"Yes, you're Uncle Nader."

"Well, I got some presents for you guys, but I must give them to you later. Is that okay?"

They looked at their mother as she nodded, and they immediately replied, "Okay."

Nader stood up; he was now facing Addis. Sarah took the opportunity to reintroduce Addis.

"Nader, do you remember my brother Addis?"

"How could I forget? He is the one who saved my behind from getting a whooping in the schoolyard!"

Addis extended his hand and shook Nader's hand. He asked, "How are you, Nader? It has been a long time!"

"It has. I've been fine, and you have not changed at all."

"Just a little older and hopefully a little wiser."

Nader smiled. "I'm not surprised. Wisdom always came easy to you. I have been reading a lot about you!"

"And I about you. I look forward to catching up."

Mustafa interrupted, saying, "You guys will have plenty of time to catch up. Addis is staying with us for the next couple of days. But right now we need to discuss making arrangements for Baba's funeral and settling his personal affairs." Their guests took that as a hint to say their goodbyes with the understanding that they would meet again for the Isha prayer that evening at the mosque. It seemed that the incoming imam, the community leaders, and family friends had made the most of the arrangements in accordance with their father's wishes.

The imam had wanted to be buried immediately after the arrival of his children as dictated by Islam. He wanted to be buried in a plot next to his beloved wife, Ahab, immediately after the Janazah (funeral) prayer with no fanfare.

After the guests had left, it was just Mustafa, Sarah, the kids, Addis, and Nader sitting in the living room, the same living room they all had been in together the last time, when the rabbi, Sarah, and Addis had been invited for Eid al-Fitr (breaking of fast) during Ramadan. The room had not changed much, except now the furniture was beginning to fray and fade from usage and the passing of time. Mustafa was silent for a few minutes as he looked around the room. A flood of memories of his father came streaming in. He was overwhelmed with grief and began sobbing uncontrollably, declaring, "I loved that man." Sarah quickly cuddled him and began to console him.

Nader was holding back the tears as his throat was tightening up and he was progressively losing his ability to breathe. He noticed how disturbed the children were becoming by seeing their father break down and cry in front of them. It was the first time they'd ever seen their father cry. To them, he'd always been strong and reliable, and that display of emotion scared them. Nader quickly distracted them, saying, "Hey, guys, let's go open my bag and see what I got you." Nader went to his bags, which had been hastily placed at the entrance of the house when he first came in. "I think they are in this one." The children were brimming with expectation, as were the other spectators in the room, who seemed for a second to have gotten caught up in the excitement as well. Nader opened his bag and pulled two boxes out. He handed a box to each of the children with their respective names on the tags.

The first to open his box was Moshe, named after his grandfather, the father of Sarah and Addis. Then Ahab, named after her grandmother, the mother of Mustafa and Nader, opened hers. Early in their marriage, Mustafa and Sarah had decided that if their first child was a boy, they would name him after Sarah's father, and if it was a girl, they would name her after Mustafa's mother.

Moshe quickly pulled the contents out, unwrapped the item, and stared at it for a moment before crying out, "Wow, it is a robot dog!"

Ahab did the same. Her dog was white instead of black. They both turned their dogs sideways, up, and down, trying to figure how they worked. Mustafa, Sarah, and Addis were looking on curiously, waiting for the toy to come alive. Nader explained, "These are robodogs developed by an MIT student. They are only available at the university bookstore. The dogs are trainable, but when you first turn them on, you must speak to them so they will recognize your voice and only obey your command."

Moshe turned his dog on and announced, "This your master, Moshe." The dog barked in conformation. Ahab followed suit and received the same response from her white dog.

Nader explained further, "These are very smart dogs. All you have to do is teach them something once, like sit. Give the command a name, and after that they will obey your command every time you ask." Moshe's and Ahab's faces lit up as they both turned around and thanked their uncle. Nader handed them the manual and challenged them, "Okay, guys, let's see who will have the better-trained dog." The kids took him up on the challenge, each going to a separate place to work on the task at hand. Nader turned around to face the adults and excused himself. "If you don't mind, guys, I'm going to rest for a few minutes before we go to the mosque."

"Of course," replied Mustafa. "I think we all will do the same. It's been a long day."

Nader grabbed his bags and proceeded to his old room. On the way, he passed his father's room and looked in. Still on the nightstand stood the picture of his father and mother, lovingly smiling at each other. All the tightly packed emotion that he successfully had kept in the recesses of his heart and mind began to bubble up as tears began streaming down his cheeks.

After a short rest, they all gathered in the dining area, where Sarah had put out some of the dishes brought to the house by friends of the imam. The children were still being entertained by their new toys, while Mustafa and Nader were rushing through their meal.

Addis politely asked, "Do you mind if I accompany you to the mosque?"

Mustafa quickly responded, "I could not think of a greater honor. And thank you for taking time from your busy schedule and traveling all the way here to pay your respects."

"I loved your father. He reminded me so much of my own. They were two beautiful souls who touched me deeply."

The three of them proceeded to the mosque, while Sarah stayed back with the children. The mosque had a respectful number of people in attendance, mainly close friends and family members of the imam and regular worshippers. Mustafa and Nader went to the front row behind the new imam. Addis choose an inconspicuous spot at the back of the mosque to sit and pay his respects in his own way. One of the parishioners made the call for prayer, followed by the new imam leading the rest of the parishioners in prayer. Addis sat quietly, closed his eyes, and listened to the sound of the Koran being recited and the rhythm of the synchronized movement of the worshippers kneeling, prostrating, and standing up. After the Isha prayer was completed, all the parishioners sat on the carpeted floor quietly, and the imam began to deliver a hypnotic and rhythmic recitation of suras (verses) from the Koran. Addis very attentively listened to the sound with closed eyes as his mind began to wander into a visual realm full of beautiful geometrical figures and mathematical equations. There was rhythmic order and balance that conjured a feeling of beauty and peace, not that much different from when he had gazed at far galaxies from some of the most famous observatories around the world. He could not help but wonder, *The laws of physics are everywhere, even in religion.*

After the service, the three of them walked the short distance back from the mosque to the imam's house. Sarah and the kids were already in bed, but Sarah had left some Middle Eastern cookies out on the dining room table for them. Addis and Nader decided to indulge their sweet tooths, but Mustafa was exhausted, so he retired to his father's bedroom.

Nader and Addis took the opportunity to catch up on their personal and professional lives since they'd seen each other last. They had had mutual admiration and a quiet unspoken fondness for each other since the days when they were schoolmates. Nader had been aware of Addis's work on the Large Hadron Collider (LHC) at CERN and was very curious about the latest developments and whether they were any closer to discovering the ever-elusive phantom particle. Addis had dedicated his professional career and research, after completing his PhD in astrophysics, to working on the particle accelerator, labeled Large Hadron Collider (LHC), one of the most complex machines ever created. Indeed, it was the world's largest particle accelerator, buried 328 feet (100 meters) under the French and Swiss countryside with a 17-mile (27 km) circumference.

Addis explained that as of late, he had been working exclusively on a miniaturized version of the LHC. Although he had been collaborating with other physicists working on the LHC project, he had been operating independently with the help of several PhD research students. The funding for the project had appeared from nowhere a few years ago, and the benefactor wanted to remain anonymous. Every year, Addis had to provide a detailed report on his progress, and in turn he received a specific mandate with certain milestones that he had to reach, along with a check for five million euros.

Nader asked, "And you are not curious about where the money is coming from?"

"I am, but I am not bucking the system. As long as I'm able to continue with the research."

"Are you prohibited from sharing your findings with the world?"

"Yeah, that is the rub. I signed a confidentiality agreement, but I stipulated a five-year noncompete after the funding stops. You cannot fault, however, someone who is spending all this capital for wanting to profit from their investment."

"I guess not!"

"By the way, I am coming to Boston in a few weeks for a symposium at MIT. Are you available to get together?"

"I would love to. It will give me the opportunity to take you around and show you Boston."

"That would be great. It has been great seeing you, Nader, but now I think I will call it a night."

"Good night."

Early the next day, Mustafa, Nader, and Addis awoke to the smell of eggs and freshly baked pita bread. The local baker and other merchants had sent their delivery boys with care packages, along with condolences to the beloved imam's family. Sarah was in the kitchen organizing breakfast, while Ahab and Moshe were arguing over which one of their robodogs was smarter. Ahab had spent the night before teaching her dog all different commands, like sitting and lying down, while Moshe had been outside playing soccer with the neighborhood kids. He was jealous of Ahab's white dog obedience training compared to his black dog, Ahab made sure to take the opportunity to tease Moshe by calling his dog stupid and a dummy.

Sarah was visibly irritated by the kids' behavior. The men seemed slightly amused by it; it reminded them of their own sibling rivalry growing up. Addis stepped in and suggested to both Ahab and Moshe, "What if we make both dogs smarter? Would you like that?"

Both kids nodded in agreement. Addis opened his laptop and connected it to the black dog first.

"You see, it is a simple artificial intelligence program. If we tweak it a little bit, the dogs will be able to learn from each other and will act like a pack."

Addis downloaded the software to his laptop and, with a few strokes, changed the code. Then he reloaded the software into each of the dogs. Now, with every command Ahab gave to her white dog, the black dog was able to replicate the behavior—and there was peace again in the room. The kids thanked their uncle Addis, and the adults gave him a look of gratitude and amazement. After breakfast, they all went back to the mosque for the Janazah prayer.

The exterior of the mosque was packed with mourners standing shoulder to shoulder with their prayer rugs placed on the bare ground. The call for prayer bellowed from the loudspeakers mounted outside the mosque. The imam began the prayer, and the hundreds of mourners echoed in one voice "Amien" after the recital of the verse from al-F tihah. They stood up and prostrated with every proclamation by the imam of "Allah akbar" (God is great). The hundreds of men and women moved in perfect synchronicity. This sea of humanity resembled the ripples on a pond gyrating from the gusting of an invisible wind.

Addis stood in the back, praying in Hebrew as he'd been taught by his father the rabbi during the many funeral services held at his synagogue. After the prayer, the coffin of the imam was hoisted on the shoulders of Mustafa, and Nader and several of the imam's closest friends. Mustafa waved Addis to come and join them, and he enthusiastically complied. Nader, creating some space in front of him for Addis to join, said, "Thank you."

Addis humbly replied, "I can't think of a greater honor."

The imam's modest casket was carried to the gravesite, followed by a procession of hundreds of mourners. The imam's casket was lowered into his grave, which had been dug previously, while the new imam and every man, woman, and child in the crowd recited al-F tihah. Mustafa grabbed a shovel and was the first to move the piled earth on the side of the grave over his father's casket. Tears were streaming down his face. He handed the shovel to Nader, who did the same. Next it was Addis's turn. He stood before Nader with a look as if to ask, *Is it okay?* Nader nodded and handed him the shovel. There was not a single dry eye in the crowd as they each grabbed a handful of dirt and lovingly threw it over the casket. The crowd began to disperse as they paid their final respects and condolences to the family.

The next day, Nader and Addis were packing their bags for their respective flights back home that afternoon. Mustafa, Sarah, and the children were staying for an additional few days, in order for Mustafa to finalize the affairs of his father. Sarah had made some sandwiches and tea for Addis and Nader before their trip. The kids and their father and mother were waiting patiently at the dining room table when both Nader and Addis emerged from their rooms with their packed bags. The kids quickly ran to their uncles and cried, "We don't want you to leave! Can't you stay a little longer?"

They both bent down and hugged the kids. Nader said, "We both are going to come and see you soon in Munich." They both sat at the table and, after thanking Sarah, began to consume the warm tea and delicious sandwiches that she had prepared for them.

Mustafa looked at Nader and declared, "Father did not leave very much except for the house and some personal items. He wanted to donate the house and its belongings to the mosque, to be used as an orphanage. If there is anything of our father's belongings you wanted to take, please go ahead. I will take care of everything else."

"The only thing I would like to take, if it is okay with you, is the picture of him and Mother that's on the nightstand."

"Please do. What would you like me to do with the small amount of cash that he had?"

"Please give my share to the orphanage."

"Thanks, Nader. Father would like that. I am going to do the same. By the way, he left this package for you with your name on it."

Nader and Addis exchanged hugs and kisses with the kids, Sarah, and Mustafa with the promise that they would all get together over the summer in Munich. There were two cabs waiting for Nader and Addis. Addis wanted to take a detour and visit his father's grave before going to the airport. As they said their goodbyes, Nader insisted on picking Addis up from the airport when he arrived in Boston the following week. Addis graciously accepted before they embraced and each embarked into his own cab.

A few hours later, Nader was sitting in his window seat on the plane. Looking at the Mediterranean Sea from thirty thousand feet, he was thinking about all that had happened in the last few days, when he remembered the package his father had left him. He reached into his backpack, pulled out the package, and opened it. There was box and a note from his father. The note read, "This was your mother's favorite medallion. Although I objected to having a physical depiction of a religious figure [Muslim edicts prohibit the depiction of a religious figure in any physical manner. It is viewed as worshipping an idol], she insisted on having it. I believe the woman in white is a connection between you and your mother, and I hope she will look over you and protect you as I know your beloved mother does. I love you, Son." Nader opened the package. It was a medallion of the Virgin Mary.

10 The Book Signing

The following week, Nader was standing in front of a monitor at Logan Airport, looking at the arrivals schedule from Geneva, Switzerland. Addis's flight had just landed, and he calculated it would probably take him another hour to collect his bags and clear customs. It was early in the morning; he had not had breakfast yet. He stopped at one of the airport's overpriced coffee shops and got himself a muffin and a much-needed cup of coffee. He checked his work email and saw that his research assistant Donna Kramer had sent him an email with a PowerPoint attachment for his presentation to the UN General Council in two weeks. He reviewed the attachment, expecting to find the need for many edits, but to his surprise, her work was impeccable and precisely what he had asked for. He responded to her email, "Thank you. It looks great. Let's schedule a time early next week to discuss. Excellent job." He was impressed with her intellect and her ability to understand complex issues very quickly.

Nader looked at his watch and realized that Addis ought to be done and exiting soon. He proceeded to the roped area outside the international arrivals gate and scanned the crowd to see if he could spot Addis. A few minutes later, Addis exited, carrying a backpack and a small garment bag. His outfit was European casual, and he walked with poise and quiet confidence. Nader had not realized how tall and physically fit Addis was until he saw him from afar. His gait was graceful and sure-footed, like that of a man who had nowhere to go in a hurry but who knew exactly where he was going.

Nader waved his hand to get Addis's attention. Addis instantaneously honed in on Nader and responded in kind. He was clearly happy to see his childhood friend as evidenced by his beaming smile. The formalities between them seeming to have dissipated, they embraced as brothers would do.

"How are you, old friend? It is nice to see you again so soon," uttered Addis.

"The pleasure is mine. I am looking forward to showing you around Boston. Consider me your guide while you're in town."

"I hope I'm not putting you out?"

"Not at all. It will be fun catching up and also remembering old times," Nader said.

They proceeded toward the short-term parking lot where Nader had parked his Camaro SS. As usual, Nader had found the most distant spot to park his car in, away from harm's way. He put the key in and opened the door for Addis, who stood for a few minutes, admiring the car.

"Wow, a classic. I don't see too many of these in Switzerland."

"You want to drive?"

"No, thanks. This beast is too much for me. I am more used to all-electric self-driving smart cars."

They both laughed and continued on their way to Addis's hotel in downtown Boston. During the short ride, Nader informed Addis that he had to go back to MIT that afternoon, but he'd pick him up around 5:00 for dinner.

At 5:00 p.m., Addis emerged from the hotel lobby. Nader was waiting outside with the car running. Addis entered the car. Nader greeted him: "I hope you got some rest?"

"Yeah, thanks. I also caught up on some work."

"I hope you're hungry. I made reservations at my favorite Italian restaurant. It's a little place not too far from here, but the food is great. I hope you like Italian?"

During the drive, Nader inquired, "Do you have any plans after dinner?"

"Not really," answered Addis.

"Great. A friend of mine is a giving a small lecture and doing a book signing at Boston College at eight. I would love it if you could join me. I think you will like her."

"I would love to."

They parked the car in front of the restaurant and proceeded inside. Nader was greeted by the maître d', who happened to be Albanian. "Welcome back, Nader."

"Salaam, Nabeel. How have you been?"

"I have been well. Your usual table for two?"

"Yes, please."

They were seated at Nader's favorite corner table by the window. The maître d' asked, "Can I get you some drinks?"

"Nabeel, this is Addis, a childhood friend who is visiting from Switzerland," Nader said.

"Welcome, Addis, to the States. I know that Nader does not drink, but can I interest you in a glass of my favorite red wine? It's on the house."

"Thank you. That would be wonderful—if it is okay with Nader."

"That's perfectly fine. And, Nabeel, I will have my usual."

"Half cranberry and half seltzer—got it. I will be right back with your drinks and some bread."

Addis began to look at the menu, but Nader did not even bother.

"It seems that you already know what you want," Addis said.

"Yeah, I'm a creature of habit. I always order the garlic soup and veal napolitana, which is to die for."

"That sounds great. I will have the same."

A waiter came back with their drinks and some bread and asked if they were ready to order. Nader gave the order for both of them. While they were sipping their drinks and buttering their bread, Nader looked up at Addis and asked, "Addis, do you remember the day in school when you stepped in and saved my ass from the three kids from the settlement who were jealous because I got accepted to MIT?"

"Yeah, I sure do."

"How did you do that?"

"Do what?"

"When you blocked the big kid's punch, it seemed like you knew exactly what was going to happen before it happened."

"That's a long story, and you might think I'm a little nutty if I tell it to you."

"That's okay, man; I think you are a little nutty already. But that is what makes you, you." They both laughed.

"Well, ever since I can remember, I've had this sixth sense," Addis explained. "I can sense things happening before they happen. At times, I can even sense what people are thinking. And this is the weird part: sometimes I have these thoughts streaming through my head as if someone is speaking to me."

"You are freaking me out."

"No, man, it is the truth. My father knew of this, and when I was a kid, I was really scared of it, but he used to tell me to embrace it and not to be afraid. He used to say that my mind is like an antenna receiving a signal from a realm that most people can't hear. I learned to accept it as I grew older. I've even developed the ability to manage it to some extent."

"What do you mean?"

"I can sense some people's intention, not all. I can see a certain aura around them. For some, it is a positive energy; for others, it is negative; and for some there is a veil that I cannot penetrate."

"Okay, I know you know my next question: What do you see around me?"

"The answer to that question will cost you dinner."

"Hey, I was going to pay for it anyway, so the way I figure it, I'm getting my fortune told for free."

"Okay, you've got such a positive aura that you emit energy rather than withdraw it from others. As a matter of fact, you've got a few guardian angels standing right next to you."

"Really?"

"Yeah. I feel your father, your mother, and even my father around you. They also seem to be asking me to keep an eye on you."

"Okay, big brother, tell everyone that I can take care of myself, thank you very much."

At that moment, the waiter arrived with their dinner. The conversation shifted to Nader and the type of work he was doing for the UN. Nader explained that his role as science and technology advisor had been recently established for the purpose of creating an international protocol for the onslaught of new technologies being developed. "A lot of these technologies do not have any guardrails, and no one has a clear understanding of the long-term social, economic, and political ramifications. My job is to create a Monte Carlo simulation of what might happen and then suggest effective operational policies. So be very nice to me, because your work on the atom collider might fall under my purview."

"In that case, maybe I should be paying for dinner."

"It's going to take a lot more than a dinner for me to be complicit."

"Nader, I have the feeling that you're the kind of man who cannot be bought for any price."

"I take that as compliment. But now I think we need to rush through the dessert in order to make it on time for the lecture." Nader waved at the waiter and asked for the bill. He left the waiter a generous tip, said his goodbyes to Nabeel, and proceeded to the car with Addis.

During the drive to the lecture hall, Addis asked, "So, tell me about your friend."

"Her name is Sacha, and she has her PhD in psychology. She did her dissertation about whether good and evil can be quantifiably measured in human beings. Her book captures her findings. It is titled *Tip of a Needle.*

"Addis, do you remember where that phrase came from?"

"That is a phrase my father used to say often. He we would often tell me, 'The universe is balanced on the tip of a needle. Every action requires a simultaneous reaction of equal force to maintain the balance. Everything we do matters.'"

"Well, one day I was telling Sacha about you and your father, Rabbi Ackerman, and I mentioned that saying. She loved it. She wanted to use it as the title of her book. Your father and mine had all these sayings that they would quote just at the right moment. They were like kindred souls."

"I guess that's why I have this constant visual of them walking together, especially when I'm around you."

"You don't know how happy that makes me feel. The other details about Sacha, I will let you find those out on your own since you have that extrasensory superpower. By the way, she reminds me so much of you. You even look alike."

"I can't wait to meet this woman."

An hour later, they were both sitting in the front row of a two-hundred-person lecture hall. There was a large screen at the back of the stage and a podium with the Boston College logo on it. The presentation was well attended except for a few empty seats at the back of the auditorium. It was an eclectic crowd with a varied dress style and of different ages. They were a culmination of the intellectually curious and the intellectual skeptics, the two clearly distinguished from one another by who was wearing a suit and a tie and who was wearing a T-shirt and jeans.

On the screen there was a picture of the cover of a book titled *Tip of a Needle* with a picture of a circular universe balanced on the tip of a needle. The picture of the title faded, and a stream of pictures depicting good and evil began to appear one after another on the screen. In the background, the sound of *Symphonie fantastique* was being piped in through the auditorium's surround-sound speakers. The lights were dim, and the crowd was getting into the desired mood. The theatrics were starting to have the desired effect, when a spotlight was turned on, pointing at its targeted subject as she appeared stage right. Every eye in the audience followed her graceful steps as she walked with confidence to the podium. On the screen behind her appeared a picture depicting the ancient Chinese symbol of yin and yang.

"Good evening. My name is Dr. Sacha Zimmerman, and today's discussion is about the balance between good and evil, which is the subject of my book *Tip of a Needle*." At that moment Sacha looked in Nader's direction and acknowledged his presence with a smile.

Nader reciprocated in kind, which elicited a response from Addis: "Wow, she is gorgeous."

"And smart," replied Nader.

The scene on the screen changed to a picture of the Hamsa, followed by a picture of the tree of life and a yin and yang version of the star of David.

After pausing for a few seconds to let the audience register these images on a conscious and subconscious level, she spoke: "All the symbols that just appeared before you are religious depictions of the balance between good and evil. Since the beginning of time, human beings have intuitively sensed that there are counterforces that are in a constant struggle to gain dominance, but only when there is a balance or equilibrium between these forces is there order. Only when these forces are kept in check can humanity exist. There is evidence of this struggle for balance throughout our history as *Homo sapiens*. As a matter of fact, I would challenge anyone in this audience to pick a history book about any time in our history, and from any region in the world, and not identify that struggle in every chapter, on every page, and in every paragraph. Religion speaks of it; philosophers and Greek mythology spoke of it; and of course folklore stories and every movie ever made speak of it. The concept of good and evil is intertwined in every part of our history because it is the dark side and light side of who we are, and because every struggle and every conflict is about maintaining the balance. The concept of balance and equilibrium is an integral part of our social, moral, and economic order. Our Judeo-Christian, Islamic, and oriental religions teach us contentment, moderation, and internal balance between our insatiable desire for more, even to the detriment of others and self-sacrifice—even to our own detriment. Even economic theories show that the desired long-term state of equilibrium is a reflection of a stable and healthy economy. However, disequilibrium or economic dislocations usually do not end up well and often result in extreme and painful corrections in order to regain the balance.

"Imagine for a second if there were no such balance. If there were no good, just evil, or if there were no evil, just good, what would the world look like? Would humanity survive either scenario? These are not extreme scenarios; humanity has faced these tipping points before. Think of World War Two and what would have happened if good had not risen to meet evil. Where would humanity be today? I submit that human survivability depends on maintaining that balance. But in the past that balance has been maintained by an invisible force, something in our DNA that causes us to right wrongs but just as often to exploit what is right. However, the state of equilibrium between good and evil is dynamic and is constantly evolving and changing from day to day and from moment to moment. That dynamic is being shaped not only by our propensity for good and evil but also by everything around us. It is the old question: Is it nature or nurture, or is it a combination of both? Of course, the Milgram experiment proved without a doubt that good people can be coerced into committing heinous acts out of fear or out of a desire to appear cooperative—even when acting against their own better judgment and desires."

On the screen behind Sacha appeared several still shots and some cartoons depicting Milgram's experiment. "So, under the right conditions, the balance we spoke about earlier can be tipped in one direction or the other. But often that change is very subtle, and we do not see it coming until it is too late. Often, we are complicit in that change because we are either gullible or silent, or because we want to believe white is black, and black is white, and gray is okay, especially when it fits our self-serving narrative. The tipping point will probably be something that we will not foresee. It is the proverbial bite of the apple! So, the question before us is, how do we monitor that balance that has been the key to our survivability? And how do we stay vigilant when the balance is being disrupted by external and internal forces? Well, imagine for a second if everyone had a gauge, a dashboard if you will, that measures your state of good and evil." In the background appeared a cartoonish figure with a gauge embedded in his forehead, with a needle pointing to the top, and with a green zone to the right labeled "Good" and a red zone to the left labeled "Evil."

"Then, clearly, we would be able to distinguish who is good and who is evil, along with the collective state of equilibrium, and possibly take some preventive measures. Well, that is exactly what my work in this area has done; it has created a dashboard to measure good and evil in individual subjects and collectively in different societies. The physiological markers for these tendencies have been identified in my research and can be quantifiably measured. They are electrochemical markers that have a physical footprint. The most obvious one of them is empathy."

On the screen there was a video of people yawning. People in the audience began to yawn.

"I see a few of you in the audience are yawning. I hope my talk is not putting you to sleep?

"What you have witnessed is an empathetic response to the subjects in the video, which is something that can clearly be observed and measured. There are many other markers that have a direct correlation to a person's current state of balance between good and evil. But to find out more about them, please meet me outside at the book signing table, where I will be more than happy to sell you an autographed copy."

The audience laughed as the lights in the auditorium brightened.

"Thank you very much. I hope to see you all at the signing table. Good night," Sacha concluded.

One gentleman in the back of the auditorium stood up and shouted, "Dr. Zimmerman, are you taking any questions?" The audience turned around to see where the question was emanating from and the presumptuous person who was asking it. It was a tall man sporting a full beard and wearing a baseball cap and dark glasses.

Sacha had to take a step back to return to the podium. She leaned into the microphone and said, "I will be happy to take a few questions." The man in the back was still standing, waiting for his cue to ask his question.

"Sir, please ask your question."

"Doctor, what do you hope to do with this finding? And is there any practical application?"

"Sir, that is a very good question. All that I can say is that I just mine the metal. Whether you turn it into a crown or a handcuff is really your choice.

"I will be happy to entertain any additional questions when we meet at the signing table. Okay, I'll see you there. Good night."

The audience chuckled as they got in to the long line behind the book signing table.

Addis and Nader took their places in the line behind the man with the baseball cap and dark glasses. Nader turned to Addis and asked, "So, what do you think?"

"Wow, she is the full package."

"Impressive, right?"

"Very. How do you know her again?"

"It's a long story. I don't want to bore you with the details."

"My sixth sense is telling me that this story is anything but boring."

"You like her?"

"What is there not to like?" Addis asked.

Nader told him, "Well, she and I are close friends, but at one time we were more than friends."

"And what happened?"

"The path I chose was not a path she wanted to follow."

Addis asked, "Do you still have feelings for her?"

"I do, but I am resigned to the fact that it could never be. She is a dear friend now, and I want nothing but the best for her as she does for me. But you seem to like her."

"I do. I just don't want to be overstepping any boundaries."

"You aren't. Let's ask her to go for coffee after the book signing."

"Oh, that would be lovely," Addis said.

At that point, the man in the baseball cap was at the front of the line addressing Sacha. "Dr. Zimmerman, I really liked your presentation. I look forward to reading your book."

"Thank you for your question. I hope I was not too vague. How would you like me to sign the book?"

"Please make it to Zack Zimmerman."

"Dad, is that you?"

Zack put his finger to his lips, indicating discretion. He had now become a very well-known public figure, and he wanted to maintain his anonymity. "Honey, I just had to come and see your book opening. I am very proud of you. We'll chat after you're done here. By the way, you have a couple of other fans standing behind me who are very anxious to talk to you. We'll speak after you are done."

Sacha was stunned when Nader and Addis stepped up the table.

"Hi, Sacha. I really enjoyed your presentation. You looked great. This is the good friend I told you so much about, Addis."

"Hi, Sacha," Addis said. "It is great to finally meet you. I have to say, Nader's glowing description did not do you justice. I would love to get an autographed copy of your book."

"Hi, Addis. It is wonderful to finally meet you as well. I will be more than happy to sign a book for you. Are you guys hanging around for a while?"

Nader replied, "Of course. Maybe we can grab coffee after you're done here."

"Yeah, that would be lovely."

Both Nader and Addis stepped aside, not too far from where the man in the baseball cap was waiting. He approached them and extended his hand to shake Nader's hand. "Hello, Dr. el Shafique. It's nice to see you gain."

Out of politeness, Nader met the man's hand in a handshake. He responded, "I'm sorry, but I don't believe I've ever had the pleasure."

"Please excuse the silly disguise, but it is getting more and more difficult to have any privacy nowadays. I'm sorry; I'm Zack Zimmerman, Sacha's father."

"Mr. Zimmerman, I didn't recognize you. How are you, sir?"

"I am well, thank you for asking. Please introduce me to your friend."

"Yes, this is Addis Ackerman, a childhood friend from Palestine."

"Hello, Addis. Are you the same Addis Ackerman who is the son of Rabbi Ackerman?"

"Yes, sir."

"I know of you and have been following your career since you left Israel. As a matter of fact, your father was a distant cousin of my father."

"It is a pleasure to meet you, sir. What a small world! I also have been reading a lot about you and, of course, your various companies."

"Don't believe everything you read in the press. You must come and see for yourself."

"I would love to, sir. That would be a wonderful opportunity."

"Great. It's settled. When are you going home?"

"The day after tomorrow, immediately after I'm done with the symposium at MIT."

"I assume you're flying commercial?"

"Yes, sir."

"Cancel it. I'll have my private plane take you back to Switzerland so you can spend the day with us at HQ. I'll have my assistant make all the arrangements. I won't take no for an answer."

Before Addis could answer, Sacha approached them, and everyone's attention was redirected to her. Zack embraced his daughter and quickly apologized: "I'm sorry, honey, to surprise you like this; I wouldn't have missed this for the world, though. Congratulations again. I hope you sell a million copies. I have invited Addis to come to see us at HQ the day after tomorrow, and he has graciously accepted. I will see you both in a few days, but now I really must run."

Zack kissed Sacha and nodded at Addis without ever acknowledging

Nader. Then he quickly exited the room. Addis turned around, looked at Nader, and asked, "What just happened?"

Sacha replied for Nader: "You just met the tsunami I call my father. Let's go get some dessert and coffee; I'm famished. I will just go collect my stuff and be back in a second."

Nader looked at Addis and asked, "What does your crystal ball tell you about this guy?"

"My observations tell me he does not like you, but my crystal ball, as you call it, is absolutely blank."

11 The Encounter

A half hour later, Addis, Sacha, and Nader were sitting at Sacha's favorite café in downtown Boston. She had just ordered a salad and a glass of chardonnay, and both Addis and Nader had ordered a cappuccino. They were sitting at a small round table. Nader was facing Sacha, and Addis was sitting opposite him, so Addis and Sacha were shoulder to shoulder. Nader was struck by the strong resemblance between them. Even some of their mannerisms were similar. The piecing blue eyes, the flowing blond hair, and even the way they tilted their heads when they were being mischievous were the same. Addis looked like the male version of Sacha, and she looked like the female version of him.

Nader sat back and watched the exchange of conversation between them as Sacha quizzed Addis about his work and his life after the death of his father. At one point they both reached for their water glasses, and their hands accidently touched. The reaction was immediate as if their hands were two live electric wires, one positive and one negative, inadvertently touching. Addis instantaneously blushed a beaming red as he tried unsuccessfully to contain his physical reaction. Sacha took notice as she was struggling to contain her own. They both avoided meeting each other's eyes and immediately tried to redirect the conversation toward Nader. Although Nader was welling with feelings of loss, envy, and regret, he generously diffused the awkward moment by asking Sacha how she liked working for her dad. She quickly jumped at the opportunity as Addis tried to regain control of himself.

"Well, it is like working for a mad scientist and a venture capitalist wrapped in one. Of course, his political ambitions add a toxic element to the whole mixture. He is a man on a mission, and the rate of change does not comport with his timetable. He wants everything done yesterday, and he becomes very impatient with the endless bureaucratic quagmires."

"That sounds like a dangerous man to me," proclaimed Nader.

"Not dangerous, just single-minded. That is how he was able to create Leapp Technologies from nothing and make it into the largest tech company in the world. He sees the current world order and our political system as dysfunctional, and he believes he is the man to right the ship."

"How is his presidential exploratory committee going?"

"I believe he is ready to announce his candidacy soon. He has been working on his platform with small a circle of very wealthy and powerful supporters. They launched a few endeavors already that will be their basis for making real change to the current political stalemate. He is just waiting for the right moment to announce."

Addis asked, "Why is he interested in me? I seem to be totally out of his league!"

"He is very interested in your work. He has been working on something really big—top secret—on a need-to-know basis. That kind of thing. I'm not even in the loop. I think your work on the Miniaturized Hadron Collider might have something to do with it."

"I'm flattered, but my work is purely theoretical at this point. All I have after several years of experimentation is a lot of failure."

"I don't know. I guess we'll know when you meet him the day after tomorrow."

Nader chimed in, "Be careful. Zack Zimmerman strikes me as a man who takes no prisoners."

"Thanks, big brother, I will. I am just happy I got to spend a lovely evening with both of you, but now I think I should retire to my hotel. It's been a long day, and I am a little jet-lagged. Nader, you and Sacha can stay and enjoy the rest of your evening. I will take a cab back to the hotel."

"I would not think of it. Sacha's apartment is on the way to your hotel. We will drop her off first, then I'll take you back to the hotel."

Nader asked for the check while Sacha was polishing off her third glass of wine. The warm flow of alcohol just washed over her body; it was well needed after a long and hectic day. Her inhibitions were down slightly, and she felt comfortable enough to lock arms with both Nader and Addis as they walked back to the car. The conversation between them was easy and natural as if they'd been friends all their lives.

Before exiting the car in front of her apartment, Sacha thanked Addis and Nader for coming to her book signing and for a wonderful evening. She reminded Addis that a limousine would be waiting for him outside his hotel lobby at 7:00 a.m. the day after tomorrow to take him to HQ and that his flight back to Switzerland would leave after lunch. She kissed Nader on the cheek and as she exited the front passenger door. Addis exited the back of the car to join Nader up front. For a few moments, he and Sacha were face-to-face, looking at each other, without being observed by Nader's curious eyes. She reached out, kissed him on the cheek, and thanked him for coming, saying how wonderful it was to have met him. Addis reciprocated the cordiality by holding her hand a few seconds longer than necessary, nodding his head, and displaying a bashful boyish smile.

Nader and Addis sat in the car for a few seconds as Sacha entered her apartment building. Once they'd begun to drive, Nader turned to Addis and asked, "How do you like her?"

"She is wonderful—smart, beautiful, and witty. What is there not to like?"

"I noticed a few sparks flying between the two of you. You really like her, don't you?"

"Nader, I know you and she have or had a thing going, and I would never do anything to hurt you. I hope you know that."

"Addis, it's okay. Whatever Sacha and I had as lovers has morphed into a strong friendship. The path I chose was not for her. I have accepted her for who she is, and she has accepted me for who I am. She is the closest thing to family I have in this country, but she has her life to lead, as I have mine. So, old friend, do not feel beholden to me. I just have to warn you, she can be a handful."

"Dude, I don't even know if she likes me."

"I know her; she likes you. You can take that to the bank."

"Are you saying it's okay with you if I ask her out?"

"Sure, it's okay. Plus, I think you will probably get a better reception from her family than the one I got."

Nader dropped Addis in front of his hotel. As they said their goodbyes, Addis invited Nader to come and visit him in Switzerland to see his work. Nader enthusiastically responded, "I would love that, especially since it will be mandated as a part of my UN report."

Nader, watching Addis enter his hotel lobby, immediately picked up his phone and texted Sacha: "You were great tonight. Addis and I were very impressed. I think he likes you a lot. It is wonderful to have my two best friends like each other. Good night, old friend."

Sacha opened the text and responded, "Thanks. You're both very kind." She knew right away that Nader was saying it was okay for her to have feelings for Addis.

Two days later, Addis checked out of his hotel at 7:00 a.m. and met his driver at the lobby. The driver picked up his bags and proceeded outside, where a stretch Mercedes-Benz limousine was waiting with the engine running. The driver opened the door to the back of the limo, and Addis was immediately taken aback by how beautifully appointed the interior was. It had been custom-designed for a person accustomed to having the best of everything and for whom price was never an issue. It was a mobile office with all the comfort and technology that one would ever need.

The driver, after rolling down the tinted glass window that separated the driver from passengers in the back, briefly explained the different gadgets to Addis and informed him that the trip to HQ in upstate New York would take approximately two hours.

Addis sat back and began to interface with the different technologies available to him, but ultimately he decided to relax and take in the view. A few hours later, the driver pulled into a sprawling campus that was well guarded by several manned and unmanned checkpoints and surveillance cameras. The campus was located on the top of a mountain with a 360-degree view of the Adirondacks valley and the surrounding snowcapped mountains. The view was breathtaking, and the main building and the several smaller satellite buildings seemed to organically complement the aesthetics of the landscape. A young woman elegantly dressed in business casual was waiting for Addis at the curb as he exited the limousine.

"Dr. Ackerman, my name is Alex. I am one of Mr. Zimmerman's assistants. Welcome to Leapp Technologies headquarters. I will escort you to Mr. Zimmerman's office. Your luggage will be taken to the helicopter for your departure this afternoon. Please follow me."

Addis followed the assistant into the lobby as she processed him through the security desk that was manned by security guards and the latest in biometric scanners. Addis was taken aback by the sprawling edifice made of honeycomb hexagonal tubular connections and glass. Natural light flooded the interior. The whole structure felt as if it were suspended in midair without the impediment of man-made walls and columns. The inside looked like a botanical garden with waterfalls and a splendid horticultural display of vibrant tropical plants and other foliage. The air felt fresh and natural with the slightest hint of humidity and floral fragrance. There were translucent large glass tubes winding through the structure filled with water, coral, and colorful fish of every kind that seemed to be flying through the air. The place was abuzz with human activity as if they were worker bees diligently going about their daily routines. People were congregating in different pods, engaged in conversations, using handheld electronic devices and hologram displays. There were others walking separately with headgear and glasses who appeared to be talking to themselves.

Addis was caught up in the beauty, the ergonomics, and the display of technology, which was so smartly integrated into the ecosystem. He wondered to himself, *Who wouldn't want to work here?* He was jarred back from his state of awe when the assistant asked him a rhetorical question.

"Impressive place, don't you think?"

"It sure is!"

"I am glad you like it. Please follow me. We are going to take the elevator to Mr. Zimmerman's office."

The elevator was concealed behind a maze of shrubbery that made the ride to the penthouse feel like a scene from the fairy-tale story "Jack and the Beanstalk." The ride to the top floor was almost instantaneous and with no appreciable effect of any g-force. The doors to the elevator opened to a large room with a glass floor and a view of the lower floor. It looked like a NASA mission control center with large screens mounted on the periphery and with more than a hundred young techies sitting or standing behind hologram screens, busy manipulating data feeds. Addis commented, "This has got to be the ultimate glass ceiling," which elicited a laugh and a response from the assistant.

"And as you can imagine, skirts don't do too well up here."

The executive floor had a large conference room with a large mahogany table and plush oversized leather chairs. The whole space was enclosed in glass that could be electronically tinted to provide privacy. The reception area was modernly decorated with tasteful and ergonomically functional furniture. The work space was large enough for the several personal assistants. The floor was adorned with imported rugs from all over the world, and the walls were hung with expensive modern art, which gave the visitor the impression that he was standing in a world-renowned museum of modern art rather than in an office space. Behind the assistants' area stood a door that spanned from ceiling to floor and opened with the push of a button.

The assistant opened the door to Zack's office and invited Addis to make himself comfortable. Addis was immediately taken aback by the view. The office was high above the tree canopy with an unob-structed view of the Adirondacks valley, the surrounding lakes, and the mountain range. It felt as if you were on the top of the world look-ing down upon humanity. The assistant briefly interrupted, asking, "Dr. Ackerman, can I interest you in something to drink?"

"No, thank you, I am fine. I think I am just going to sit here and take in this view."

"Well, enjoy, sir. Mr. Zimmerman will be with you shortly."

A few minutes later Sacha walked in. Addis immediately stood up to greet her.

"Hi, Addis. It is so wonderful of you to come and visit. I didn't know if you were going to change your mind and not come."

She kissed him on the cheek, and Addis again felt the same con-nection he had had with her a few days earlier.

"I would not have missed this for the world."

"Well, I'm glad you're here."

Sacha dropped all business formalities and sat next to Addis on the couch, instead of sitting in one of the chairs across the table from him. They were laughing about some of the comments made during their evening together with Nader, when Zack walked in. Zack, im-mediately noticing the familiarity between Sacha and Addis, thought, *That's my girl.*

"Hello, Addis. It is nice of you to come."

"It's my pleasure, sir. It is an impressive place you've got here."

"Thank you. The beauty is not only skin deep. I will have Sacha show you around before your departure and have you kick the tires, as they say."

"I would enjoy that."

"Addis, I know our time is short, so let me cut to the chase. As you are one of the top astrophysicists in the world, I have naturally taken an interest in your work. I became aware of our family connection after I heard of your father's assassination when you were only fifteen years old. Since then, I have kept an eye on you and your sister, Sarah, from afar, just in case you needed my help. I am glad to see that both of you have made it on your own without any assistance. Your work is of great interest to me since we are both attempting to solve the same problem, albeit from a different angle. Sacha's experiments have yielded tremendous insight into how the human body works, especially in the area of kinetic energy and the electrochemical response living organisms have to external and internal stimuli. It appears that living organisms have an infinite capacity to produce organic energy. We have an energy division at Leapp Technologies that has as its sole focus how to control and harness that energy. From what I know of your work on the Miniaturized Hadron Collider, it appears that there is a lot of redundancy in our respective work. So, I would like to suggest joining forces and giving you access to our intellectual and financial capital in order to achieve the desired results. Before you give me your answer, I would like you to take some time to think about it. I am very aware of how fiercely independent you are and that what you do is not necessarily motivated by profit. I want to assure you that our goals are not that much different. And if you do decide to join us, you will be given full independence. As for the profit motive, all I can tell you at this point in my life is that wealth no longer has the utility value it once had. However, making the world a better place does. I hope this point is further validated when the company makes a major announcement in a few weeks."

Zack paused for a few seconds, allowing Addis to respond.

"Sir, that is a very tempting offer. And thank you for keeping a watchful eye over me and my sister during a very difficult time. I would like to take you up on your suggestion of taking some time to give your offer some serious thought."

"That is wise. In the meantime, I just had an idea that I hope is okay with you and Sacha. If it is okay with both of you, I would like to suggest that Sacha join you on your trip back to Switzerland and possibly take a tour of your facility to see how best we can accommodate your needs, in case you decide to join us."

Addis and Sacha were both stunned. They felt too awkward to do or say anything to refuse the suggestion. Deep inside they both welcomed the idea of spending some more time with each other, and Zack knew it. Zack didn't give them the chance to respond. He quickly said, "Well, that's settled. However, now, unfortunately, I must put out a few fires. Addis, I hope you enjoy the tour of our campus. If there is anything you need, please let my assistant know. Both of you, have a great trip. Sacha, I will see you in a few days." Zack extended his hand to bid Addis goodbye. Addis responded in kind and thanked him.

As Addis and Sacha were walking out the door, Sacha excused herself. "Addis, can you give me a few seconds?"

"Sure. I'll wait for you outside."

Once the door had closed, Sacha turned around and looked at her father. Pointedly, she asked, "What was that all about?"

"What? I thought it was an excellent idea. You get a couple of days off and help us out in case he agrees to join the company. Plus, he seems like a very charming fellow."

"I am not your girl for hire. Don't ever put me in this position again." She turned around and stormed out of the office.

When Sacha emerged from the office, Addis looked at her and asked, "Is everything okay?"

"Yes, everything is great. I just had to work out a few logistics with Zack. Let me take you on that tour, then we can have lunch on the plane."

"Okay. You lead, and I'll follow."

Sacha turned around. She looked at Addis and said, "You don't seem to be the kind who likes to be led."

"I can always make an exception."

She smiled at him, picked up her phone, and called her assistant. "I'm going on a trip for a few days. Please pack a bag for me. Casual clothing is fine." Once she'd hung up, she grabbed Addis by the forearm and said, "Okay, let's go spend some of the company's money."

Right after the door to his office had closed, Zack called his assistant and directed her to ask Tom to come to his office right away. A few minutes later, the chief financial officer walked into Zack's office.

"Tom, please grab a seat."

"Good morning, Zack. Is everything okay?"

"Everything is fine. Tom, you know the research grant that we provide anonymously to Addis Ackerman for his research on the Miniaturized Hadron Collider project?"

"Yes. What about it?"

"When is the funding due?"

"I will check with my staff, but I believe his request has been submitted for this year's funding. And my staff is preparing the paperwork for your approval."

"Deny it."

"May I ask why? His work has been yielding some interesting results, and our scientists have been able to decipher from his annual submissions some interesting clues."

"Let's just say that I want to motivate him to make a certain decision sooner rather than later. Give him a few weeks before you send the denial letter. State as the reason lack of funding."

"Okay, Zack, will do."

"Tom, make sure you bury any information about this endeavor. I don't want any of this to leak out."

12 The Tour

After the tour of the complex, Sacha and Addis drove a golf cart to a helipad located on the outskirts of the complex. There were two Sikorsky helicopters parked on the pad. One had its engine running, and the other was all black with no specific markings, sitting idly. Sacha pointed to the black helicopter and commented, "This is how Zack drives himself to work every day. It even has a coffee cup holder."

Addis asked, "Where does he park this thing?"

"On the roof of either his high-rise building in Manhattan or his estate in Long Island."

"He seems to like to be on top of the world."

"You can say that again!"

Sacha and Addis climbed into the helicopter, where their bags already had been loaded and tucked away in a separate compartment. The ride to the private airport took less than five minutes. Addis wished it had taken longer; this was his first time in a helicopter, and the speed rush and the view from ten thousand feet was breathtaking.

The helicopter landed next to a Bombardier Global Express jet waiting on the tarmac with its engines roaring. Sacha and Addis climbed onto the jet as a male attendant brought their bags from the helicopter. The inside of the jet was plush with twelve oversized all-white leather chairs that could swivel in order to create multiple seating arrangements. The two front seats already had been arranged by the hostess to receive her two important passengers. The hostess greeted Sacha and Addis as they entered the airplane. Showing them to their designated seats, she asked her guests if they would be interested in a drink. Sacha replied first: "Joyce, I will have my usual."

"And what can I get for you, Mr. Ackerman?"

"I will have whatever Ms. Zimmerman is having."

"Absolutely. I will be right back with your drinks."

The male attendant closed the door to the airplane. Immediately afterward, the jet began to taxi onto the runway. The pilot got on the intercom and announced, "Ms. Zimmerman, we're clear for takeoff. Would you like to take 'er up?"

Sacha stood up and walked through the open door to the cockpit. She assumed her seat in the pilot's chair, put her headset on, and announced to the air traffic controller, "This is flight Bravo–Victor–5–7–9 requesting permission for takeoff."

The response came immediately: "Flight Bravo–Victor–5–7–9, permission granted." Sacha pushed the throttle, and the engines came to life as the jet raced down the runway. The takeoff was as smooth as any Addis had experienced. The jet climbed to thirty thousand feet, when Sacha relinquished control back to the pilot. "Sam, you take it from here. I'm going to entertain our guest." Addis looked in awe and wondered, *Is there anything this woman can't do?* Sacha returned to her seat, facing Addis. She took her shoes off and asked, "I hope I didn't make you too nervous?"

"That was very impressive. Is there anything you can't do?"

"I can't cook to save my life."

"Well, that I can do. Maybe I will get the opportunity to cook for you sometime."

"I would love that."

Joyce was back with a vintage bottle of Dom Pérignon champagne, two glasses, and hors d'oeuvres. She immediately announced, "Lunch will be served shortly. Is there anything else I can get for you?"

Both Addis and Sacha responded, "Thank you, Joy. We're fine."

Joyce quickly disappeared behind a partitioned space in the back of the plane, giving her guests their privacy. Sacha poured the champagne into both their glasses, grabbed a piece of hors d'oeuvre, and sat back in her chair with her legs folded under her.

Addis grabbed his glass, took a sip of his champagne, looked at Sacha, and stated, "This has definitely been an interesting day so far, but somehow I get the strong feeling that being around you is never dull."

"Is this one of your pickup lines, Addis?"

"Frankly, I never mastered that skill. My life, so far, has always revolved around my studies and work."

"You mean to tell me that a handsome, smart, and charming man like yourself doesn't have a significant other?"

"Well, thank you for those kind words, but no, I don't have a significant—or, for that matter, not even an insignificant—other."

"Well, we'll have to do something about that."

"Ms. Zimmerman, is this one of your pickup lines?"

"Not at all. I have a lot of single friends whom I can introduce you to."

"Thanks for the offer, but I always had the feeling that my significant other, as you call them, would be someone I'm destined to meet, and it will be something that is totally out of my control."

"You're a romantic who believes in destiny. I like that. Nader told me about your sixth sense. So, what do you think of my father?"

"Your father is an enigma. There is a veil around him that is difficult to penetrate, but I feel that there are conflicting energies around him that are in constant struggle with each other."

"How about me?"

"You're an old soul. I have the uncanny feeling that I knew you from before. Like I knew you in a previous life."

"Now that is definitely a pickup line."

They both laughed. Joyce appeared again with their lunch of miso soup and an assortment of sushi and sashimi. For the next seven hours, until they landed in a private airport outside Geneva,

Switzerland, their conversation revolved around their work and Leapp Technologies' capabilities.

It was two o'clock in the morning; they both had been up for close to twenty-four hours. Sacha asked if it was possible for her to freshen up at Addis's apartment before they visited his lab in the morning since her assistant had neglected to make a hotel reservation. Addis gladly agreed. They hopped into the waiting limousine as the male attendant loaded their luggage into the trunk. The ride to Addis's apartment in a small hamlet outside Geneva took less than an hour. Addis took both their sets of luggage to his upstairs apartment, where opened the door to a functionally decorated space and invited Sacha in. He placed her luggage in the single bedroom. Fearing his action might be interpreted as presumptuous, he quickly explained: "Please make yourself comfortable. I'm sure you are very tired. I will grab a pillow and a blanket and will be right outside on the couch. The bathroom is right there, and anything you need is in this linen closet."

"Thank you," replied Sacha.

Addis grabbed a pillow and a blanket from the closet and exited the room, saying good night as he closed the door. Then he started a fire to warm the living room. He arranged the pillow and blanket on the couch, then undressed down to his boxer shorts. He sat on the couch for a while, watching the fire and replaying in his head the day's events, when the door to the bedroom opened. The glow from the bedroom light shone on her beautifully defined porcelain shoulders. She had a towel wrapped around her hair and another draped just below her arms. Her silhouette, amplified by the light emanating from the bedroom, made her appear as if she were an angelic mirage. She approached Addis slowly as he stood up in complete surprise. Without exchanging words, she stood before him, grabbed his hands, and wrapped them around her waist as she freed both towels. She gently reached in and passionately kissed him on the lips. As her plump breasts met his chest and their bodies tightly embraced, Addis became immediately aroused. With his arms tightly holding her, not wanting to let go, he opened his eyes. With an almost apologetic look, he said, "I'm afraid I might disappoint you."

"Addis, I don't think you will ever disappoint me."

"I just don't have a lot of experience making love."

"Am I your first?"

"Yes!"

She smiled at him and gently kissed him again as she slowly removed the last garment between them. She gently sat him on the couch and slowly mounted him. He immediately orgasmed, his body beginning to quiver uncontrollably. She held him tightly while stroking his hair and kissing every part of his face. He was still inside her when he regained a full erection. This time she guided his rhythm and they moved as one.

Sacha began to feel something unique about being intimately connected to Addis. It felt blissful and spiritual at the same time, unlike anything she had experienced before. As Addis orgasmed again, his body began to quiver more intensely than it had the first time. Sacha held him tightly as if she were protecting the most vulnerable living thing in her life. They both sat blissfully on the couch for a few minutes, quietly holding hands and watching the fire, when Addis turned around, kissed her, gently laid her on the couch, and penetrated her. This time their bodies moved as one, the ebb and flow of their rhythm like a well-choreographed ballet. The intensity of their rhythm and of their breathing was rising simultaneously as they orgasmed at the same time. Both their bodies were quivering intensely as they held each other for the longest time.

Addis stood up and carried Sacha to the bedroom, admiring every contour of her body. Her beauty and the intensity of the feelings he had for her made him ache inside. He felt as if this were a fleeing moment that was too perfect to possibly last.

He softly laid Sacha on his bed as he stood above her, admiring her beauty, her flowing blonde hair, her piercing blue eyes, the perfection of every curve in her body. He lay next to her as she intertwined every part of her body around him, saying, "Do you remember when you said that I'm an old soul and you have the feeling that you knew me from a previous life?"

"Yes."

"I think I know now what you mean."

He kissed her. They both peacefully fell asleep.

In the morning, Sacha woke up to the smell of eggs and coffee emanating from the kitchen. She wrapped the bedsheet around her naked body and walked to the kitchen, finding Addis standing behind the counter with only his boxer shorts on. He greeted her, "Good morning, love." Without responding, she undraped the bedsheet, wrapped it around both of them, and kissed him with the passion of a lover reuniting with a soldier returning from a long war. They were back in bed making love as the eggs and coffee went cold.

As they were having breakfast, Addis asked, "I don't want to be presumptuous, and I'm relatively new to this, but what happened between us, is it the beginning of something? Or is it something that I should be grateful for without any expectations?"

"Addis, all I can tell you is that I never experienced anything like this with any man before. I would love to continue to see you, if you will have me."

"You don't know how happy that makes me. I was afraid I disappointed you."

She stood up and went to sit on his lap. "The only disappointment I have is that I didn't meet you a long time ago." Then she kissed him.

"What about Nader?" he asked.

"I know. I think we should tell him together."

"I think you're right. Do you think he will mind?"

"I know that Nader loves us both. I think he will understand."

13 Hadron Collider Project

Addis and Sacha arrived at the lab in the early afternoon. There were several research assistants scurrying around the lab, diligently setting up another test of the Miniaturized Hadron Collider (MHC). They had been patiently awaiting Addis's return; the anticipation that this test might finally yield the results that they were all hoping for was palpable. The collider was encased in a glass room with video feeds streaming from every direction and appearing on the assistants' computer terminals.

Addis gave the command for the countdown. One of the assistants began the countdown from ten to one. "Ten, nine, eight ..." On the count of one, the machine came to life, emitting a loud screeching sound. Atoms began racing around a circular tube. As their speed increased, so did the sound. The sound, reaching its crescendo, turned into a loud bang, followed by a flicker of light captured in a glass bell jar that only lasted for a few seconds. It was not to be. Another failure. The faces of the assistants visibly displayed their disappointment.

Addis looked at the results on his screen with the objectivity of a well-trained scientist, and declared, "Okay, we're good. Both the duration and intensity were appreciably higher than last time. Please

identify the variables and have them on my desk as soon as possible."
The assistants' focus turned to the task at hand. They began to look
at the string of data being spewed out by the in-house supercomputer.
Addis looked at Sacha and said, "One small step for man, one giant
leap for mankind."

Sacha looked at him with an amused expression and replied,
"Very original."

"I know. Scientists are not known for their poetic creativity."

"I beg to differ!"

Addis turned around, looked at Sacha, and smiled. A PhD research assistant approached the open door to Addis's office and waited
patiently to be invited in. Addis looked up and invited his student to
come in as Sacha looked on.

"Hi, David. What do you have for me?"

"Sorry to bother you, Professor, but there seems to be something
wrong with the recent data we have been receiving about the black hole
in our Milky Way, MS13."

"What seems to be the problem?"

"Well, the gravitational pull and the size of the black hole
both seem to be growing at a faster rate than any of our previous
measurements."

"Let me look at the data."

Addis looked at the data feed. He considered the different itera-
tions before he spoke.

"This can't possibly be right. There must be something wrong
with the calculations. David, please check the program and calculations again. It's most probably a programming error."

"Okay, Professor, thanks. Will do."

Sacha's curiosity was piqued by the conversation between Addis
and his student. She asked Addis, "What was that all about?"

"Well, David is an astrophysics PhD candidate who also helps our
research team. In turn, I give him access to our supercomputer and
help him with his thesis."

"He seemed genuinely scared by his finding."

"I would be scared as well if it weren't highly improbable."

A few minutes later, Addis was startled by the sound of Sacha's voice repeatedly saying his name and tightly holding his hand.

"Addis, are you okay?"

"Hi. I'm fine. What happened?"

"I don't know. You seem to have been transported to some distant place. Your eyes were open, but you were looking past me as if I were not there. You scared me."

"I had a vision."

"What vision?"

"I initially saw absolute darkness. Then two lights appeared from nowhere, then a third. The energy between them was disturbing. When the three lights touched, there was a burst of energy that was blinding. Then I started hearing you calling my name."

"Was this what Nader was talking about when he said you have a sixth sense?"

"I guess. I've had these visions ever since I was a child. Something always triggers it. I think it was the discussion about the black hole."

"So, what does that make of my chances of cheating on you and getting away with it?"

"Hopefully we will never have to find out."

They both laughed. She kissed him. Then he looked at her watch and apologetically said, "Wow, I wish we could spend more time together, but I really have to get back. Do you think you can spare some time and take a ride with me back to the airport?"

"I wouldn't miss it for the world."

Sacha got out her highly secure corporate satellite phone and called the pilot. "Jim, please get the plane ready for takeoff. I will be at the airport in an hour."

Sacha and Addis opted to take Addis's car to the airport, an all-electric smart car that was barely big enough to accommodate two passengers and her luggage. Sacha didn't mind; she just wanted to spend more private time with Addis. And the car matched his eccentric personality, which she loved. The confined space in the car suited Sacha and Addis just fine; they were shoulder to shoulder and held hands for the whole ride back to the airport. She felt closer to him than she had to any other human being in her life. They felt genuine and pure love for each other, which made their inevitable separation unbearable. They wished they could run away together to a deserted island untouched by humanity, but the world had its demands on them, and that fact was unescapable.

At the airport, Addis handed Sacha's bags to the male attendant waiting at the foot of the airplane stairs. Then he turned to Sacha and said, "I will miss you, love. When can I see you again?"

"Soon. How about next weekend, dinner in Paris? I will make all the arrangements."

"I would love that. This will be the longest week of my life."

Sacha embraced him and kissed him passionately, not wanting to let go of the moment. Addis stood at the tarmac as he watched her climb the stairs to the airplane. At the top of the stairs, she turned around and threw him a kiss before entering the plane. The stairs coiled back into the plane, and the door closed. Addis felt as if a piece of his heart had been ripped out. He got back in his car, drove a safe distance from the jet, and parked, not wanting to miss a moment of seeing her depart, as if hoping that the jet would stop taxiing down the runway, the door would open, and she would disembark, running back to him.

The jet took flight. He sat in his car for a few minutes, trying to bring his emotions under control.

14 The Presentation

Donna Kramer arrived for her meeting with Nader a few minutes earlier than scheduled. The door to his office was open. Nader was placing his prayer rug, readying himself for the Fajr (morning) prayer. His back was to the door, facing east in the direction of the Kaaba, the holiest of Muslim sites, toward which all Muslims face when they're fulfilling their obligatory prayers five times a day. Donna stood quietly outside the door, watching with great curiosity. This man whom she sought was an intellectual giant, a man of science who seemed to be in a state of utter and complete humility and submission to an invisible God. It didn't comport with her that this man of science could also be a devout man of religion. She also had a spiritual craving that recently had been in conflict with her love for science and her need for factual validation. It was the reason she had chosen to attend Nader's class Evidence of Science in Scripture. She had been reading a lot about Islam lately, especially after meeting Nader and taking a personal interest in him.

Nader prostrated for the final time and turned his head to the right and then to the left as if he were greeting a would-be worshipper on each side during a group prayer with God's mercy and blessing. He stood up to find Donna waiting patiently outside his office door.

"Ms. Kramer, how long have you been waiting?"

"Not long."

"Please come in. Good morning."

"Good morning, Professor."

"I looked at the presentation you emailed for the UN General Council Science Advisory Board meeting, and frankly it really captures the essence of what I am—what we are—trying to communicate. Your quick grasp of this rather complex issue is really very impressive. We just need to make a few cosmetic changes."

"Thanks, Professor."

"Please call me Nader."

"Okay, Nader. Do you really believe that humanity is doomed if we don't slow down the technological rate of change?"

"What I believe is that diving headfirst from a hundred-foot cliff into a pool of water without knowing how deep the water is, is an act of insanity."

"But is it not that our history on this planet has always been about pushing the inside of the envelope, trying to discover the next distant shore in the hopes of finding riches? Where would we be if the explorers of old hadn't tested their fate by going on voyages whose outcome, and even their own survival, was never ensured?"

"True, but those adventurous types were the canaries in the coal mines. If the canary didn't come back, no one would follow. Today, we're all the canaries."

"I see. Since we're being philosophical, do you mind if I ask you a personal question?"

"How personal?"

"I think it's very personal."

"Go ahead, ask. But I reserve the right not to answer."

"Is this apocalyptical view you have of the future driven by faith or by science?"

"Well, Ms. Kramer—"

"Please call me Donna."

"Well, Donna, that is a great question. The answer is, maybe both. But that is the beauty of combining the two; they change your perspective from a single dimension to a multidimensional view. But now we really have to finish this presentation."

For the next few hours, Nader and Donna worked on the presentation sitting side by side. Their collaborative efforts seemed seamless. They were like a tag team, feeding off each other's thoughts, even to the point of heightening each other's creativity. It was like a two-piece jazz band improvising highly melodic sounds on the fly. From time to time, Nader would catch Donna gazing at him with an endearing look, but he would always look away and avoid any direct eye contact. He couldn't help but feel flattered. He even felt a sense of attraction toward her. After all, she was a very physically attractive young woman, but more importantly, he found her intellectually attractive. The rhythm between them was natural and unencumbered.

After agreeing on the final version for the presentation, they decided to role-play in preparation for the actual presentation before the UN General Council. As hard as Donna tried to stay focused on Nader's delivery, she couldn't help but slip into a daydream of herself in the company of Nader amid several intimate and private settings.

After trying different approaches, they both agreed on the final version of their presentation. Nader graciously thanked Donna for her assistance.

"Donna, you have been of great help to me. I was wondering if you would be interested in joining me for the presentation at the UN?"

"Nader, it would be a great honor."

"Great. I will make the necessary arrangements. In the meantime, you must be starving. Can I interest you in lunch?"

"Sure."

"Well, there is a great café not too far from campus that has great soup and sandwiches. And their lattes are to die for. I'll drive."

On the way to the café, Donna took the liberty of engaging in further conversation.

"Nader, I hope you don't mind, but I'd like to ask you another personal question."

"Sure, but I reserve the same right as before."

"What right is that?"

"Not to answer."

"When I came to your office earlier, I noticed that you were praying. Are you a devout Muslim?"

"I would like to think so, but being devoted to anything is a journey of self-discovery. It's not a final state. Why do you ask?"

"Well, although I'm Jewish by birth," Donna said, "I grew up in an atheist household. Both my parents were very liberal and despised any and all organized religions."

"And you?"

"I have a strong craving for spiritual discovery. That is one of the reasons I took your class."

"One of the reasons? What are the others?" Nader asked.

"I reserve the right not to answer that question."

Nader smiled as he replied, "Fair enough. Have you found what you are looking for?"

"No, but I have been experimenting and reading about a lot of different religions and spiritual practices. But I end up having more questions than answers. I know the answer is there, but it keeps on eluding me. I think when I find it, if I ever find it, it will be so profound and will touch me so deeply that I will have no doubt that it is the right thing for me."

"Well, my late father, peace be upon him, used to say, 'Religion is not the word of man; it's the Word of God that is encoded in every person's soul. Never confuse the two.' If you keep on seeking the truth, the truth will find you."

"I hope so. I have been reading a lot about Islam and the Koran lately since I met you. Will you allow me to ask you about some of the texts and rituals that I found confusing?"

"I will gladly do my best. I just hope that I don't confuse you more."

They parked the car and proceeded to the café. For the next two hours, Donna grilled Nader on different verses of the Koran, asking, "Why do Muslims pray five times a day?" "Why do they fast during the month of Ramadan?" and "Why do Muslim women wear the hijab?" She clearly had done her research. Nader was more than happy to oblige.

As Nader was about to drop her off at campus for her three o'clock class, Donna turned around, looked at him, and said, "I really enjoyed this day, and I learned so much. Thank you for lunch. I just have one final request. Will you teach me how to pray?"

Nader was taken aback by the request, but deep inside, he was intrigued by her intellectual honesty. And he couldn't help but being physically attracted to her in spite of his reluctance to feel that urge.

"Sure, I will be happy to."

"Thanks. I will text you later to see when you're available. Bye."

"Bye."

Nader sat in the car for a few minutes, not knowing how to feel. He was very conflicted about his attraction to Donna and about his conduct as a Muslim and as her professor. In the end, he decided to focus on the work at hand. However, as hard as he tried, he couldn't get her out of his mind.

The sudden ringing of his cell phone jarred him back to reality. He looked at the caller ID. It was Sacha.

"Hi, sunshine. How was your trip?"

"It was great. Is this a good time?" Sacha asked.

"Sure. I have a few hours before my class starts. What's up?"

"I need to talk to you. Are you available for dinner tonight?"

"I will make myself available. Is everything okay?"

"Yes, everything is fine," she responded. "How about your favorite Italian restaurant at eight o'clock?"

At 8:00, Nader was sitting at his favorite corner table, chatting with Nabeel, the maître d', when Sacha walked in. Nader stood up to greet her as Nabeel pulled out the chair adjacent to Nader and warmly welcomed Sacha.

"Hello, Ms. Zimmerman. It's nice seeing you again. Can I get you your usual drink?"

"Yes, Nabeel, that'd be great. And it's nice to see you again. I hope business is doing well?"

"Yes, thanks to God. I will be right back with your drink."

Nader leaned over and kissed Sacha on both cheeks. He stared at her for a second and proclaimed, "You look different!"

"Different, how?"

"There is a glow about you."

"I could say the same about you."

"Well, there is a lot I have to tell you, as I'm sure you have a lot to tell me. Is this about your trip with Addis?"

"Yes, kind of."

"Sacha, it's okay. I noticed the attraction between you the first time you met. I love you both. I couldn't be happier for the two of you."

"Do you really feel that way? Because we were both afraid that you might see it differently."

"Not at all. What you and I once had has evolved into a strong friendship. Now you're like family to me. I wouldn't give up my friendship with you or with Addis for the world."

"I'm so happy to hear you say that. You're my dearest friend. I was so afraid I might lose you."

"Never. You're stuck with me."

She leaned over and kissed him on the cheek, saying, "Well now, let's talk about your glow."

For the next hour as they ate dinner, Nader talked about Donna and his attraction to her, saying that he was very conflicted about many things.

Sacha listened attentively. She responded, "Do you remember once you told me about a text that your father sent you? It went like this: 'Love is the euphoric state that results from mutual satisfaction of needs. Tainted love is the by-product of tainted needs.' That saying always stuck with me. I guess it is the ultimate litmus test. I started to look inward to find out what I really was looking for in a relationship. The contrast of what I thought I needed and what I really needed was disturbing. So, I started to focus on those tainted needs. Thanks to you—you were my compass. Without knowing it, you made me a better person and maybe helped me finally become ready to have a meaningful relationship with some-one like Addis."

"You know the other thing my father used to say? 'Life is a journey of self-discovery. What you learn about yourself will enlighten you more than what you learn about others.'"

"I wish I'd known your father; he sounds like a very kind and wise man."

"He was. I wish I had appreciated him more when I was younger and had spent more time with him."

For the rest of the evening they discussed their work, the presentation to the UN, and some of the more mundane aspects of their lives. Later Nader dropped Sacha off at her apartment and walked her to the door. She reached over, kissed him on both cheeks, and said, "You know I will always love you."

"I know you do. And I also know you know I will always love you."

15 Jeopardy!

It was eight o'clock in the morning. Zack was having a meeting in his office with one of his top engineers. Both Zack and Sanja were nervous about tonight and wanted to make sure they dotted all their *i*'s and crossed all their *t*'s before tonight's event. Sanja knew that their scheme must be executed flawlessly; nothing less would be tolerated by Zack.

"Have you checked the equipment?"

"Yes, Zack. I tested and retested it several times."

"Who else knows about this?"

"Just you and me, no one else."

"Keep it that way. The day after the event, I will announce your dismissal from the company. Immediately afterward, you and your family are to relocate back to India. Make sure none of your travel plans are discussed or prearranged with anyone. You're not to have any discussions with the media afterward. A Swiss account will be opened, and a two-million-dollar deposit will be made in your name. After your six-month sabbatical, I will reinstate you with the company as an outside consultant. All this is predicated on your keeping your mouth shut and never uttering a word to anyone about this, including your family. Is this understood?"

"Yes, sir."

"Good. Good luck tonight. We will chat again in six months."

"Thank you, sir. I will not fail you."

"I'm counting on it."

Sanja proceeded to exit Zack's office. As he was opening the door, Sacha walked in.

"Good morning, Ms. Zimmerman."

"Good morning, Sanja."

Sacha grabbed a seat on the couch as her father quickly closed the electronic file displayed on the virtual screen. "Good morning, honey. You want some coffee?"

"Good morning. No thanks."

"How was your trip to Switzerland?"

"It was great. I got to see Addis's operation. I think we will be able to accommodate him, if he ever decides to join the firm."

"Anything else happen?"

"What do you mean?"

"I mean, how was it on a personal level?"

"Dad, I don't know how many times I have to say this, but my personal life is my own business. I don't appreciate your question."

"In this case, your personal life is becoming intertwined with a key business decision, which gives me the right to ask."

"I don't want to discuss this any further. What was Sanja doing here?"

"Oh, he requested to meet me because he is disgruntled about the strategic direction we're taking with one of his pet projects."

"Which project is that?"

"I'm afraid I can't discuss it at this time, but you will be in the loop soon enough. When is your next meeting with Addis?"

"I might see him next weekend in Paris."

"Great. I can't stress strongly enough how much of an asset he will be to this company if he decides to join us."

"I got that loud and clear."

"Okay. But now I really have to excuse myself. I have so much to take care of this morning. Keep me posted."

"Okay. I will speak to you later."

Sacha left the office feeling as if she'd been put in a very precarious position, between her personal relationship with Addis and the professional demands her father was making on her.

That evening, Zack was sitting in his office with a glass of 150-year-old scotch that cost more than the average salary that one of his rank-and-file workers made in a week. He turned on the hundred-inch monitor embedded in one of his office walls. The screen and sound came alive with the iconic soundtrack of the game show *Jeopardy!* The announcer's voice came on:

"This is *Jeopardy!* Let's meet today's contestants: a compliance officer, Alex Jones, from Denver, Colorado; a patent attorney, Angela Lester, from Chicago, Illinois; and Sanja Gupta, a computer engineer from upstate New York. And now here is the host of *Jeopardy!*, Rex Tridua."

"Thank you, ladies and gentlemen. We have all new but formidable contestants today, so good luck to all. Here we go. Let's look at the categories, shall we, starting with the Sweet Science of Wrestling, followed by Blank of Blank, then a Very Versatile Rule, then Eggnog by Any Other Name, followed by Habitats for Serenity. Sanja, go."

"Blank of Blank for two hundred."

"Because they hunt and feed on other animals, hawks and eagles are classified as these."

Sanja answered, "What are birds of prey?"

Sanja's adrenalin was in a heightened state; his reaction time was instantaneous. The answers to the questions were coming into his head before the host was halfway through the questions. Category after category, Sanja spewed the answers before the two other contestants had had a chance even to process the information. He was executing with the precision of a supercomputer. Every now and then, Sanja would allow one of the other contestants to answer the question, just to make it less obvious what he was doing. With every Daily Double, Sanja wagered his total winnings, doubling his winnings every time.

It was now the final question. The score showed Sanja with $63,900; Alex with $1,400; and Angela with $2,600. The host announced, "International Airports is the topic of today's final question.

"From the name of the world capital it serves, HRE is the three-letter code for the African airport named for her." The *Jeopardy!* theme song began playing as the contestants began to write their answers.

"Alex, you seem to be struggling with this question. And your answer is?"

"No answer!"

"You wagered $1,399, leaving you with only $1."

"Angela, your answer is?"

"Harare, Zimbabwe."

"That is correct. You wagered all $2,600, making your total winnings $5,200."

"Finally, Sanja, you also gave the correct answer, 'Harare, Zimbabwe,' and you wagered the total amount of $63,900, making your total winnings for today a whopping $127,800. Congratulations to all." Again the theme song came on as the host walked over to congratulate the individual contestants.

Zack melted into his leather chair, comfortably drinking his 150-year-old scotch and entertaining a devilish smirk. He had a self-congratulatory thought: *I love it when a plan falls into place.*

The next morning, he turned on the hologram projector in his bedroom and began to manipulate the data feed with a wave of his finger, until he found what he was looking for.

"*Jeopardy!* contestant admits to cheating." Another headline read, "A tech engineer games the game." Yet another read, "A *Jeopardy!* contestant admits to pulling a fast one," and the last he saw said, "Technology one, humanity zero. A software engineer at Leapp Technologies uses a new technology to gain an advantage over other *Jeopardy!* contestants."

Zack clicked on one of the news stories. It read as follows:

Sanja Gupta, a computer engineer employed by Leapp Technologies, admitted to wearing a new tech device that allowed him to receive answers to *Jeopardy!* questions instantaneously, giving him an advantage over other contestants. He voluntarily admitted that fact to *Jeopardy!* producers at the end of the show and forfeited all his winnings. When asked why he'd done it, he indicated that he was disappointed by the company's decision not to commercialize this technology, which he was instrumental in developing, and he wanted to show them the error of their ways. He described the technology as an inconspicuous earpiece that is connected to the World Wide Web through a network of satellites that can decode thought patterns and respond back to the user in a split second. By simply hearing or reading a question, the user is communicating that information to the device through his thought process, and in turn the device searches the Web and communicates the answer back to the user.

Zack shifted to one of the morning shows and listened to the hostess comment on the story as they replayed scenes from last night's *Jeopardy!* episode. One of the commentators proclaimed, "If this technology truly exists, it could be a game changer."

Zack looked at his phone, which he had muted the night before. It had over a hundred calls and messages. He thought, *The game is on. Let them stew for a while before I respond.*

He showered, got dressed, and had a light breakfast before he departed for the office. It was already 10:00 a.m. He normally was in the office by 7:30, but today was different; he wanted to let the suspense build a little longer until it reached its intended climax. He knew the longer he waited, the greater the frenzy and the more the media would have this story on a constant news loop. He looked at his handheld device to see how many hits the story already had, and the number was already in excess of ten million. He looked at his phone again and saw that Sacha already had called him three times and had left him several text messages, which he decided to ignore. As soon as he walked into his office, using the private entrance, his assistant frantically approached him.

"Sir, you have received over a hundred calls this morning. The news media, the board members, and the managing directors are requesting to talk to you. How do you want me to handle them?"

"Sort all the calls alphabetically and send the list to me ASAP. Also, I don't want to be disturbed for the rest of the morning, unless I tell you otherwise—regardless who it is."

"Even your daughter, sir?"

"Even my daughter."

He went into his office and closed the door behind him, waiting impatiently for the list to be compiled. His assistant walked in with the list a few minutes later. He scanned the list and found the two calls he was hoping for. The list contained calls from top investment bankers, wanting to discuss taking his company public; news media executives; marketing companies requesting to place ads on his network of browsers for their top Fortune 500 companies; and members of his political exploratory committee. On the list, too, was a call from *Jeopardy!* executive producers wanting to discuss last night's events, and a call from the executive producers of the news show *60 Minutes*, requesting an interview.

Zack's first call was to the *Jeopardy!* executive producer. "Mr. Wolf, this is Zack Zimmerman returning your call."

"Mr. Zimmerman, thank you for returning my call. I want to discuss with you the events of last night."

"About that. I wanted to personally apologize for the conduct of Mr. Gupta and for any damage it might have caused your network. Mr. Gupta will be dealt with swiftly, and I assure you, we are ready to compensate your network for any damage."

"Frankly, I'm surprised that you and your company are willing to take personal responsibility for this when it was the act of a lone wolf."

'Well, Mr. Gupta has been a longtime loyal employee and has contributed greatly to my organization. However, he was disgruntled about our strategic direction regarding this technology. After all, this was one of his top initiatives at the firm."

"Well, Mr. Gupta was very forthcoming after the show and made no attempt to hide the fact that he had used this technology to gain an edge over the other contestants. He also voluntarily forfeited all his winnings. At the end of the day, the show has gained tremendous free advertising as a by-product of this stunt. People all over the world are replaying footage of the show, trying to see if they can identify the earpiece or any odd tics in Mr. Gupta's performance. Our advertisers couldn't be more pleased.

"Zack, we've decided not to make any formal charges with the authorities. What you do with Mr. Gupta, as far as we are concerned, is purely an internal matter for you and your company."

"Mr. Wolf, I greatly appreciate your decision. I assure you that we will be dealing with this matter swiftly. Good day to you, sir."

"Good day."

Zack sat back in his chair and thought, *That went well.*

His next call was to the producers of *60 Minutes.*

"Mr. Zurzuinski, this is Zack Zimmerman, returning your call."

"Mr. Zimmerman, thank you very much for returning my call. I'm sure you're a very busy man, especially this morning, so I will get to the point. Given last night's events and our knowledge of your political interest in running for the presidency of the United States in the next election, we would like to interview you for one of our upcoming shows."

"If I may ask, how much airtime would this interview get? And how soon will it be televised?"

"Well, because of the great public interest that has been generated by the events of last night, and if we're guaranteed to be the first exclusive interview, we're willing to devote half the show to your interview, and possibly air it as early as next week."

"Mr. Zurzuinski, thank you for your interest. I find the terms of your offer to be acceptable. Please have one of your producers make arrangements with my office with regard to the venue and other logistics. I would also appreciate a list of your questions submitted to my office prior to the interview, and the name of the designated interviewer."

"Mr. Zimmerman, we will be more than happy to do as you ask. I look forward to meeting you in a few days. Have a good day."

Zack hung up the phone, stood up, and walked to the seamless glass wall overlooking the Adirondacks from high above. He felt like the master of the universe.

That evening Sanja informed his young wife of the plan to leave the country as soon as possible. She was reluctant at first, but he assured her that it would be a short-term sabbatical, without elaborating further on his plan with Zack. The following day, he booked two one-way tickets to India, departing the day after that; listed his condominium with a real estate agent; and made arrangements with a moving company to pack his belongings and place them in storage. For the duration of the next day, he and his wife stayed indoors, avoiding the horde of reporters waiting outside their complex.

The company had made arrangements for a private security company with top security clearance to sneak them out of their condominium in the middle of the night and escort them to their flight the next day. Sanja and his wife were both dressed in disguises. They went unrecognized as they embarked the plane and assumed their first-class seats. Sanja sighed in relief only when the jet finally took flight. After a flight lasting longer than fifteen hours, they landed in New Delhi, India. As they were taxiing to the gate, the flight attendant announced, "You are now free to use your electronic devices." Sanja turned on his phone, waited for a few seconds to get a signal, and logged securely into his new Swiss bank account. The first thing to appear on the screen was the balance: $2,000,000. He made sure to count all the zeros a few times before allowing himself to break into a smile.

After several rebuffed attempts to see her father, Sacha finally had been given access to see him. She stormed into Zack's office as he was casually turning away from the screen to face her.

"Hi, honey. How is your day going?"

"How is my day going? That is rich! A better question is, how is yours? What is going on with this whole fiasco with Sanja and *Jeopardy!?*"

"You heard the news."

"Heard the news? It's what everybody is talking about. I'm getting a lot of calls from the media and, more importantly, from employees who are wondering what hell is going on. Frankly, I don't have any answers for them. I'm in the dark as much as they are. What is going on?"

"I'm very sorry about that, honey, but we had to keep any information about this project very close to the vest, in fear of potential leaks."

"Well, I guess that strategy didn't work too well."

"Apparently not."

"So, what is it exactly that we're talking about here, and how is the company intending to use it?"

"It is a wearable device that can be inconspicuously worn inside the ear canal. Using nanotechnology, our scientists and engineers were able to create a device that is connected to the user's internal nervous system and cerebrum, thus allowing it to decode the user's thoughts and communicate back in kind. It is simply a search engine that scans the World Wide Web using very sophisticated algorithms. As of our last test, it was able to produce the right answer 99.9 percent of the time in a matter of seconds. It is also wirelessly connected to the thousands of miniature satellites we have orbiting the earth."

"We have a satellite company?"

"Yes. It's a company that I bought three years ago for this purpose."

"So, let me understand this correctly. By the user's just thinking up a question, the device will pick up on it, search the Web for an answer, and communicate it back to the user?"

"Yes, and it will do it in less than a second."

"That sounds too good to be true. There must be some kind flaw?"

"One, it has a battery life of less than an hour, and we can't figure out how to improve it."

"Wow, that is impressive. But more importantly, why are you being so secretive about this?"

"I have a big announcement to make, which I wanted to make

under the right circumstances. This brings me to another topic that we urgently need to discuss."

"What is that?"

"You know that I have been thinking very seriously about running for the office of president. You also know that I have formed an exploratory committee to formulate a policy agenda and assess my chances of winning based on this platform, the potential contenders, and the current political environment. So far, the feedback has been very positive. It would appear I have a fighting chance of winning. I'm doing this not for the accolades and platitudes, but because I believe I can effect real change in a very tumultuous time. If I'm successful in getting elected in two years, I need to know that I can hand over this company to you to run it, for as long as I'm in office."

"Me?"

"Yes, you. That's why I was never interested in taking this company public. This is a legacy company, and you're my legacy."

"So, the reason for your vote of confidence and the right to run this multibillion-dollar conglomerate is just because I happen to be your kid?"

"You're not just my kid; you're the smartest, most astute woman I know. Plus, we have two years to get you up to speed. But in the meantime, you have to do a lot of growing up to do very quickly."

"This is a lot to think about. This was never on my radar, and frankly, it is a huge responsibility."

"Take your time to think about it. But right now I want you to think about coordinating my interview with *60 Minutes* this upcoming Thursday."

"My goodness, you're full of surprises today."

"I want you to coordinate all the details with my assistant. And no fuck-ups! I want the venue to be at my father's old hunting cabin at Lake Placid. The setting is to be casual, modest, and comfortable. Fireside chat is the look I'm going for. And I want you to be there."

"But that place is very small and modest. The only reason you kept it is that it was the only thing Grandpa left you. I don't think you've been there in years."

"I don't want a display of wealth and opulence, just a salt-of-the-earth type of look."

"Got it. I will take care of it. Salt of the earth. Wow, those are words I would never have chosen to describe you."

"Okay, we're done here. I've got a lot of stuff to take care of. Thank you. And give some serious thought to what we discussed."

16 60 Minutes

The *60 Minutes* crew was scurrying around the cabin, setting up the lighting and cameras, as Sacha micromanaged every detail with the show producers. The oversized stone fireplace was ablaze, emitting a warm and comfortable glow. Zack's chair was placed just right, so the camera shots would capture the extensive wood paneling and bookshelves, stacked with an extensive collection of literary works. She had debated whether to have the gun rack with its expensive collection of rifles, shotguns, and handguns on display or to remove it from the scene altogether. She had decided to leave it in place, minus the handguns. The crew and host were ready for the interview, when Zack walked in wearing jeans, a navy-blue blazer, and a crisp white shirt. He gave Sacha a look of approval and assumed his seat in the modest leather chair adjacent to the fireplace.

The host, Scot Stanley, greeted Zack and signaled to the producer that he was ready. He took another look at his notes before he sat upright, readying himself for the cameras to be turned on. The producer counted backward, "Three, two, one," and waved her hand for the interview to begin.

"Mr. Zimmerman, thank you very much for agreeing to this interview. Let me begin with the question that is obviously on everyone's mind. One of your top engineers has admitted to using a wearable technology that allowed him to gain an advantage over other contestants during a recent *Jeopardy!* contest. Can you tell us more about that?"

"Well, Scot, the ex-employee in question had been employed with our firm since he graduated from college five years ago. He is a very bright individual who has contributed greatly to advancing several initiatives that we're actively pursuing. The technology in question is in the later stages of development, and there was a strategic decision that went contrary to his desire to advance this techware going forward. He used the *Jeopardy!* stunt to validate the market interest in this technology, which frankly he was successful in doing, but our decision remains the same. He has since been dismissed from the company."

"So, what is this technology, and when will it be introduced to the public?"

"All I can say, Scot, is please stay tuned; the firm will be making a major announcement next week that ought to shed greater light on what we intend to do with this technology."

"Well, we will all be anxiously looking forward to that, Mr. Zimmerman."

"Please call me Zack."

"Zack, you have made no secret of your interest in running for political office, and not just any office, but the office of the president of the United Sates. Can you tell us when we can expect a formal announcement with regard to your intentions?"

"Scot, I think now is as good a time as any. I'm formally announcing my candidacy for the presidency of the United States, effective immediately. My campaign will be totally self-funded except for individual donations. Individuals interested in making a donation can go to zzforpresident.com."

"Zack, this begs the question, what is your political affiliation? Are you running as a Democrat or a Republican?"

"Neither. I'm forming a new party called the National Independent Socially Responsible Party, or NSIRP."

"Do you believe forming a new party is a winning strategy?"

"I believe the current two-party system has morphed into something that our founders never intended. The current system is self-serving and self-promoting and has become utterly partisan and dysfunctional. The survivability of one party, or close to 50 percent of the population it represents, oughtn't be based on the ultimate destruction of the other party and the other 50 percent they represent. Vote pandering in order to stay in power shouldn't be the goal of a civil servant. The goal of a civil servant should be to serve our national interest for the sake of all our people at all times."

"That sounds pretty lofty. But what is the specific agenda of this new party?"

"NSIRP will advocate for socially responsible policies that are based on the tenets of free enterprise. These two objectives, I would argue, are not mutually exclusive but compatible. Our goal is to create not only financial wealth, but also emotional and social wealth."

"And how exactly do you do that?"

"Take for example health care. Both parties are using this issue to pander to their constituents, hoping to garner more votes and strengthen their hold on power. Well, clearly that ought not to be the driver. It ought to be, let's identify the problem without all the political noise, then collectively put our heads together and find the right solutions. In fact, that is what my committee has actually done. And it is not based on a bloated bureaucratic government solution that is under the control of a few and that will put our kids and grandkids under a mountain of debt. It is a private market solution. To that end, I have formed an exploratory committee of business leaders, nonprofit organizations, and charitable foundations that together formulated a plan to launch the new nonprofit health exchange. First, the exchange will be operated by businesses that will opt to internalize their cost of health care rather than purchase it from a for-profit health insurance company, thus eliminating the profit motive. This will be a substantial win-win for both the company and its employees. All businesses regardless of size will be invited to join. We believe the large pool of participants will dilute the risk and further reduce the cost. Further, it will allow us to aggressively negotiate medical and pharmaceutical costs.

"Second, we will be working with nonprofit organizations, medical associations, and charitable foundations to launch a nationwide network of free clinics to serve rural and poor areas, and of course the uninsured, free of charge. Third, we will be launching a program similar to the Reserve Officers' Training Corps—ROTC—but for doctors. The program will be funded by private endowments and will provide free medical school education to those willing to serve the poor and needy in our free clinics for five years after graduating."

"What will the government's role in all this be?"

"Simply put, to facilitate these endeavors by removing burdensome regulations, and incentivizing and rewarding organizations that serve a social need."

"As you know, Zack, the issue of income inequality has been one of the issues that many of your opponents have made into the centerpiece of their campaign. What is your solution to this potentially explosive problem?"

"Well, I don't believe that income redistribution or socialist policies is the answer to this problem. This is not a zero-sum game, where the success of one guarantees the failure of another. We all can succeed in varying degrees based on our own individual abilities. Those who peddle that other garbage are only looking to divide us into haves and have-nots in order to gain control of the purse. What I'm interested in is raising the standard of living for all and making poverty a choice, not a predetermined outcome. We have seen millions of examples in this country of people who were able to rise from poverty and create substantial wealth for themselves and their families. In fact, I would argue that the source of most of the wealth in this country started from nothing and was made through hard work and tenacity. I want to cultivate an environment that promotes that type of entrepreneurship, nothing less. I can't think of a better way of achieving that goal than to make our education system the envy of the world.

"I believe the lack of comprehensive education in impoverished areas is the civil rights issue of our time. Again, I'm enlisting the help of the private and nonprofit sectors to create an economically feasible solution to this problem. Companies are struggling to find skilled labor and, in many cases, spend billions of dollars educating, retraining, and retooling their workforce. I'm proposing investing some of those funds at the front end of the problem by creating a charter school system designed to train the workforce of the future. Everyone who graduates with a high school diploma, a bachelor's degree, a master's degree, or a PhD is ultimately looking to use that degree to get a job, but somehow the education system shuts out those who are providing those jobs. It is time to integrate their needs and their strategic plans for the future into our education system. It's time to create a curriculum that is needs-based, a system that demands accountability. But instead of fighting endless political battles to reform the current system, we are creating a parallel choice, especially in the inner cities and the underserved communities, which are caught in this inept system."

"Another very hot issue is global warming and the introduction of new legislation to reduce our carbon footprint. So, to start, do you believe in global warming?"

"With all due respect, Scot, I believe that is the wrong question to ask. Debating this issue only detracts from coming up with a commonsense solution. Let's start with the premise that both sides of this argument are correct, and based on that, let's come up with policies that plan for both contingencies."

"And how do you do that?"

"Again, market-based solutions. Let's create alternatives to old technologies that are contributing to our carbon footprint. The trick is to make these technologies competitive both in price and in functionality. Consumers will make that choice, free of heavy-handed and burdensome regulations that impede economic growth. I would argue that the best antidote to the problem of global warming is economic prosperity. The biggest contributors to global warming are poor countries with a large proportion of their populations struggling just to survive. You can't expect them to have this issue at the top of their priority list. Like the industrial psychologist Maslow implied in his famous theory about the hierarchy of needs, and I paraphrase, the luxury of being altruistic occurs only when all your other basic needs are satisfied."

"In every presidential campaign, we see the debate between Democrats and Republican evolve around the size of government and the tax code. Which camp do you advocate for?"

"Neither," Zack responded. "I'm a federalist who believes the federal government should be tasked with only those things that states cannot do for themselves, like national defense and interstate commerce. The farther the decision is from the person who will be most impacted by it, the less democratic we become as a society. We should be thinking very seriously about decentralizing the federal government and moving a lot of those functions back to the states, including the IRS. I will propose a tax system that taxes the states based on the size of the population and their per capita income rather than taxing the individual. Let the states create their own tax policies that best suit their needs, and let their citizens vote on these tax policies through the ballot box and with their feet. I don't think a lot of these senators and congresspeople will be voting for a lot of these pork belly projects once they realize it will impact their state tax rate directly."

"Another issue that has divided the country is immigration," Scot said. "What will your approach be to this intractable problem?"

"I would say that this problem is analogous to being in a boat that is taking on water, with 50 percent of the occupants arguing about how much water the boat can take on and the other 50 percent fervently trying to the bail the water out. This is insane. The first thing you do is plug the source of the problem. Then you start bailing the water out while you argue about how much water the boat can retain without drowning all the occupants. We have to secure our borders and control the flow of immigrants first. After that we can debate our immigration policies to our hearts' content. I will recommend legislation to make it illegal for any employer to hire an undocumented worker. I also recognize that there is a need for migrant workers that is currently not being met be our indigenous workforce. To that end, I will demand countries of origin such as Mexico and Guatemala to establish employment agencies to process these migrant workers. US employers must first list their unfulfilled positions on a national registry, meeting all required labor laws for three months. If the position remains unfilled, then they're free to list the position with a foreign employment agency. Certain exemptions to our labor laws, such as unemployment, Social Security, and FICA taxes, will be granted; however, these agencies will be responsible for financing their employees' medical insurance plans, paying for background checks, and paying costs of incarceration and repatriation if the employee commits a crime while they're here. If the job is eliminated, the employee will have one month to retain another. Otherwise they have to return to their country of origin. As to the rest of our immigration policies, I believe immigration should be merit based."

"Finally, where do you stand on a woman's right to choose an abortion?"

"This is one issue that has divided our country for too long. This issue shouldn't be politicized or decided by weaponizing our court system. This is a moral decision that ought to be decided by us collectively as a society. I believe in a woman's right to choose and to have control over her own body. However, we as a society have to make a moral decision about the point when a vital fetus becomes a separate entity with its own inalienable rights, including the right to exist, the right not to feel pain, and the right to have the same rights as others, along with the full protection that is granted to all human beings in a civil society. To that end, there will be two initiatives that I will be advocating during my first ninety days in office, if I'm fortunate enough to be elected. One, a public referendum deciding the issue of at what stage of gestation a fetus becomes an independent entity with its own inalienable rights. Let us all openly and honestly debate the science, legality, and morality of this issue and once and for all make it the law of the land without vilifying the other point of view. In addition to that, I will be recommending the passing of a law requiring the biological father to pay child support if the woman decides to have the child.

"The second public referendum will be to institute term limits, limiting senators and congresspeople to two terms in office. Candidates for these offices should be driven by the need to serve their country, not their own self-interests. We've got to eliminate the profit motive that has corrupted so many of these public officials."

"Zack, these are very lofty goals indeed. I'm very confident in saying that you will be facing an unsurmountable hill to climb. What do you think is your chance of winning?"

"All I can say to that question is that people will always surprise you, so stay tuned. I can promise that it will not be boring."

The host ended the interview by extending his hand to shake Zack's hand and wishing him good luck. As the crew began to dismantle their equipment, Zack stood up and walked toward Sacha. She had a smile on her face. He asked her, "How did I do?"

"You looked very presidential. I didn't realize how much thought you have given to all these very difficult issues."

"I have been working on this platform for a while with some of the people you met at my fiftieth birthday party."

"Zack, you never cease to amaze me. You will have the snot kicked out of you, but I wouldn't be surprised if you came up on top. This will be fun to watch."

"Well, thanks for the vote of confidence. I hope you're ready to roll up your sleeves, because I'm going to be heavily depending on you."

"Come again? I didn't know that I was a part of this."

"You're a part of everything I do. You're the only one in the world whom I trust and who gives it to me straight and without equivocation. If I can't lean on you, whom can I lean on? And by the way, thank you for taking care of the setup for the interview. It was perfect."

"Okay, Zack."

17 Paris

Addis arrived at his office early Friday morning. He had a lot of data to analyze from the last test they had run on the MHC the day before. His desk had a stack of letters that he needed to go through before his trip to Paris that afternoon. He couldn't stop thinking about spending the weekend with Sacha. Everything else was just a distraction. He wasn't accustomed to being distracted; he usually was laser focused on his work and research. But thinking about her made him feel complete, more alive than he'd ever felt before. There was even a strange sense of contentment, as if there was nothing else he wanted at this moment except to be with her. That feeling of not longing for anything, not wanting anything except for what he already had, left him with a profound sense of bliss.

He noticed among the pile of letters the official-looking envelope that he had become accustomed to seeing every year at this time. He knew what the envelope contained, a congratulatory letter from the anonymous foundation approving his research grant for the upcoming year and a check for five million euros.

The letter seemed lighter than usual. He opened the envelope, expecting to see the attached check first, but there was no check, only a one-page letter. He unfolded the page, which contained one sentence:

Dear Mr. Ackerman,
     We regret to inform you that we will no longer provide funding for your research.

Best regards.

There was no signature, no address to reply to, no contact information of any kind.

Addis was stunned by the news. It was the last thing he had expected. Receiving his grant annually was a given; he'd never contemplated the possibility of not receiving it. He racked his brain, trying to think of what he had done wrong—after all, his research had been progressing as promised—but he was at a loss for an answer. This news was dampening his mood and his excitement about the weekend with Sacha. He thought about writing back, arguing the merits of his research and asking for further clarification, but the letter he'd just read had a degree of finality to it. He decided to defer on the issue until Monday. After all, he had no other options. He grabbed his bag, got in the car, and embarked on the five-hour ride to Paris. He only wanted to think about the weekend with Sacha, her embrace when he first saw her, their conversations, and of course the intimate hours to come, but the thoughts of the denied grant kept on creeping into his mind.

He waited anxiously at the private airport outside Paris for her plane to arrive. At approximately 5:00 p.m. local time, her private jet touched down. It took the plane a few minutes to taxi to the hangar where Addis was waiting. The door opened, and Sacha emerged carrying her own weekend travel bag. The sight of her made Addis's heart beat faster. She looked very beautiful. He had to do a quick reality check to see if this goddess really belonged to him or if this whole thing was a figment of his imagination. Sacha descended the stairs with the grace of an athlete, without ever taking her eyes off him. As soon as she landed at the foot of the stairs, she dropped her bag and ran to him with a beaming face and a smile. They embraced passionately. She whispered in his ear, "I missed you."

He replied, "Oh God, you have no idea." She laughed and kissed him again.

Sacha had had her assistant reserve a suite at the Hôtel Plaza Athénée for the weekend and a table for dinner this evening at La Grande Cascade. During their half-hour drive to Paris, Addis and Sacha frequently kissed, held hands, and laughed with the familiarity of old lovers and the exuberance of teenage infatuation. For the next two days, they mostly stayed in their suite, enjoying each other's company and shutting the outside world out, except for the occasional walk through the streets of Paris and a quick stop at a local café.

It was now Sunday evening, and they were both dreading the end to this perfect weekend. They decided to have dinner brought to them in their room so they could just spend a quiet evening together. Plus, Sacha wanted to catch the *60 Minutes* broadcast featuring the interview with Zack.

Addis seemed slightly distracted during dinner, which Sacha picked up on very quickly. "What's wrong?" she asked.

"Nothing, really. I just want to enjoy the few hours I have left with you."

"Please tell me. I want you to feel like you can tell me anything at any time. I don't want any secrets, unknowns, or white lies between us. Please tell me."

"Well, I got some bad news on Friday."

"What is it?"

"The funding for my research has been denied, and I have no way of contacting the anonymous donor and arguing my case. I'm screwed."

"Not necessarily!"

"What do you mean?"

"I have a strong recollection that my father offered to fund your research," Sacha reminded him.

"I never gave the offer any serious thought. I just wanted to spend the day with you!"

"Well, you will get to spend more than one day with me, and

I wouldn't have to take an eight-hour plane ride to see you if we're both working in the same place. We could even have lunch together every day."

"As tempting as that sounds, I still have some reservations about your father. I don't know if he is as altruistic as he made himself out to be the last time we met."

"The word *altruistic* doesn't come close to describing Zack. But you and I are a tag team, and I know how to keep him in check. Would you please give it some thought? It would be lovely if we didn't have to have an intercontinental relationship."

He reached out and kissed her, and said, "I will." At that moment, his phone rang. They both had ignored their phones all weekend long, but as the weekend was coming to a close, they were both anxious to find out if there were any fires that they would have to put out.

Addis looked at the caller ID and saw it was Nader. It also showed that he had called two times since Friday. Addis showed the phone to Sacha, asking her, "What do you think?"

"I don't know. I don't think this is about us being here. It would be totally out of character. Give him a call."

Addis opened the missed call notification and clicked on the call icon. After two rings, Nader answered.

"Hey, man, where have you been? I called a few times."

"Sorry, I had my phone off."

"Where are you?"

Addis paused for a second. "I'm in Paris."

"Paris? Now I know why you had the phone off. Is my girl there?"

"Sacha? Yes."

"Put her on."

Addis handed the phone to Sacha with a confounded look on his face.

"Nader, hi," Sacha said.

"Hi, sunshine. I called you a few times. I wanted your opinion on something, but it can wait. Paris must be wonderful this time of the year. I'm very happy for you."

"Thanks, Nader. What is it you wanted to ask me?"

"You know I have this big presentation before the UN General Council tomorrow. I was notified by email a few days ago that my presentation time has been reduced by thirty minutes. Apparently, your dad is presenting as well, and it is all a big secret. Do you know what it is all about?"

"I have no idea. It might have to do with the new techware that was worn by one of our engineers on *Jeopardy!* You know he is going to be on *60 Minutes* tonight?"

"Yeah, I know. Hey, thanks. You've got better things to do than talking to me. Can you put Addis back on the phone? I have a quick question for him. Then, I promise, I will leave you guys alone. I love you."

"I love you too. Here is Addis."

"Hey, man. I'm really sorry to interrupt," Nader said to Addis, "but there are some facts about your research that I'm including in my report to the UN that I wanted to verify with you before the presentation. Listen, I will put it in an email, and if I'm not stating anything blatantly wrong, you don't have to respond. And again, I'm so sorry."

"No worries, man; it's all good. Yeah, go ahead and send it to me. I will look it over."

"Thanks, Addis. Give my girl a hug from me." He hung up.

"Wow, that was a little awkward, but he seems okay with everything," Addis said to Sacha. "I think he might be genuinely happy for us."

"I know he is," responded Sacha. "He is the sweetest man I know. How did I get so lucky to have two men like you two in my life?"

"It must be karma, something you did in your previous life."

"Whatever it is, I'm so happy to be here with you now." She put her arms around Addis's neck and whispered, "I think I'm getting into very dangerous territory, but I have no resistance."

"That is a journey I want to take with you, and maybe one day soon we will call it by its true name."

She reached out and kissed him.

They had their dinner brought up to their room. For the rest of the evening, they talked and cuddled, occasionally making love. It was 12:00 midnight Paris time when Sacha turned on her computer and began streaming the *60 Minutes* show. The iconic clock and tick-tock sound came on as short teaser videos introduced the different segments. One of the segments showed Zack sitting in a comfortable leather chair with a large stone fireplace emitting the warm amber glow of a picturesque fire. The reporter's voice came on: "He is considered one of the most successful tech moguls of our time, who has amassed one of the largest technology companies in the world from a one-man start-up when he was a freshman in college. Today, at the age of fifty, he believes that he can translate that same business acumen into a political movement that will transcend the current political gridlock."

The bottom thirty minutes of the episode exclusively featured the interview with Zack. Sacha and Addis sat quietly, watching the interaction on the screen between the host and Zack. Zack was in his apartment in New York City doing the same. At the end of the show, Sacha turned to Addis and asked, "What do you think?"

"I think he came across as very presidential. I don't know if I agree with all his initiatives, but it seems like it was devoid of politics. He didn't go after any of his opponents; he just focused on policies and his agenda. He seemed genuinely concerned about issues that are socially conscious. I didn't pick up on that side of him in our last meeting."

"Yeah, he will surprise you like that. Do you think he has a chance of winning?"

"I don't know, but I have this nagging feeling that he is destined for something profound and that somehow I will be caught up in it."

"Addis, were you ever considered a star baby?"

"You mean like the Greek myth about Astraeus, the adopted child of the Greek philosopher and mathematician Pythagoras, who invented the Pythagorean theorem?"

"Yes, that one."

"Baby, you flatter me, but you can call me your star baby anytime you want."

"How about SB for short?"

They both laughed as they began to pack for the drive back to the airport.

18 The UN

It was still dark outside. The early morning chill had not yet dissipated from the air. Donna was already standing on the train platform for the 6:06 a.m. train at Boston's Back Bay Station, traveling to Penn Station in New York City. She looked at her watch. It was 5:15 a.m. Clearly the platform was still devoid of travelers. She was so nervous about missing the train that she had set her alarm for 3:30 a.m., although her apartment was only a fifteen-minute walk to the station. A few days earlier, during her meeting with Nader to finalize the presentation to the UN, he impromptu had asked her if she would be interested in attending the meeting with him. It had taken every ounce of control for her to contain her excitement, but her answer was an immediate yes.

Donna felt a gentle tap on her left shoulder and immediately turned around to find Nader standing in front of her with a tray holding two cups of coffee. She stood for a second, scanning him from top to bottom without being overtly obvious about it. He was dressed in a well-fitted light gray suit, a crisp white shirt, and a solid black tie. Both his beard and his hair were well-groomed; a snapshot of him could have easily made the cover of an issue of *GQ*. She had never seen him this well-kept and formally dressed before. Now it was blatantly obvious to her how other women and even men on the platform were taking notice of him. It took Donna a few seconds to respond to Nader's "Good morning."

"Good morning, Nader."

"I got you a cup of coffee. If I remember correctly, you take your coffee with milk and one spoon of sugar."

"Yes, thank you. I could use one right about now."

"You look lovely. I hope I didn't get you up too early this morning."

"Not at all. And I must say, you clean up very nicely."

"Thanks. It's not too often that I get the opportunity to put a suit and tie on."

"Well, no pun intended, but you should do it more often; it suits you."

He chuckled. "Thanks. So, are you ready for this afternoon?"

"I'm just an observer, but I'm ready to provide any support you need."

"Thanks. I really appreciate your help with this. Here is our train. Let's go through the presentation one more time during the ride."

For the next three hours, Donna and Nader rehearsed his presentation before the UN council. Her astute observations about his intonation, his body language, and his ums and ahs were very helpful to Nader, but they made him feel like he was the student and she was the teacher. Somehow their relationship was morphing into a relationship of equals, but he didn't mind. As a matter of fact, it was a relief. He didn't have to maintain an air of superiority, and finally he could be himself.

The later part of the ride was mostly about their respective childhoods and their relationships with their parents, with some being about his journey from an atheist to a man of faith. Donna was in awe and wished the train ride would have lasted a lot longer, but the train conductor's voice came on the intercom announcing the next stop: "Penn Station, next and final stop. Please exit to the right."

They had over an hour before their meeting, so they decided to walk the twenty blocks to the UN headquarters on Forty-Seventh Street and First Avenue. It was a beautiful day. They both enjoyed the energy and the hustle and bustle of New York City—it made them feel alive and invigorated. The exchange between them felt natural and comfortable. The only thing that was missing was for them to be holding hands like all the other lovers walking the streets of New York City.

It was approximately 9:45 a.m. when they reached the entrance to the UN headquarters complex. Zack's limousine pulled in at the same time and parked directly in front of the main entrance. His chauffer immediately exited the car and walked to the back of the limousine, ceremoniously opening the back door for Zack. Zack exited, followed by an entourage of assistants carrying several large suitcases. Both Nader and Donna took notice of the fanfare as Donna commented, "This must be a very important person. Who is it?"

"He is the main headliner for today's meeting, Zack Zimmerman, the tech mogul who owns Leapp Technologies."

"Do you know him?"

"Yeah, we've had a few run-ins before."

"It sounds like you don't like him."

"I don't trust him. He always has a self-serving ulterior motive for everything he does."

The meeting was in a large conference room on the twenty-third floor of the UN building. The view of the NYC skyline was spectacular. Present were the scientific attachés from the five permanent members (United States, China, Russia, France, and England) and ten nonpermanent members from various African, Asian, and Latin American countries. They were all sitting around a large circular table with their respective assistants sitting directly behind them. Zack was sitting diagonally across from Nader. They cordially acknowledged each other's presence by politely nodding their heads in a manner that was akin to two prizefighters touching gloves.

The residing chairman of the meeting from the small African nation of Zushaka immediately took control of the gathering by announcing the purpose of the meeting, the agenda, and the presenters.

"Ladies and gentlemen, the purpose of today's meeting is to begin the process of creating an international protocol for managing very complex issues involving existing and new technologies that have the potential for short- and long-term distributive ramifications. In today's global world, where technology knows no physical borders, our aim is to create an international policy that safeguards against potential unintended consequences.

"Although today's meeting was intended for discussing the general framework of the task before us, we have received and have granted the request of Mr. Zimmerman, the head of Leapp Technologies, to address our committee. That will be followed by a brief opening statement from our scientific advisor, Dr. Nader el-Shafique from MIT. With that, let me introduce Mr. Zimmerman.

"Mr. Zimmerman, the floor is all yours."

"Good morning, ladies and gentlemen, and thank you for the opportunity to address this distinguished committee," Zack began. "As part of the designated international regulatory body tasked with creating a framework by which existing and new technologies can be vetted for any potential short- and long-term negative impacts on public health, safety, and security, I'm respectfully here to say that you need to add another mandate to this list, and that mandate is income and social equality. Technology is a tool like many of the other tools humans have created during our history on this planet. Like any other tool, placed in the right hands, it can bring about positive change. However, when it's placed in the wrong hands, it can be a destructive force. Also, history has shown us time and time again that those who possess these tools can have a clear and quantifiable advantage over others. It can literally mean the difference between prosperity and poverty. I submit to you that technology is the great equalizer that allows nations to leapfrog from poverty to prosperity, from illiteracy and disease to education and health. To that end, I'm asking you to consider this question when you are creating and placing these rules: Who on the economic and social ladder will you most likely impact or disenfranchise?

"Today, I have such a tool." Zack instructed his assistant to distribute the specially designed boxes with the Leapp Technologies logo to the fifteen members of the advisory board and one for Nader. "Please take a few minutes to open the boxes. As you can see, the box contains a smaller box and three envelopes. In the smaller box you will find a small device that we at Leapp Technologies have affectionately named Grok. Grok is an earpiece that can be comfortably inserted in either ear. You might have heard of this device a few weeks back when one of our engineers demonstrated its use on the *Jeopardy!* game show without the company's authorization. Please go ahead and insert the earpiece in your ear. I assure you, it is safe and has been vigorously tested."

The members hesitantly opened the small boxes and carefully inspected the devices. It seemed that no one wanted to be the first to insert it in their ear, until the chairman took the plunge first; then the others followed.

Zack said, "Please say, 'Grok, on.' Or better yet, I want you to just think it."

A few seconds later, all the members, including Nader, had a look of wonder as if a door to another realm of reality had just opened.

Zack continued speaking: "Ladies and gentlemen, what you're experiencing is the euphoric state of being directly connected to the internet. Your brain is reacting to the flood of new stimuli by producing endorphins and increasing metabolism and heart rate. Please give your body a few minutes to adjust. Before you, you will also find three envelopes. Please open the envelope labeled number 1."

Members opened the suggested envelope, and inside there was a card with the following algebraic formula written on it:

$$z_1 = a + 3i, z_2 = 4 + bi, z_3 = 6 + 10i$$

Next was a problem: Find the value of a and b if $z_3 = z_1 + z_2$.

Zack said, "Please write your answers now on the back of the card, and raise it up for everyone to see."

It took the members two seconds to write their answers on the back of the cards. As if they were in a contest, they all wanted to be the first to raise their card with the answer. All the cards had the number 7.

Zack said, "Ladies and gentlemen, you all have the right answer. Now, please open envelope number 2."

They all excitedly opened envelope number 2, to find a Sudoku puzzle labeled "very difficult."

Zack said, "Please take as much time as you need to solve this rather difficult puzzle."

It took each of the members less than one minute to complete the puzzle. Zack was timing them using a stopwatch.

Zack said, "I see that all members were able to complete the puzzle successfully in under one minute."

The members began to look at each other with amazement and with the giddiness of a child discovering a new experience for the first time.

Zack said, "Finally, ladies and gentlemen, please open the last envelope."

They all did so, with newfound excitement. The card inside read, "Calidam mingō quod frīgidam bibī." When the members looked at the phrase, they all chuckled.

Zack said, "I see from your reaction that all of you understand what the literal translation of this phrase is. However, the literal translation being one thing, the more common meaning is 'Do the best you can in a bad situations,' but obviously you knew that.

"Congratulations, ladies and gentlemen. Based on your performance on this rather simplistic yet indicative quiz, if all of you were to take an IQ test right now, you would all have a score that would categorize you as geniuses. Although I know for a fact that this is the case without the aid of Grok, you must admit that this little device was of some help."

They all chuckled at the underhanded flattery.

Zack said, "Now I want you to think *health monitor*."

Members began to visualize their own actual heart rates, internal temperatures, blood sugar levels, and other vital signs.

Zack said, "Yes, that is also one of the other capabilities of this device—a very sophisticated health monitor that allows the user to monitor and manage his or her health. Just imagine how many heart attacks this device will be able to prevent, not to mention the numerous other health conditions that can be avoided through early detection and preventive action. This device is not only a conduit that allows the user to be fully connected to the World Wide Web; it also embodies a sophisticated software that utilizes artificial intelligence to learn and grow in tandem with the user's needs and the demands on it.

"So, I can imagine what all of you are asking yourselves at this point: *What's the catch?* Well, here is the catch: There is no catch. I have been a very successful entrepreneur and have been fortunate to have accumulated substantial wealth—frankly, more than any one person should or ought to have in one lifetime. At this time in my life, I don't need or care for more dollar signs with many zeros next to them. Ladies and gentlemen, this device is the great equalizer, making possible the leapfrog effect with the potential for creating social and economic equality throughout the world. It is the device that would allow a Third World country, with its average citizen living on what we here in this country pay for a cup of coffee, to leap into the twenty-first century. At this juncture in my life, I would like to serve all of humanity by providing this device to every man, woman, and child for free, and I need your help to make that dream possible. Thank you for your time."

Zack immediately sat down and bowed his head in a gesture of humility as members looked on in a state of disbelief. Nader, on the other hand, was not buying it. He knew the man too well to know that with him nothing was for free. Members quickly regained their focus when the chairman began to speak.

"Mr. Zimmerman, thank you very much for your enlightening presentation. I'm sure I'm speaking on behalf of all our members when I say that your offer is most generous. And I'm sure it's at great cost to you and your company. Frankly, the information you provided is a lot to digest during this session; however, this board will give it its utmost attention and consideration. At this time, we would like to hear from Dr. Nader el-Shafique. Mr. Zimmerman, you're welcome to stay if you wish."

Zack said, "Thank you. I would."

The chairman knew Nader well enough to know that a debate was ensuing, and he wanted Zack to hear the counterargument.

Nader immediately stood up to address the board. "Distinguished members, thank you very much for the opportunity to address the board. I couldn't agree more with everything that Mr. Zimmerman has said. However, the question before us is, at what cost? Technological advancement has been singularly the most impactful factor in human advancement and the creator of the greatest economic wealth that humankind has ever seen. Albeit that wealth hasn't necessarily been evenly distributed and, for that matter, has been one of the factors in the widening economic and income disparity between the haves and the have-nots. Nevertheless, the cost of the negative unintended consequences of the rapid and unencumbered technological changes will be less discriminating and will be felt by all. Human history dates back two hundred thousand years. However, over 90 percent of all technological changes have occurred in the last hundred years—and that percentage is growing exponentially. One thing we know for sure is that none of these technological changes comes without a cost, both known and unknown. Frankly, as a scientist, the thing that keeps me up at night is all the unknowns. Our capitalistic corporate structure, which is driven by short-term profit motives, combined with a human population that is predominantly interested in instant gratification, has hastened the introduction of these new technologies without any checks and balances. My colleague and I, Ms. Donna Kramer, have developed a model that we call the Spike. This model attempts to look at all the technological changes that have occurred in the last hundred years and the future trajectory of additional changes anticipated to occur in the next twenty to thirty years. We also looked at the social, economic, and environmental consequences to our world of recent technological changes. We used very sophisticated mathematical and forecasting algorithms to extrapolate what our world would look like thirty years from now if these technological changes go unchecked. Frankly, I was shocked but not surprised by our findings. But first, let me set up the theoretical framework of this study."

Nader said, "Ms. Kramer, will you please launch the presentation on the overhead projector?"

The first slide was a list of all the major technological discoveries that had occurred in the last hundred years. Nader let the information sink in for a moment before signaling to Donna to click on the next slide. Information began to populate next to each listed discovery with known negative consequences. Nader signaled Donna again, and another column began to populate with potential unintended consequences. The information was overwhelming and clearly had a sobering effect on the audience. Nader quietly stood next to the screen as the audience was taking in the magnitude of the data. Their facial expressions were changing constantly: some were nodding in agreement; others were shaking their heads at human complacency; and still others were overtaken by the enormity of the task before them.

Nader said, "As you can see, each innovation has brought with it a whole new set of challenges that were either unanticipated or simply ignored for economic, social, and/or political reasons. The technological dogma is that the benefits will always outweigh the costs. This mindset underscores the complexity of the issue and the lack of social will to bridle or curtail past technological advancements for the sake of short-term gains and with a total indifference to the impact on future generations. As a scientist and advisor to this board, my focus is on the science and the potential risk if we continue on this path without any checks and balances. I leave it to this committee to factor in the political, social, and economic will to do what is necessary to negate this risk.

"Take, for example, genetically modified food, which is a technology that has been widely and commonly used in almost every food product that we all consume on a daily basis, albeit unknowingly. This is a technology that typifies the debate over short-term economic benefits versus long-term potential problems. Genetically engineered food is a product of transitional 'life science' corporations such as Monsanto and Novartis. Basically, this is the science of altering the genetic blueprint of living organisms—plants, animals, and possibly humans—for the purpose of improving their individual properties. The improvement, of course, is in the eye of the beholder. Some argue that these alterations will create agricultural sustainability, eliminate world hunger, cure diseases, and vastly improve public health. Others argue that this technology is a means by which international corporations with a strong profit motive can dominate and monopolize the global market for seeds, food fiber, and medical products. However, the most concerning argument is raised by environmentalists who have sounded the alarm about this technology, linking it to potential health risks, infertility, immune problems, accelerated aging, faulty insulin regulation, and changes in major organs and the gastrointestinal system, in addition to a multitude of other food-related illnesses. Also, there is the well-founded concern that this technology will cause a rise in antibiotic-resistant bacteria and microbes, the inadvertent creation of genetically engineered superweeds and superpests, and possibly the degradation of soil.

"Ladies and gentlemen, the more than one hundred potential negative by-products of this technology, listed on the screen before you, are just some of the Armageddon-type scenarios that could be the unintended consequence.

"With all these competing voices vying for public attention, it appears that the one with the biggest megaphone is drowning out all other voices. That megaphone belongs to the large 'life science' multinational corporations and their lobbyists, in concert with public officials who continue to ignore this problem. In the meantime, genetically engineered food has been pervasively integrated into our food supply with minimal resistance. Today, supermarket shelves are stacked with a plethora of genetically modified food, and consumers have been purchasing these products with limited or no knowledge of their origins or potential risks. Efforts to label these products or curtail their use have been relatively muted or simply ignored for the purpose of short-term and shortsighted gains. Even government agencies such as the FDA have been complicit by not providing the necessary oversight.

"This is just one example of one technology, but it's not the exception; it is the norm. As you can see on the screen before you, every technology ever created by humankind creates a whole set of new problems. However, what is not immediately apparent is when these problems will come to fruition. In this study, we refer to this dilemma as the 'lager effect.' Looking at old technologies, we were able to statistically ascertain the average time it takes for these consequences to occur and the average number of unintended negative consequences brought on by every new technology."

Nader nodded at a Donna, and a new slide appeared on the screen, showing a graph of two lines moving in tandem at first in a slow and linear fashion, then splitting and ascending straight up. The first line represented rate of technological changes (TC); the second, potential unintended consequences (UC). The y-axis represented the rate of change, and the x-axis represented time. The graph dramatically depicted how the (UC) line overtakes the (TC) line in as short as a few decades.

"As you can see, ladies and gentlemen, there will come a time, if we don't act today, when we will not be able to innovate quickly enough to mitigate the negative impact of these unintended consequences. As you can see, this problem is not unique to genetic-engineering technology but is the prevailing status quo for the predominant number of technologies created in the last hundreds of years. Whether it's the combustion engine, social media, or the internet, they all represent a tipping point with a clear and present danger to future generations and our way of life. Imagine for a second if we had the foresight to see the impact the combustion engine would make on global warming, urban sprawl, and deforestation. Would we have done things differently? As a matter of public policy, would we have focused more on environmentally friendly urban planning, efficient mass transportation, and green forms of energy? I believe the task before us is to be the agency with that foresight. In closing, as a scientist, I have to caution all who care to listen: Beware of the false prophecy that technology promises. In the promised world of technological utopia, the serpent can't be lurking too far away."

Nader turned around and directly looked at Zack as he uttered that last statement. Both Zack and the chairman took notice of the direct dig. Zack had a subtle smile but was fuming inside.

Nader said, "Ladies and gentlemen, I will be submitting my full study for the record. I look forward to working with you to remedy this impending humanitarian crisis. At this time, I'm recommending that the board halt any new approvals for new technology intended for mass distribution until said technology has been fully vetted. I'm forming a committee of top scientists from different disciplines to assist with this endeavor and to advise the board accordingly. Thank you for your time."

Nader took his seat next to Donna as board members applauded. Zack was also applauding politely while maintaining direct eye contact with Nader. The animus between the two of them didn't go unnoticed by the chairman. They were both readying themselves for the battles to come.

The chairman said, "With that, we will be concluding the presentation portion of this meeting. We will take a short break and reconvene in ten minutes. The board would also like to thank our distinguished guest, Mr. Zimmerman, for his presentation and offer."

Board members applauded Zack as he stood up and exited the boardroom with his assistants. His facial expression immediately changed as he exited the door. His assistants immediately knew to maintain their distance. Nader knew that this shot across the bow would not go unanswered.

19 The Fix

The next morning, Zack was in his office streaming all the news feeds on his wall-mounted screen, when he found what he was looking for. The headline read, "Tech mogul and presidential candidate Zack Zimmerman makes an offer to the United Nations Scientific and Technology Board that apparently they can refuse." Zack began to read the article: "Mr. Zimmerman had offered to distribute his latest techware, which recently had been displayed on the game show *Jeopardy!*, to the world for free, but the UNSTB rejected his offer, citing the need for further tests and ample time to vet the technology." The article went further to say, "The majority of the board voted to delay the acceptance of Mr. Zimmerman's offer until further review, based on the recommendation of their scientific advisor, Dr. Nader el-Shafique."

Zack was enraged, his anger reaching the boiling point. He didn't like to lose, especially to someone who he thought was considerably beneath him. His deep dislike for Nader had been seeded the first time he met him with Sacha at his birthday party four years ago.

While Zack was reading the full article on the screen, Sacha was making an attempt to enter his office, but she was blocked by one of his assistants.

The assistant said, "Ms. Zimmerman, your dad asked not be disturbed. And I have to warn you, he is in a very foul mood."

Sacha responded, "That's all right, Alex. Don't worry, I will tell him that I forced my way in."

Sacha proceeded to Zack's office. As she opened the door, her athletic reflexes took over, causing her to duck when she saw in her peripheral vision a projectile speeding toward her head. The figurine crashed and shattered against the wall behind her.

"What the fuck is going on, Zack?"

"Sorry, I was aiming at the monitor."

"God, I hope that what you lack in athleticism, you make up for in brains."

"I'm not in the mood for your sarcasm. Your ex-boyfriend screwed me at the UN," Zack said to her.

"You mean Nader?"

"Yeah, that piece of shit. I never liked that goddamn petulant Arab."

"Nader is a dear friend of mine, and I would appreciate it if you didn't refer to him in those derogatory terms," Sacha said sternly. "I heard about what happened yesterday at the UN. When did you decide to give Grok to the world for free, and why was I not told about it?"

"I have been thinking about it for a while. I didn't make my final decision until recently."

"Well, the news of your offer managed to impress someone else very much."

"Yeah? Who is that?"

"Addis called me this morning after reading about your offer to the UN. He was so impressed with your generosity and sense of philanthropy that he decided to take you up on your offer to join the firm."

"Well, finally, that is good news. When is he ready to make the move?"

"I guess as soon as it's conveniently possible," Sacha replied.

Zack said, "We are all set up to receive him. Make it happen sooner rather than later."

"Why do I get the feeling that you already anticipated his decision?"

"Call it intuition," Zack responded.

"Too bad you didn't have that so-called intuition when it came to Nader."

"This is round one. Don't discount your father yet."

"I never do, Zack. What you're capable of never ceases to surprise me," Sacha said to her father.

"Well, I will take that as a compliment. In the meantime, have Alex make the necessary arrangements for the transportation of Addis's equipment and his lodging. I have his lab and staff already arranged and in place. I will call him a little later to congratulate him and welcome him to the firm. And congratulations to you as well."

"What do you mean?" Sacha asked.

"Well, at least now you don't have to have a long-distance relationship!"

"Zack, I told you many times before, stay out of my personal business."

"Okay," Zack answered. "You have a lot to do, and I have a few matters to take care of. We'll talk later."

Sacha proceeded to walk out of Zack's office, but she had this nagging feeling that when it came to her father, she was never in control. Somehow he was always pulling the strings, and she didn't like it.

Zack picked up the phone and called his head of human resources, Tom Schafer. "Tom, I want you to look at our employment data bank and see if we've ever received an employment application from a one Ms. Donna Kramer, a graduate student at MIT. I will hold."

After Tom came back on the line, he said, "Yes, we did. She was looking for an internship position a few summers ago. She has very good credentials, and from what I see on her résumé, she appears to be very bright. Is there a reason you're asking?"

"I want you to ask her to come in for an interview. If she agrees, offer her a position as a research assistant at a salary she can't refuse. Tell her that it's a very sensitive position involving proprietary information and that she must sign a confidentiality agreement vowing not to discuss the nature of her work or employment with Leapp Technologies. If she agrees, tell her we need her to start right away. Also tell her that she will be issued a highly secure laptop and cell phone that she must exclusively use for all business and personal-related activity. I will have these items ready for you if she accepts."

"Okay, Zack, I will have my assistant get on it right away," Tom replied.

"No, I want you to do it. No one else can know about this. Make this happen, and let me know as soon as you get it done."

Tom knew that this was not a request but an order; there would be negative consequences if he were to fail.

Zack dialed Addis's cell number next. After a few rings, Addis answered. "Hello?"

"Hello, Addis, this is Zack."

"Hello, Mr. Zimmerman. It is nice to hear from you."

"Likewise, Addis. I heard the great news from Sacha that you have agreed to join the firm. I'm very excited about the prospects of working together and the potential revolutionary work you will be able to produce with the right support."

"Sir, I just want to be very clear that my work is very experimental at this stage. I don't know if it will ever yield any commercial benefits."

"I'm well aware of that, Addis, and I want to assure you that you will not be under any time or financial pressure to produce."

"Thank you for that assurance. I'm also looking forward to working with you and Sacha."

Zack couldn't help but let a little smirk develop on his face.

"That's great. I will put the firm resources and my assistant at your disposal. A corporate jet will be available for your relocation as soon as you are ready. As for your housing, the firm will take care of that as well. Just let my assistant know your specs, and she will take care of everything. Also feel free to recruit any of your staff whom you deem are important to your work."

"Sir, that is very generous."

"We want to make sure that you are comfortable, so you can focus on the important stuff. When are you able to make the move?"

"I guess there is nothing holding me back. As soon as possible."

"No problem. I will have my assistant reach out to you to coordinate all the logistics. And, of course, use Sacha as a resource as well. Again, congratulations, and welcome to Leapp Technologies. Have a great day."

"Thank you."

They hung up.

A few minutes later, Alex came on the video telecom: "Mr. Zimmerman, I have Chairman Aboudi from the UN on hold for you."

"Put him through."

"Chairman Aboudi, it is a pleasure to hear from you. I'm sorry to hear about the decision of the UNSTB."

"Mr. Zimmerman, I'm sorry that you had to hear about our decision through the media first. Unfortunately, the information was leaked before I was able to contact you. I wanted to take this opportunity to discuss with you another option. Although I don't fully agree with the board's decision, I see the merit in being cautious given Dr. el-Shafique's compelling presentation and the current environment. However, I also believe that the best way to validate your technology to the world is by having it tested in a real-world situation. To that end, I have spoken to my government, and they have agreed to allow you to distribute your techware to the citizens of Zushaka."

"Chairman Aboudi, that is a great news. But wouldn't that put you in an awkward position with the board?"

"I convinced the board, as a compromise and as an interim step, to use my country as a genie peg, if you will."

"Well, sir, I commend you and your government on your foresight and progressive thinking."

"Mr. Zimmerman, I also have to be forthright and mention that there are certain caveats and demands that have to be agreed to first."

"Okay. And what are those?"

"First and foremost, a mechanism to render the device inoperable must be created, and control of this option must be in the hands of our government. Second, all data feeds from the device must be channeled through our intelligence agency. Third, compensation for the government's time and effort to promote this concept to its citizens is required. There are some other, minor items that I will send you a list of, but these are the main demands."

"Well, Chairman Aboudi, I have to give these demands some thought. In the meantime, please send me the other things on the list. I will give you my answer in a few days. Thank you, sir."

"Thank you. Good day."

A few minutes later, an email notification flashed on Zack's screen indicating the arrival of an email from Chairman Aboudi. Zack quickly opened the email and the attachment and read through the contents. Aboudi's government's demands included filters to block antigovernment sites and content and an algorithm to control the narrative in the public square. Zack looked at the list and smiled. He had fully expected these demands and had already designed the necessary provisions for them in the software. That was the price of admission, but it was not necessarily all bad. Becoming the political and propaganda arm of this government meant that their own survival would come to depend on the flow of information that he controlled—and that was a drug too powerful to be weaned off of.

Zack had the urge to respond immediately to the chairman and accept his demands, but he knew it would be more prudent to let him wait for a few days. In spite of the setback from UNSTB, his plan appeared to be coming to fruition, albeit a little slower than he wished. The task before him was to make this opportunity a resounding success. He sat back in his chair and thought, *This has turned out to be a great day after all,* but he vowed to make sure that Nader would never again be a thorn in his side.

A few days later, Tom was sitting at his desk when his secretary escorted Donna Kramer into his office. Donna was dressed in a navy-blue suit and was holding a small leather briefcase. She was both nervous and excited about the opportunity to work for the premier tech company in the world. She was frankly surprised to have gotten the call from the head of human resources. She wondered why her and why now, and did it have anything to do with her work with Nader, but this was a once-in-a-lifetime opportunity that she couldn't miss.

"Ms. Kramer, please make yourself comfortable. Thank you for agreeing to the interview. As I mentioned during our phone conversation, this is a very sensitive position that deals with security protocols and the protection of the firm's proprietary information. Keeping your role a secret will be of paramount importance in order to protect you and the firm from the potential ransomware and hacking. It's imperative that you exercise extreme discretion as to your role with the firm if you were to be hired. Have you mentioned this interview to anyone?"

"No, sir."

"Good. Ms. Kramer, we have scoured our résumé data bank in hopes of finding the right candidate for this position, and frankly, your résumé was one of five résumés that made the final cut. So far, I have interviewed all the other candidates. You're the final interview. Given the sensitivity of this position, the interviewing process is limited only to me, and I'm hoping to finalize my decision in the next few days."

Tom went through the formalities, asking the typical interview questions such as "Where do you see yourself in five years?" and "What personal skill sets do you have that, you believe, will make you a strong candidate for this position?" Donna delivered the standard answers, but Tom was not even listening. He just wanted to go through the formalities in order not to make it obvious that she already had the position.

After the half-hour interview, Tom took a theatrical pause as if he were contemplating his decision. He lifted his head and directly looked at Donna. After what seemed like a long and uncomfortable pause, he said, "Ms. Kramer, at this moment, I feel very comfortable making my decision right now. Out of the five candidates, you, I strongly believe, are the most qualified. I would like to offer you the position right now. Unfortunately, I'm under some time pressure to get this position filled, so if you're unable to accept at this time, I will have to offer the position to the next qualified candidate. Before you answer, I would like to address some issues that I'm sure you have some questions about, for example, salary, benefits, and work hours. Your starting salary will be $125,000, and you will receive full benefits on day one, which are very generous and include medical, dental, vision, and a 401(k) with a match. You will not be required to report to work and can work from home, unless you're requested to attend a meeting. You will receive both a secure laptop and a secure cellular phone that we will insist that you use exclusively as a condition of your employment."

Donna was flabbergasted at the offer. This was more money than she'd ever hoped for. She had anticipated the typical internship salary of $40,000 a year and no benefits. This offer would go pretty far in solving her financial problems and paying off her student loans.

"Mr. Schafer, this is a great opportunity. To be working for the premier tech company in the world, and in such an interesting position, is an honor. I'm ready to give you my answer now, and that answer is a resounding yes."

"Ms. Kramer, I'm very happy to hear that. Congratulations! As I mentioned before, this is a highly sensitive position, and as a part of your employment agreement, you cannot make your position with Leapp Technologies public. You must sign a nondisclosure agreement memorializing that fact. Your start date will be this following Monday. Both the laptop and phone will be overnighted to you in the next few days. I will have my assistant prepare all the necessary paperwork for you to sign. Again, congratulations! Welcome to Leapp Technologies."

Tom stood up and shook Donna's hand as he escorted her to the door. He opened the door and instructed his assistant to prepare the necessary paperwork. He again extended his hand to Donna as he wished her the best of luck. Once she had gone, he immediately went to his phone and called Zack.

"Zack, this is Tom. I just met with Donna Kramer, and she

accepted the position. Her start date is next Monday. She is signing all the agreements you requested as we speak."

"Great job, Tom. You made it clear to her that she cannot make her employment with Leapp Technologies public?"

"Yes, sir, crystal clear."

"Thanks, Tom. I will have the laptop and phone sent to your office for delivery. Great job."

"Thanks, Zack. Glad to be of help."

They hung up.

That same day, Zack contacted Chairman Aboudi and accepted his demands with the promise to have over one hundred thousand Grok techware units delivered to his country by the end of the month, accompanied by a team of technicians.

20 The Relocation

Addis was standing in the middle of his new lab, a sprawling seventy-thousand-square-foot complex made of glass, steel, and concrete. The building was annexed on a separate gated lot a few miles away from headquarters with its own private security detail. The lab was already operational with the most advanced lab equipment, computers, and robotics, all housed in an ergonomically designed space that was both functional and aesthetically pleasing. The whole complex was energy independent with enough juice to power a small city and was totally off the grid. Addis turned around and looked at Sacha.

"Wow, this is a lot more than I expected. How did you manage to do all of this in such a short period of time?"

"I didn't. This was all Zack. He seems to anticipate everything and execute his plans with the accuracy of a well-tuned Swiss watch. He must have known somehow that you were going to say yes!"

"I don't how he would know; I didn't even know myself. All my equipment is here, and the relocation was done with the precision of a well-rehearsed and well-executed military operation. Even my apartment location, as well as the decor and amenities, is perfect."

"Well, that was me."

"You're both very impressive. I hope I don't disappoint."

"Well, there is one person whom you will never disappoint."

165

"Who is that?"

"Me, silly." After a quick smile, Sacha said, "Let me introduce you to your staff. After that we have to head back to headquarters to meet with Zack and all the department heads. He wants to make a formal introduction and make sure that you get all the support you need."

Sacha and Addis walked into the main reception hall with its glass dome that flooded the space with natural sunlight. The space was tastefully designed, combining horticulture, sunlight, and functionality, which conjured the feeling of both warmth and comfort. The entrance didn't look anything like the entrance to a physics lab, but more like the entrance to a natural art museum. Addis looked at the awaiting crowd, all dressed in white lab coats. He noticed a few of his colleagues from the Geneva lab. They were the brightest of all his interns, handpicked by him for this new opportunity. They all had received an offer that they couldn't refuse: the chance to work for such a prestigious and renowned firm with deep pockets. The rest of the staff had been hand selected by Zack and Sacha.

The staff stood quietly, attentively waiting for their leader to articulate his vision and their mission for this enigmatic project. Most of them had not been fully briefed on the details of their new positions, only told that they had been assigned to a new project and to report to the new complex on this specific date. There was a lot of chatter among the reassigned staff prior to their first day on the job, which became faster and more audible when they saw the complex for the first time. Most of them hadn't known it even existed and were taken aback by the size and sophistication of the complex. There was excitement and anticipation in the air as they could sense this was something very important that the company was backing with a substantial amount of capital and toward which it had committed an inordinate amount of resources for the long term.

Addis took a second to digest the intellectual power that was standing before him and the enormity of the task before him. All these highly motivated type A personalities were depending on him to lead them. For a second, he questioned whether he had what it took and whether this endeavor would be a colossal failure. He willed those negative thoughts out of his mind and began to address the crowd.

"Ladies and gentlemen, I'm very fortunate to have the opportunity to work with such a talented group of individuals. All of you bring a set of skills that are unique and complementary to our overall mission. For those I'm meeting for the first time, I had the opportunity to review all your résumés and credentials, and frankly, I couldn't be more impressed. You're all experts in your respective fields. I'm going to depend on you heavily to help me steer this ship in the right direction. There are some among you whom I have known and worked with for a while, who have graciously decided to embark on this journey and open this new chapter with me and relocate here from my previous lab in Switzerland. Regardless of whether you're new to this project or have been working with me for a while, we're all one team working to achieve the same goal. That goal is to discover and harness the infinite source of natural energy—energy that is clean, boundless, and sustainable, to ensure the planet's and humans' survivability and our ability to reach the stars. Ladies and gentlemen, this is our mission, and it's no small task. But what we endeavor to create here is the frontier of science and something that will change the world forever. We're all very fortunate to be a part of this tipping point in the history of humankind. I congratulate you and look forward to working with you and being on this fantastic adventure with you. It has been a pleasure meeting all of you. I look forward to getting to know each of you on an individual basis. However, at this time, I have to attend to a more mundane corporate task back in headquarters. But I suggest that you spend the rest of the morning getting to know each other on an individual basis. Thank you. Again, I look forward to working with all of you."

There was applause from the staff as Addis and Sacha proceeded to exit the building for their meeting back at HQ. An all-electric vehicle that looked like something from the future was waiting for them with the driver patiently standing by the open rear door. The vehicle didn't make any noise or give out any emission. As Addis assumed his seat next to Sacha, he wondered if the engine was even turned on. The acceleration of the vehicle was instantaneous; it felt as if they were floating on air. The interior was appointed with all the amenities of an expensive limo rather than a souped-up golf cart. Addis looked at Sacha and said, "Wow this feels like something out of *Star Wars!*"

"It is one of Zack's inventions. It recycles its own energy, and it's solar powered by miniature cells embedded in the paint. Its battery is the size of a car battery."

"Is there anything this man can't do? He seems to have endless energy and creativity."

"His problem is, he can't master the simplest of things. They're too mundane for him."

"What are those?"

"Interpersonal interaction with others and empathy for human feebleness."

"That must have been tough for you growing up?"

"I learned to deal with it. I just hope the apple fell far, far away from the tree."

"You're my apple. I want you to take shade under my tree," Addis said flirtatiously.

"You're so corny, but I love you for it."

"You love me?"

"I do," Sacha replied.

Sacha and Addis walked into the conference room. All the department heads were seated at the twenty-foot-long mahogany conference table, patiently awaiting their arrival. Zack, standing at the head of the table, immediately turned around and looked at Sacha with an expression of disdain. It was a look that she was clearly familiar with, but it had never had its intended effect on her. She had learned early in her teens not to let anything that Zack said or did intimidate her, or at least she thought she had mastered that skill. Zack was clearly annoyed by their lack of punctuality, and everyone in the room knew it. He quickly acknowledged their presence and began to speak.

"Ladies and gentlemen, we're all very busy. Out of respect for your time, let me cut the formalities and begin by saying we're very glad, and indeed fortunate, to have Dr. Ackerman join our firm. The good doctor doesn't need an introduction. I'm positive everyone in this room is keenly aware of his work and his research papers. If you're not, I suggest you bring yourself up to speed ASAP. I want to make this perfectly clear and without any equivocation: you're to make yourselves available to Dr. Ackerman and to any requests he has for information or assistance—no exceptions. With that, I want each department head to stand up and give a brief description of their project. Let's start with this side of the table. Jack!"

Jack Levine, the head of the satellite and communications division, stood up to address the audience, but he maintained his focus on Zack and Addis.

"My division has been tasked with creating a network of satellites that will ultimately provide global coverage and access to every human being on the planet. We endeavor to accomplish this goal in two years' time. We are aided in this effort by our proprietary satellite technology. Thanks to Zack's vision and pioneering spirit, we were able to develop the most advanced miniaturized satellites that are the size of a small microwave. We're able to launch these satellites to their designated orbits in a cluster—a hundred at a time. Our target is to have a launch every quarter, for a total of eight launches at the end of two years. Please consider me and my staff as a resource, Doctor. We look forward to collaborating with you and your staff on all future endeavors."

Next, the head of the nanotechnology division stood up. "We're glad to have you as a part of the team, Dr. Ackerman. Our work has yielded some fantastic innovations that are at the cutting edge of technology and that have the potential to transform medicine, manufacturing, communication, and more importantly, human existence. With your help, we will finally have the missing element that will make this transformation, finally, a reality. I'm very much looking forward to working with you to make sure this vision becomes a reality."

Addis immediately turned around and whispered to Sacha,

"What does he mean?" Zack took notice, but he decided to ignore the obvious surprise of Addis at the closing statement of the last speaker. He wanted Addis to feel like he didn't have a mandate for any deliverables, but that illusion was quickly shattered by the previous speaker. Zack, clearly annoyed at this inadvertent slip of the tongue, directed a stern look toward the man as he assumed his seat.

It was Sacha's turn to speak.

"Ladies and gentlemen, you're all familiar with my work. It's the cross-pollination of everything we do in this firm. Because of our extensive user interface with the public, and soon to be with the world, we're the largest megadata center with access to trillions of touch points. Our proprietary data evaluation algorithm coined 'Tip of the Needle' allows us to ascertain the collective health of the human psyche as a society. As importantly, we are determining the trends that are becoming pervasive as society collectively interfaces with cultural, social, and economic contemporary changes occurring in real time. These analyses will allow us to react to changes as they occur and to modify our deliverables accordingly. This is analogous to having a moral compass to will aid us in navigating these uncharted waters."

Zack couldn't help but find this last statement too altruistic for his own liking, but the perception of being a good corporate citizen served his political and corporate ambitions well.

Other division heads continued with their well-rehearsed commercials about their respective missions. At the end, Zack stood up, thanked all his division heads, and summarily dismissed them by stating, "Okay, folks, we all have a lot to do, so I won't take any more of your time." As they began to stream out of the conference room, Zack asked Addis and Sacha to stay behind. After everyone had left, Zack looked at Addis and asked, "I hope you found everything up to your standards?"

"Yes, sir, everything is more than sufficient. But of course, I have not had the chance to test-drive it yet."

"I'm sure you will not be disappointed. I took a personal interest in making sure that your lab has everything you need for your research and more. Talking about more, I would really appreciate it if in your spare time you would be able to help us with a technical problem that has stifled our ability to advance the Grok technology to the next level."

"What problem is that, sir?"

"Well, our nanotechnology division has been working on creating a miniaturized version of our Grok device, converting it from a wearable to an injectable. The problem we are facing is how to power the device once it's injected into the host. Obviously, the size of the device makes it virtually impossible for us to power it using a conventional power source like a battery. We're looking for an infinite source of energy that renders the device energy self-sufficient and viable for the life of the host. I would greatly appreciate it if you would give this dilemma some thought."

"Sir, this is no small task, but I will be happy to give it some thought. Some of my current research has yielded some findings that might shed light on this enigma. And of course there's Sacha's research, especially in the area of kinetic energy and the electrochemical response living organs have to external and internal stimuli. From what I understand from Sacha's research, it appears that living organisms have an infinite capacity to produce organic energy. Maybe this is something that Sacha and I can collaborate on. I will be happy to give this some thought."

"Thanks, Addis," Zack responded. "And remember that you have open-door access when it comes to me and my office. Welcome again to Leapp Technologies. Sacha, make sure you show him the ropes."

"Thank you, sir," Addis said.

Both Sacha and Addis departed the boardroom. Sacha immediately turned around and sarcastically uttered, "Wow, open-door policy. I don't even have that kind of access. It must be those blue eyes?"

"The only thing these blue eyes want to look at right now is you. Can we play hooky? You can come to my apartment and give me some pointers on how best to arrange my furniture, especially in the bedroom."

Sacha looked at him and, without saying a word, lifted her phone and called her assistant. "Please cancel my appointments for the day and have my car ready and waiting downstairs."

Two hours later Addis was getting his wish, the world outside be damned. The only thing that mattered to Addis and Sacha was the moment and each other.

That evening Sacha and Addis met Nader and Donna for dinner at Nader's favorite Italian restaurant. Addis and Sacha ordered an expensive bottle of Malbec, a red wine, for the table, but neither Donna nor Nader partook in its consumption. Instead, they both ordered Nader's favorite drink, a glass of half cranberry juice and half seltzer. Sacha took notice and couldn't help but feel slightly jealous. She knew it wasn't about rekindling her relationship with Nader but about how this woman had succeeded where she herself had failed. *What does she have that I don't have?* After all, Sacha had always been fiercely competitive, and the idea of failing didn't comport well with her sense of identity.

Throughout the evening, Sacha observed Donna's every move and every word, attempting to develop a psychological profile and answer the question that had been eluding her all night: *Why her?* Her curiosity getting the best of her, she no longer cared about being politically correct or gracious. She just wanted answers.

"So, Donna, Nader tells me that you're helping him with his work for the UN."

"Yes, and it has been a pleasure. I have learned so much from Nader."

"Did you grow up in this area?"

"No, I actually grew up in Long Island, New York."

"Oh, I know Long Island well. Where?"

"Old Westbury."

"That is a very affluent area. So are you the daughter of David Kramer the hedge fund manager?"

"Yes, but since my parents' divorce seven years ago, I had a falling-out with the both of them over their personal choices. I have not spoken to them for a while."

"I'm sorry to hear that. Were you raised Jewish?"

"Both my parents are Jewish by birth, but they are devout atheists, and any religious talk was strictly forbidden in the house when I was growing up. It was the antithesis of anything that resembled religion."

"But you seem like a very spiritual person."

"I would like to think so, but until now, I have been on a spiritual journey trying to cut through the noise, in hopes of finding the right message for me."

"You're speaking in the past tense, and you said 'until now.' Have you found what you're looking for?"

Donna became flushed and visibly uncomfortable with the question. She paused for a second to contemplate whether this was the right setting to declare that she had made one of the most important decisions of her life. Her intent was to do so in a private setting with only Nader present. She knew that Sacha intentionally had pinned her into this corner, but she was happy to get this load off her mind. She had been trying all day to find the right moment to tell Nader, but the setting was never right.

"I guess this is as good a time as any. As a matter of fact, I have been thinking about this decision for a long time. With the help of Nader, I have been learning and reading a lot about Islam. I have made the decision to convert."

There was absolute silence at the table as Addis and Sacha watched Nader's facial expression. He was clearly in shock. It took him a few seconds to gather his wits. He looked at Donna and asked, "When did you arrive at this decision?"

"Last night!"

21 The Tech Invasion

A military detail of ten armored cars was parked at the end of the tarmac of a military airfield on the outskirts of the capital of Zushaka. Fifty paramilitary soldiers were standing in formation, commanded by a five-star general dressed in battle fatigues and donning aviator sunglasses that appeared too small for his full face. Next to him stood Ambassador Aboudi. In the distance, up in the sky, appeared two gleaming lights that were approaching quickly, heading for the empty runway. A chartered Boeing 747 and a C-17 Globemaster III military cargo plane touched down one after the other and taxied to the end of the runway, where the general and the ambassador were waiting at full attention. On the side of the planes, the logo of Leapp Technologies was conspicuously emblazoned for all to see.

An airport vehicle moved the mobile stairs and aligned them perfectly to the jet's front door. The front door to the lead jet opened, and emerging from behind it was Sacha, dressed in khaki cargo pants, military-style boots, and a long-sleeved hiking shirt. Her blonde hair was tucked under a baseball cap and tied in a ponytail. She was the woman in command; there was no confusion about her role as she descended the stairs with an army of technicians and engineers emerging from both planes. The general looked at Ambassador Aboudi with an expression of surprise, clearly taken aback by the size of the entourage. It looked like a mini invasion of his small country. Four armored vehicles emerged from the back of the C-17 and surrounded the entourage on both sides, directly facing the general and his troops. There were four occupants in each of the armored cars dressed in military fatigues and bulletproof vests. They were armed with M4 CQBR machine guns and SIG Sauer P226 sidearms. They were all a well-trained ex–Special Forces security detail who'd been hand selected by the head of security at Leapp Technologies for this mission. Among them was one individual who stood out from the rest. He had Middle Eastern features and a thick mane of black hair. He was the same individual who had been involved in the botched assassination of the imam, Nader's father, several years earlier in Palestine.

The ex–paramilitary soldiers disembarked their vehicles and quickly positioned themselves in front of the entourage of civilians whom they were in charge of protecting. Sacha approached the ambassador and introduced herself.

"Ambassador Aboudi, I'm Sacha Zimmerman. I'm in charge of this operation. It's a pleasure to finally meet you."

"Ms. Zimmerman, the pleasure is mine. This is General Imani, who is in charge of this mission."

"General, it is a pleasure to meet you as well. We appreciate any assistance you can provide."

"Ms. Zimmerman, welcome to my beautiful country. You and your entourage are more than welcome to spend as much time as you like enjoying our beautiful city and countryside, but we will take it from here. A few technicians embedded with my troops will be more than sufficient to get the job done."

"General, with all due respect, we are here to get a job done, not to behave as tourists," Sacha said. "The delivery and training on the use of this techware will be completed by me and my staff and directly to the people of Zushaka. If the government of Zushaka have any ideas to the contrary, I will be more than happy to get back on the plane with my staff and head back to where I came from with the two suitcases of US currency I brought with me."

The general slowly took off his sunglasses off and directly looked at Sacha with a stern and aggressive expression. Sacha responded with the slightest of smiles. He immediately knew, *This one is not easily intimidated.* The ambassador, noting the tension, quickly intervened.

"Well, maybe it would be best if I spoke directly to Mr. Zimmerman?"

"Be my guest!" Sacha quickly pulled out her satellite phone and speed-dialed her father. "Zack, Ambassador Aboudi would like to speak to you. It seems that we have a slight misunderstanding."

She handed the phone to the ambassador.

"Ambassador, this is Zack. I hope you're well. My daughter informs me that there is a slight misunderstanding. How can I be of assistance?"

"Your daughter?"

"Yes."

"Well, Zack, my government would like to take charge of this delivery, and I'm afraid your daughter has some misgivings about how this thing is supposed to go down. My government isn't comfortable giving up control of our internal affairs. I'm sure you understand."

"Ambassador, Sacha is in charge of this field operation, and I have the utmost confidence in her leadership. It's her call. I would like to remind you of our original agreement, that this techware is for the direct benefit of the people of Zushaka. Good day, sir. I hope you're able to resolve this misunderstanding amicably."

The ambassador was taken aback by the finality and the tone of Zack's statement. It was clear he was not willing to negotiate. It was also clear that Sacha was fully in charge. The ambassador looked at Sacha and at the general, clearly disappointed in his inability to negotiate a different outcome.

"Well, Ms. Zimmerman, this decision is above my pay grade. I will need to discuss it with the president."

"Ambassador, I perfectly understand. My crew and I will return to our planes and await your decision," Sacha replied.

She directed her crew to return to the planes and asked her assistant to have the pilots fire up the engines.

Both the general and the ambassador were perplexed by her indifference. As she began to head back to the plane, she turned around and addressed the ambassador one last time. "Mr. Ambassador, if I can be presumptuous, I had my public relations department draft a speech to be delivered by your government to the people of Zushaka. I believe it will serve your president's public standing well. May I send it to you?"

"Yes, please go ahead."

The general didn't like that he had been sidelined. His facial expression reflected his disgruntled mood. He was not accustomed to not being in charge in front of his men. And the fact that he had been emasculated by a foreign white woman didn't sit well with him.

The ambassador went back to his car, leaving the general waiting on the runway with his troops like a dog that had been commanded to stay and was obediently awaiting his master's signal to move. Aboudi opened his secure phone and immediately was pinged by the sound of an incoming email. He opened the email and quickly skimmed the contents. He took a few minutes to visualize the optics of his president delivering the speech to the people of Zushaka. Liking what he saw in his mind's eye, he immediately picked up the phone and called his president.

"Mr. President, this is Ambassador Aboudi. It appears that the head of Leapp Technologies and his team on the ground are not willing to let us take control of the distribution of the Grok techware. They seem very adamant about reaching the people directly and controlling every facet of the distribution. They have threatened to pack up and head back to the States. As a matter of fact, they're currently waiting in their planes with the engines running, in case you decide not to comply with their wishes."

"Who the hell do they think they are? Ground the planes, and have the general confiscate their equipment. I will not have some bunch of American cowboys tell me how to run my affairs."

"If I may suggest, Mr. President, the equipment is useless without their technical know-how and training. Plus, taking them as hostages will create an international incident that will not bode well for your government's domestic and international image. They have provided me with a politically well-thought-out speech to be delivered by you to the people of Zushaka, which I believe will reflect very well on you and your administration. I have sent the speech to your office for your review. Please take a few minutes to look it over, and then let me know your final decision. In my humble opinion, the messaging of the speech, combined with the net benefits to the people of Zushaka, will position you as a man of the people and as the most progressive leader in Africa. I suggest that we be magnanimous and let the Leapp Technologies team proceed as requested. Plus, there are two large bags of US currency that will go very far in soothing any bruised egos, including that of the general."

"Let me read the speech. I will take your suggestion under consideration. I'll let you know my answer."

A few minutes later, the general received a call. As he was attentively listening to the voice on the other end of the line, the ambassador watched his facial expression. It went from a frown to a subtle smile. The ambassador knew full well what had prompted the change in mood. He thought, *Nothing like greasing the palm to get the wheels of progress in motion.* The general pocketed his cell phone, turned to the ambassador, and with a nod of his head indicated that it was a go. The ambassador retrieved his cell phone from his pocket and immediately called Sacha.

"Ms. Zimmerman, my president has agreed to your terms. You're now free to initiate your operation. The general will provide you with a security detail of twenty of his best men and several translators to assist you with your operation. Please let me know if you need anything else."

"Thank you, Ambassador Aboudi. We look forward to working with you and the general. I will have my security detail deliver the two suitcases to you immediately. I look forward to making this operation a success."

The ambassador hung up the phone. Within a few minutes, an armored vehicle with two men from Sacha's security detail emerged from the back of the C-17 military cargo plane. They drove over to the ambassador's and the general's entourage and handed the two large metal storage cases, which were each the size of a small refrigerator, to the awaiting soldiers. The soldiers quickly placed the boxes in the general's armored vehicle.

Sacha wasted no time in ordering the two planes to taxi to the inconspicuous air force hangar at the far end of the airport. That was to be her command center for the next several weeks. The technicians immediately set up her command center inside the Boeing 747. The setup resembled that of Air Force One with monitors streaming real-time satellite videos of every providence and city in Zushaka. Another monitor listed every school, university, hospital, and community center, with names and contact information of the individuals in charge. On the other plane there were hordes of technicians unpacking the techware and readying it for activation. Grok security protocol allowed only one user to activate the device through voice recognition with the voice being as unique to the user as his or her fingerprint. Sacha's heat map, displayed on another large monitor, showed the location of every device, the current Web activity, and the user's physical and mental vital signs. Her state-of-the-art Tip of the Needle, or TIP for short, algorithm was aggregating and monitoring intellectual, physical, and behavioral activity in real time.

Sacha ordered an immediate strategy meeting of all thirty team leaders. Each team had three technicians, an engineer, several assistants, a translator, and a security detail. They were all given their designated locations, their points of distribution, and the names and contact information of the community leaders within those areas. Her target was to have all the devices distributed and operational within the next two weeks.

That evening, before the next day's launch, she and her staff watched the streaming news telecast of the president of Zushaka delivering his scripted speech to the people of his country.

The head of this small African nation was seated behind an ornate desk in the Presidential Palace, dressed in a traditional tunic. He directly looked at the camera with a beaming facial expression as he addressed his nation.

"I'm proud to announce today the partnership of our great nation with Leapp Technologies, one of the most prominent technology companies in the world. It has been my mission as the president of this country to raise the standard of living for every man, woman, and child in our beloved Zushaka. I can't think of a more effective way of accomplishing this goal than through knowledge and education. It's my aspiration for our people to substantially reduce illiteracy in every corner of our beautiful and proud country and to wipe out the scourge of diseases such as malaria, Ebola, and AIDS, among many others, that have taken so many of the sons and daughters of this country. We aim to create an economic engine that will be the envy of Africa and will make us the Silicon Valley of this continent. To this end, I have instructed my administration to acquire and distribute to the people of Zushaka, for free, Leapp Technologies' latest techware, named Grok. We will be the first nation in the world to provide this technology to its citizens for free." His speech went on to describe his accomplishments and his progressive agenda, along with his glaring vision for the future of his country under his tutelage and leadership. His speech was verbatim as scripted by Leapp Technologies' public relations department.

Sacha watched the screen with a coy smile. At the end of the speech, she concluded the meeting by dismissing her staff.

"Okay, troops, we're done for the day. Let's all get a good night's sleep and hit the ground running early tomorrow. Everything as planned. And no fuck-ups!"

The next day before sunrise, all thirty teams were positioned outside the aircraft hangar, ready for their marching orders. Sacha stood before them, ready to deliver her motivational speech.

"Ladies and gentlemen, today we're changing the world. You will be known as the team that broke the barrier of inequality and leapfrogged a small Third World country from the obscurity of the Dark Ages to the twenty-first century. You should all be very proud of yourselves. The legacy and footprint that you will indelibly leave on this small, distant country will live on for generations to come. I congratulate you on your future success and wish you good fortune. Go get it done; the world is watching."

There was a roar among the crowd as they started their engines and began streaming out of the airport in single file. Sacha joined her staff back in the command center on the 747 and watched the thirty dots on her screen diverge in every which direction.

There were lines of people in every village waiting for this new present from their president. They didn't know what it was or how it worked, but it was free and it came in a shiny box with an embossed logo of Leapp Technologies with gold lettering. The first to receive the techware were teachers, doctors, and professional organizations. The second wave went to students ranging in age from five to twenty-five. The remaining devices were given to NGOs and community leaders, to be distributed on an as-needed basis.

Within the next several days, training sessions were being held in schools, universities, hospitals, and community centers. Before long, the presence of the device was everywhere. People were visibly interacting with the device, oblivious to their surroundings. They were talking to themselves out loud as if they had gone insane, but they were merely immersed in this new universe of their own making.

Sacha was in her control room watching the heat map and the corresponding TIP dashboard. On it there was a slew of electronic gauges measuring everything from IQ, to empathy, to the emotional and physical vital statistics of the end users. More importantly, the gauges were measuring how the AI programming was evolving as the end users became more engaged with the device and proficient in its use. The heat map was lighting up like a Christmas tree or a satellite image of New York City at night.

The change in the people of Zushaka was immediate and profound. Children were learning their alphabet and their multiplication tables in a matter of days. Their mastery of new languages was immediate and unprecedented. Teachers had to change their course plans and curriculums by condensing what once took their students a year to learn into weeks. Physicians were collaborating with the best specialists all over the world and were performing the most advanced technical surgeries locally. Innovations were being created by entrepreneurs at a pace never seen before. The cross-pollination of ideas was instantaneous, and it took weeks instead of years to turn an idea into a marketable product. The country's gross domestic product (GDP) was growing exponentially, and investable capital was flooding into the country from investors from all over the world seeking to capitalize on returns that dwarfed opportunities anywhere else in the world. Zushaka's stock exchange was listing several new initial public offerings (IPOs) on a daily basis. Wealth was being created up and down the economic ladder and was visible throughout the country. New cities were popping up all across the countryside with new luxury malls and residential properties. Luxury cars could be seen on the streets in abundance, whereas not too long ago there were donkeys and horses and the occasional car built in the fifties.

Back at HQ, the staff in charge of mining the influx of data streaming in from Zushaka were busy compartmentalizing all the information and tweaking the algorithm. The government and the president of Zushaka were provided with a daily briefing, summarizing public sentiment and sites frequently trafficked by users in their country. The president couldn't have been more pleased; this initiative had worked better than he ever dreamed, and his public approval rating was within the ninetieth percentile. Sacha was also monitoring all these changes and activities on TIP and was becoming more and more concerned. All these changes were not occurring without a cost.

22 The Man of the Year

The cover of *Time* magazine featured a picture of Zack dressed in a black turtleneck sweater and jeans, standing in his office next to a window overlooking the vast Adirondack Mountains. The pose was intentionally designed to show him as a very reflective man with a far-reaching vision for the future. The caption read, "A combination of Steve Jobs, Bill Gates, and Elon Musk in one." Zack was sitting behind his oversized desk, awaiting the airing of his interview with Jim Johansson, the lead reporter for the most watched morning business show. The reporter began by introducing Zack as the most impactful technology visionary of our time. He began his questioning by saying, "Zack, let me ask the most obvious question that is on everyone's mind: When should we expect Leapp Technologies to go public?"

"Well, Jim, I don't expect to take my company public anytime soon."

"Why is that? Given your company's resounding success in launching the Grok wearable technology in Zushaka, and given the worldwide interest in having access to this technology, one would think you'd be considering going public."

"I have to admit, the profit motives are very compelling, but this is all the more reason to keep the company privately held. A public company believes that increasing shareholders' value is the main driver behind every decision. I'm at a stage in my life where my sole motivation is not money. I have been fortunate enough to have amassed enough wealth to last a hundred lifetimes. It is time to give back to causes that I believe will serve humanity. I can't do that by being a public company."

"Zack, that sounds very noble, but I have to ask this question: Does your political ambition to become the president of the United States have anything to do with your new sense of philanthropy? Are you mainly using your financial power to gain another form of power?"

"That is a fair question. I'm only interested in the power of new ideas that will serve this country's national interests, by improving the quality of life for every American as well as for our neighbors."

"Based on the popularity of your political rallies and on recent polls, it appears that your message is resonating well with a wide swath of potential voters, especially with younger people. Why do you think that is happening?"

"Young people understand the power of technology and how transformative it can be," Zack replied. "Using technological advances not as a product to be sold for a profit, but as a service to improve the quality of life for those who are less fortunate, is a mission statement that young people can identify with and have an affinity for. Plus, my platform of new ideas, which focuses on finding solutions rather than endless bickering and laying blame, differs greatly from that of the other two parties. They have focused on destroying each other for political gain, with reckless abandon of what we have elected them to do, which is to serve the people who elected them and to attend to the issues that matter to them most. They see me as the antithesis of that, an individual who is not interested in using his political office to enrich himself but who is willing to sacrifice much personal gain to do what is right for every man, woman, and child in this country."

"I have to admit, Zack, you're different from the typical politician we have become accustomed to seeing, and your message differs greatly from the extreme position of the other two parties."

"Jim, I will take that as a compliment. I don't consider myself an ideologue but a pragmatist. And those who believe that their way is the only way, frankly, scare me. Extremists will always sell their twisted ideology by using the emotional power of fear and greed. Pragmatists will give you the facts and strive to find bipartisan solutions to every complicated problem. I believe the current two-party system is polarizing our country and, for that matter, the world. We have to come up with a different way, or divided we will all fall."

"Well, sir, I'm looking forward to watching your debate tonight with the other two parties' candidates and covering your future rallies. Good luck."

"Thank you, Jim."

That evening Sacha and Addis were standing in the kitchen of Addis's apartment, preparing a Greek recipe that Sacha had found online for their dinner guests. Addis wanted to spend the evening watching the debate with his closest friends. He had suggested the idea to Nader and Sacha, and they thought it would definitely make for an interesting evening. By this time, the relationship between Nader and Donna had become exclusive. It had been several months since Donna declared her desire to convert to Islam, and her intent to do so remained unwavering, in spite of strong objections from her family and friends. Her father was so enraged by her decision that he threatened to disown her and sever any future contact. But Donna had made up her mind, and she was never one to be swayed by other people's opinions. She felt like a woman in control of her own destiny, and that new sense of freedom, from a life charted by others to one charted by her, caused her to make another declaration. That night while Nader was dropping her off in front of her apartment, and after she'd declared her intentions to convert in front of Nader, Sacha, and Addis a few months earlier, she reached out and kissed Nader on the lips. Afterward, she stated, "I love you. I don't know if you have the same feeling for me, but it's okay if you don't. I want you to know that I'm not converting to Islam because I'm in love with you, but because you showed me how it's to be a good Muslim. I fell in love with that as well."

Nader looked at Donna for a few seconds before speaking. When he finally spoke, his words came out as if he had been holding them back for a long time. It was a relief to finally get them off his chest.

"Donna, you have no idea how happy you have made me. I have been so conflicted about my feelings for you and my need to stay true to myself and what I believe in. I didn't think a long-term relationship between us would work out given our differences, and I didn't want to put our friendship in jeopardy by declaring my feelings for you."

"You said something interesting before about long-term relationships. What did you mean?"

"Well, it is forbidden for us to cohabitate or engage in an intimate relationship unless we're married. And I've often fantasized about us being married. I hope I didn't frighten you."

"Is it okay to be intimate and kiss you although we are not married? Well, I don't care; I have not converted yet."

She reached out and kissed him again, more deeply and affectionately this time, and whispered in his ear, "If this is your way of proposing to me, I accept."

The next day, Donna and Nader went to the same mosque that Nader had gone to, to renew his faith a few years earlier. Donna declared before the imam three times, "Ash-hadu alla ilaha illallah, wa ash-hadu anna Muhammadar rasulullah" (There is only one God, and the Prophet Muhammad is his messenger). That afternoon while having lunch, Nader formally proposed to Donna. He got down on one knee and handed her his beloved deceased mother's engagement ring. He had had the ring for some time, since the passing of his father; it was one of the items that his brother, Mustafa, had insisted he take. He never thought he would ever get to use it, having resolved himself to the idea that he would be a bachelor for life.

Nader and Donna kept the news of their engagement secret in fear that their relationship would be frowned upon by MIT administrators. After all, she was still his research assistant and he was still her professor. However, that charade was soon to be over, after Donna's graduation in May. However, this evening Donna and Nader were planning to reveal their plans of marriage to Addis and Sacha during dinner.

Nader and Donna arrived at Addis's apartment promptly at 7:00 p.m. as directed. They rang the doorbell. A few seconds later, Sacha opened the door, wearing an apron over her tight-fitting sweater and jeans. She was always impeccably dressed and always looked as if she had just emerged from a photo shoot. The first thing that Sacha noticed was that Nader and Donna were holding hands and that there was a gleeful look about them. She reached out and kissed them both on the cheeks. "Come on in. Can I get you something to drink?"

They both responded in unison, "Sparkling water would be great."

"We got you your favorite dessert, pumpkin pie and homemade whipped cream."

Sacha looked at Nader with a remorseful smile. "You remember!"

Nader responded, "Of course I do."

Donna quickly picked up on the suppressed feelings between Nader and Sacha and knew that there was some history between them that she didn't fully grasp. She intended to find out what it was after this evening was over.

At that awkward moment, Addis emerged from the kitchen, looking a little disheveled. "Hi, guys. Thanks for coming. Sorry for the look, but cooking hasn't ever been one of my strong suits."

"That's okay, honey. Why don't you get Donna and Nader some sparkling water while I finish dinner? We should be eating in about fifteen minutes."

"Thanks for saving me, honey. I definitely can pour a mean glass of sparkling water better than I can cook."

Addis's apartment overlooked the Boston Harbor. The view was breathtaking. As Nader and Donna were enjoying the view, Addis was starting a fire that perfectly complemented the beautiful view and the overall relaxed ambiance. A few minutes later, Sacha summoned her guests to the dinner table. As always, every detail had been impeccably arranged. She was a perfectionist even when it came to the most mundane tasks. There was a beautiful floral arrangement in the center of the table, and the combination of the tablecloth, silverware, and expensive chinaware made the setting appear as if they were dinning at the most expensive five-star restaurant in the city.

Addis uncorked the wine and poured a glass for Sacha and one for himself. He raised his glass and toasted his guests: "To my closest friend, whom I consider as my family. May we have many moments like this to share in the future." They all clinked their glasses. Nader turned his head and looked at Donna as if he were asking for permission. Donna, knowing exactly what the look meant, nodded.

Nader raised his glass of sparkling water again and declared, "Well, I also would like to make a toast. I would like to make a special announcement before my closest friends and the only family I have in this country. I'm very happy to say that I have asked for Donna's hand in marriage, and surprisingly and graciously she has accepted."

Addis jumped from his chair and grabbed Nader in a tight embrace. "Man, that is great news! I'm very happy for both of you," which was followed by an equally affectionate embrace of Donna as he looked her in the eyes and said, "You're marrying the most genuinely good man I have ever had the blessing and good fortune of meeting and knowing. I wish you both all the happiness in the world."

Sacha sat quietly, clearly shocked by the news. All three directed their gaze at her for a few uncomfortable seconds, waiting for her response. She finally realized that she had to say something. Her response came out as somewhat canned and detached: "That is great news. I'm really happy for you guys." All three picked up on Sacha's tone but decided to redirect the conversation back between them. The rest of the dinner conversation was about Nader and Donna's future plans, Donna's family's objections to her conversion and her marriage to Nader, and how difficult it was to keep their relationship secret during work at MIT. Sacha mostly sat quietly, contributing to the conversation every now and then just to show that she was engaged. Her demeanor didn't go unnoticed by all three.

After dessert, they all retired to the living room to watch the debate.

Zack was standing behind the podium stage, on the left, next to his two opponents, the nominees from the Democratic Party and the Republican Party. By way of contrast, he was younger by several decades than both his female and male opponent. He was considerably better-looking, better dressed, and fitter than the other contenders for the office of the president. His two opponents were well-established career politicians who had risen through the ranks of their parties, initially as local politicians, followed by a stint as congresspeople, then senators of the states of Texas and California, respectively. Their faces, as well as their politics, were well-known to anyone who had the slightest interest in politics. They both had been groomed for the office, and their respective parties' vast capital and political machinery was fully vested in their winning the ultimate prize of becoming the leader of their respective political party and the president of the United States.

Zack, on the other hand, had made it very clear at the beginning of his campaign that he would not accept any PAC or corporate money. The only fundraising he was willing to accept was through his campaign website, and it would be limited to individual contributors and to an amount no greater than $100 per contribution. His campaign was primarily funded from his own wealth in order to avoid the appearance of any conflict of interest.

The moderator, from a relatively liberal news outlet, opened the debate by announcing the rules of engagement and the debate format. He prohibited the audience from clapping, jeering, or booing during the hour-and-a-half debate. He quickly explained that each candidate would make an opening statement, followed by a question and answer session where each candidate was limited to two minutes to articulate and deliver his or her answer. The subject matter would cover both domestic and international policies. The moderator added that the questions were formulated by him and his colleagues without any input or prior knowledge from any of the candidates.

"Ladies and gentlemen, we will now begin by having each candidate deliver a five-minute opening statement. The first candidate to deliver his opening statement was chosen by an electronic lottery system. It's Mr. Zimmerman. Mr. Zimmerman, the floor is yours."

Zack began by thanking the moderator for hosting the event; the American people for the opportunity to be their servant; his family for their support; and all the $100 contributors for their votes of confidence and their hard-earned money.

"Let me begin by saying who I'm not: I'm not a politician. I'm not interested in using the office of the presidency to feather my own nest. I'm not an ideologue hell-bent on changing the world into my own image. I'm not about winning at any cost, even if it destroys the thing that I love the most: my country. I'm not here to give anything, sell anything, or buy your votes.

"What I am is a proud American; a proud father and a husband grateful for the love of his spouse and child; an entrepreneur; and a businessman with a track record of solving problems and creating value for his constituents.

"This is what the American people ought to expect from me and my campaign: I will not engage in slandering, digging, or fabricating dirt on my opponents, nor will I perpetuate such behavior by spending my time talking about gossip and false accusations, rather than policies. My life is an open book. I will demand full transparency from my staff and, more importantly, from myself. Anything the public needs to know will be on full display on my website, including all the specifics of my proposed policy initiatives. These mission statements will not be hyperbole or grandiose ideas that are not based in fact. Instead they are actual models on how we, collectively, are going to make them work and, more importantly, how we are going to pay for them.

"What I am is a pragmatist, a problem solver, and a realist, but most of all I am a grateful American who wants to give back rather than take. If this type of person is what you want as your voice in Washington, then I would be honored to receive your vote. If I'm so honored, we will reconstruct this country and make it again what the founders had intended: a free, independent, and self-reliant people looking for a governing body to do for them only what they can't do individually or collectively for themselves. And to the greatest extent possible, any decisions impacting us individually ought to meet the litmus test as to whether it ought to emanate from our own communities where we, as individuals, have the greatest control or from a bloated, bureaucratic, and—may I even daresay—often corrupt central government that is more often interested in protecting their own interests rather than the interests of the people they serve.

"Thank you, and God bless this country, its people, and everyone we touch throughout the world. Thank you."

"Mr. Zimmerman, you still have a few minutes left for your opening remarks," the moderator said.

"Sir, it is not how much you say that matters; it's what you say," Zack responded.

The debate began with a succession of questions from the moderator, covering a wide range of topics dealing with the economy, international policies, and social issues such as income inequality, abortion, gun control, crime, climate control, and immigration.

Zack came across as well prepared with facts and figures to support his positions. His arguments were salient and well thought out, while his opponents often spewed incoherent policies that sounded like a long list of giveaways (free health care, free education, guaranteed retirement income, etc.) that they had a difficult time supporting with any facts or figures when the moderator asked for specifics. They often refuted Zack's policy initiatives by attacking him personally as being a billionaire who was out of touch with the common person.

Zack had no problem deflecting these criticisms, by pointing out that he was a common man who had come from nothing and was able to build an empire because of the American dream. He said that if he were to be elected as president, his goal would be to make that dream available and accessible to everyone. Zack's command of facts and dates often caused his opponents to go on the defensive.

He would often point out their hypocrisies by stating the dates and circumstances surrounding when they had espoused policy positions different from the ones they were advocating now just to win votes. He would often contrast their actions after they'd been elected to public office and how dramatically these differed from their campaign promises. His opponents appeared emotionally and physically flustered, having to spend most of their time defending their track records versus selling their agendas.

At the end of the debate, Zack emerged as the clear winner, both in style and in substance. His opponents appeared totally disoriented and physically shaken during their closing remarks as they realized that the substance of most of their prepared remarks had already been artfully debunked by Zack.

Back in Addis's apartment, Addis, Sacha, Nader, and Donna sat quietly as they watched Zack's performance before the nation. There were no cheers and no jeers, just absolute silence as if they were impartial judges at a spelling bee contest. None of them were emotionally or intellectually vested in any of the candidates, including Zack. They all seemed guarded and held their opinions close to the vest in fear of offending their guests or their hosts, whichever the case may be. Addis finally broke the silence by stating that he thought Zack had emerged as the clear winner. He asked, "What do you guys think?"

Donna was the first to reply. "Yeah, I think he came across as being very presidential with a clear vision of what is needed to fix this country. I don't agree with everything he said, but at least he didn't come across as a typical politician or a used car salesman like the other two."

Nader and Sacha exchanged a look as if they knew what each other was thinking. She knew that he was deeply suspicious of Zack, given their history, and she didn't fault him for it. She also knew Zack better than anyone in the room, and she was not buying his shtick. It seemed to her that his delivery was too mechanical, was too well rehearsed, and lacked the idiosyncrasies, tone, and intonations that she was accustomed to seeing in her father as early as she could remember. At times there were silent pauses in his delivery during the debate that struck her as awkward.

Addis redirected his attention to Sacha and asked, "So, what do you think, darling?"

"I think he did well, but something about his delivery seemed unnatural to me."

Addis said, "Really? It's funny you say that, because I noticed that as well."

The rest of the evening, they enjoyed each other's company and discussed Nader's and Donna's future plans, being careful not to ask the obvious question that was on everybody's mind: when was Addis going to propose to Sacha, or possibly the other way around?

While Sacha and Addis were in bed that evening, Sacha woke up in the middle of the night to Addis screaming in his sleep with his hand reaching out to an imaginary figure in his dream. "Give me your hand. Give me your hand."

He was sweating profusely. Sacha was hesitant to wake him up; he was clearly having a nightmare. Sacha gently rubbed his arm. "Addis, wake up. Addis, wake up."

When he finally awoke from his nightmare, he sat up in bed, clearly shaken by his vision.

"Honey, are you okay?"

"Yes. I had a dream or a vision—I don't know which."

"What was it?"

"My father the rabbi, and Nader's father the imam, were standing at the edge of a black whirlpool. The thick black liquid was churning violently, and there was a figure on the other side of the pool whose face I couldn't see, watching. He had on a hoodie and was dressed in a black robe. I couldn't see his face, just his eyes—and they were very evil. There was a person in the whirlpool who was being sucked down. Both my father and the imam where urging me to save him, but every time I reached out and grabbed his hand, my hand would slip. Then I woke up."

"What do you think it means?"

"I don't know. I have a feeling that the person drowning is Nader."

The next morning after the debate, Zack was in his office, when his expected guest knocked on the door.

"Come on in."

"Good morning, sir. How did Grok 2.0 work?"

"Well. Except the damn thing kept on blacking out."

"Yes, sir. The power source is not very stable and seems to react negatively to biological changes in the body, like an increase in body temperature or heartbeat."

"Okay. Just get this thing out of my neck."

23 The Setup

After the resounding success of the Grok device in Zushaka, many countries were clamoring to get access to the same technology. They exerted substantial pressure on their UN ambassadors to mount a concerted effort on the UN General Council Science Advisory Board to give their stamp of approval for the deployment and distribution of the device worldwide. Under substantial pressure, the council ultimately acquiesced to the demand and scheduled an impromptu meeting, requesting the attendance of both Zack Zimmerman and Nader el-Shafique. This time the chairman of the board, Ambassador Aboudi, recused himself as the residing chairman, and instead became an expert witness, having firsthand knowledge of the technology deployment in his country. The new residing chairman was the ambassador from Romania. It was no coincidence that he was the one who had been handpicked by Ambassador Aboudi. The selection of the new residing chairman was a result of Zack's arm-twisting, his making a direct request of Ambassador Aboudi to specifically pick the Romanian ambassador. The Romanian government was widely known as the most corrupt government in eastern Europe, and the oligarchs running the country had been cleverly manipulated by Zack to become his allies in this fight. The quid pro quo was that if they helped him, he would enter into a joint venture agreement to manufacture parts for his products in Romania, using factories owned by these oligarchs.

The new chairman had wasted no time in scheduling a meeting of the full board for another presentation with Zack. Zack was not going to make the same mistake this time. Using back channels to the new chairman, he had made sure that he was in full control of the meeting agenda, especially the time allotted to Nader to rebut any of his proposals. Not leaving anything to chance, he also had an insurance policy permanently eliminating his nemesis once and for all.

Zack still harbored deep animosity toward Nader from the last time they'd gone before the board. This time he was not about to repeat the same mistake. He didn't believe in taking prisoners. If there was an obstacle in his way, his modus operandi was to remove it permanently. Nader was no exception, regardless of his history with Sacha. Not only had Zack stacked the board in his favor, but also he had made sure that he had an insurance policy as a backup.

The meeting with the board was scheduled to take place in two weeks. It was time for Zack to put his plan into action. He was sitting in a nondescript joint in Bay Ridge, Brooklyn, that was known as a bar that catered to alcoholics who liked to start their daily ritual as early as ten in the morning. The place was dark and damp, and reeked of alcohol and sawdust, the latter of which was intended to mask the putrid smell of vomit.

Zack drove his rented Nissan Altima to the location. He was wearing a baseball cap, jeans, a lumberjack jacket, and construction boots. He looked the part of an unemployed construction worker who was looking for an inconspicuous bar to drown his sorrows. His intended guest arrived a few minutes after Zack. Zack was at a corner table with his back to the wall, at the far end of the bar and next to the back exit. All the details of their meeting location, including the specific table and the escape route, had been planned by Zack's guest. After all, he was a man who had formidable training in covert operations and knew well how to be stealthy and have contingency plans in case of any surprises.

The Middle Eastern–looking man with a full mane of black hair approached Zack slowly, casing the joint, eyeing every patron, every nook and cranny, trying to identify anything or anyone out of the ordinary. When he was finally comfortable with his surroundings, he grabbed the chair next to Zack and extended his hand to shake Zack's hand.

"Mr. Zimmerman, it's a pleasure to finally meet you."

"Please sit down. Is everything in place?"

"Yes, sir. We were able to use the laptop provided to Ms. Kramer by Leapp Technologies to hack into Nader's computer. The fact that she was searching many Islamic sites made it easy for us to download links to terrorist sites on her computer and, in turn, on Nader's computer. The links and cookies are encrypted, so they're not visible to the user. Frankly, the fabricated chats and conversations embedded on their laptops with these sites are pretty damning, and they're totally unaware of it."

"When are we going operational?"

"Well, sir, everything is in place, as I said. I have been coordinating with the Israeli intelligence, and they are ready to alert US authorities when you give the go-ahead. We made the threat very credible and made the plot to execute a terrorist attack in NYC seem imminent."

"I expect this to go down flawlessly—and no fuck-ups this time."

"Of course, sir. What do you mean, this time?"

"This is not your first foray with el-Shafique. Last time, you ended up killing Rabbi Ackerman instead of the intended target, Nader's father, the imam."

"How did you know about that?"

"Who do you think prompted your prime minster to launch the assassination plot, and who do you think yanked you from the Israeli intelligence service, brought you here, and gave you a job?"

"Well, sir, I wasn't aware of that information, but thank you for the opportunity. I assure you, this time I will not fail you."

"I want you to launch the operation this weekend, and after that I want you to go on a long vacation outside the country. Don't contact me; if I need you, I will contact you."

Zack got up and exited through the back door. His guest made sure to finish the two beers he had ordered for the two of them so as not to look suspicious. Wiping the table and bottles clean of any fingerprints, he disposed of the bottles and left the bartender a dollar tip on his way out the front door. The tip was neither too large nor too small, just enough to make sure that his encounter with the bartender was not a memorable one.

The Friday before the campaign against Nader was to go live, Zack was having a meeting in his office with Addis, Sacha, and the head engineer in charge of the Grok techware. The head engineer had a perplexing problem that he couldn't solve, in spite of assembling the best engineers and scientists in the firm and expending an inordinate amount of time and capital to come up with a solution. The conversion of Grok techware from a wearable to an injectable was a herculean task that Zack had designated as the sole priority of the firm for the last six months. Every PhD in the firm knew that this was priority number one. They also knew that, to a great extent, their careers and future employment with the firm were dependent on their success. Many of them worked around the clock to complete the task at hand within the ambitious timetable established by Zack. However, there was one vexing problem that, as hard as they tried, they couldn't solve. The nanotechnology design of the device made it difficult to create a sustainable and reliable source of energy. The device was unpredictable and would often shut down at the most inopportune time. That was what Zack had experienced during the presidential debate; his level of frustration was well-known to everyone involved with the project. He had placed his last hope on Addis to figure out the solution. He knew that Addis was fearlessly independent, so he'd had to present this problem to him not as a mandate or as condition for his continued employment with the firm, but as an intellectual challenge.

Addis was intrigued by the challenge; he had been working on capturing the elusive phantom particle for the last three years, to no avail. Although his recent experiments were able to capture it on several occasions, it would only last for a split second. His recent collaboration with scientists of diverse disciplines within Leapp Technologies had convinced him that the elusive phantom particle naturally existed within the human body and was produced in abundance. The premise was that humans didn't need an external source of energy and didn't operate on batteries or have to be hooked up to an electric outlet. The challenge was how to have the injectable Grok device tap into this infinite source of power, thus making it a permanent part of the host.

As the four of them were discussing all the relevant issues, Addis became distant and less and less interactive. It became very obvious to the rest of them that he wasn't even listening to their conversation. His face was becoming noticeably pale, and he began to sweat profusely. There was a slight but noticeable tremor in his hand and legs. Sacha became very alarmed and went to sit next to him on the couch. She began to wipe the sweat off his forehead with her handkerchief as she stroked his hand and asked repeatedly, "Addis, are you all right? Addis, are you all right?" Zack immediately got on the phone and instructed one of his assistants to dispatch his personal physician on staff and his team. Leapp Technologies had their own medical facilities on the premises with some of the best physicians in their respective fields on retainer.

Addis's eyes began to roll back in his head. The tremors were getting convulsive, and the veins in his neck were pulsating at an inordinately high rate.

Zack yelled, "I think he is having a stroke." He opened the door to his office, yelling at his assistant, "Get those fucking doctors here now!"

Sacha was beside herself. She grabbed Addis and brought him closer to her chest, trying to do whatever she could to comfort him. She didn't know what to do. The thought of not being able to help him, and worse yet the possibility of losing him, was emotionally unbearable.

Sacha noticed immediately after embracing Addis that his pulse was slowing, color was coming back to his face, and the tremors were becoming less noticeable. He opened his eyes and looked at her, quickly whispering in her ear, "Get me out of here now, please." There was no debating his request. She knew him well enough to know from the tone of his voice that this was a request that she needed to comply with—and with haste. She got up, helped him off the couch, and began to escort him to the door.

Zack and the engineer immediately protested, Zack saying, "Addis is not well; he needs to be thoroughly checked by the doctors. He could have had a stroke. Moving him is not wise."

Sacha ordered Zack's assistant to have her car brought to the front entrance. Then she looked at Zack and, with a firm voice, said, "I know what I'm doing. I will take care of him from here. We are not debating this. I will call you in a few hours."

Addis leaned on Sacha as she gingerly walked him to the elevator. A few minutes later, they were in Sacha's car for the two-hour drive back to Boston. Addis sat in the passenger seat quietly for the first half hour of the drive. Sacha held his hand, not only to comfort him, but also to monitor his pulse, the tremors, and his body temperature. She would frequently turn her head and look at him; he looked calm, just quietly staring at the view in front him as if he were trying to decipher what had just happened to him.

When he finally spoke, he turned around and looked at Sacha. "We need to call Nader right now. He and Donna are in grave danger." His voice was firm and resolute.

"What do you mean, they're in danger?"

"I will explain later. Please call him on your secure phone right now."

Sacha grabbed her satchel from the back seat, opened it, and pulled out her secure satellite phone. She put the phone on speaker and dialed Nader's number, which she knew by heart. After the second ring, Nader answered.

"Hi, sunshine. I was about to call you. Donna and I wanted to thank you and Addis for the wonderful dinner and the—"

Addis interrupted, saying, "Nader, this is Addis. I need you to listen to me very carefully. We don't have time to discuss or debate what I'm about to tell you."

"Addis, you're scaring me!"

"Fear is exactly what you should feel. Both your life and Donna's life are in grave danger. Listen to me very carefully: You need to get out of your apartment immediately. Put on very loose clothing—a hoodie, a hat, and sunglasses, anything that will disguise your look. Use the back entrance to your apartment, and avoid all cameras. Don't take your phone, wallet, or laptop. No electronics of any kind."

"What is this all about?"

"I will tell you all about it when I see you. Where is Donna right now?"

"She should be finishing her last class and starting to walk back to her apartment."

"What is her cell number?"

Nader rattled off the number, beginning with the 617 area code.

"There is an old abandoned warehouse a few blocks from my apartment building. Do you know the one I'm talking about?"

"Yes, I do," Nader responded.

"Good. I will meet you there in about an hour. I will call Donna and arrange with her to meet us there as well."

"Addis, this is all very strange. And I really have a very busy day today."

"Nader, you need to trust me on this. Please know that this is very serious. I need you to follow my directions exactly. I will explain it all when I see you."

"Addis, I trust you implicitly. I guess I will see you in an hour!"

Addis dialed Donna's number. The conversation went very much as the one with Nader had gone, except she needed a lot more persuading.

On the drive to the abandoned building, Addis began to describe to Sacha what he had experienced in Zack's office.

"I was overwhelmed by this evil presence that seemed to want to pull me down into a dark pit. Then I began to have a vision of Nader and Donna being seized by a large company of armed men dressed in black. I could also hear voices in the background urging me to help them.

This is when you hugged me and brought me back. This is not the first time I had a vision about Nader. When we were kids back in Israel, we both attended the same school. One day after class, walking back to my sister's car, which was waiting to take me home, I had a vision of Nader getting beaten up by couple of school bullies. I knew exactly where he was on the school grounds, and I sprang to help him out. I found him being pushed around by three thugs, and I intervened."

An hour later Addis and Sacha arrived at the abandoned building, where Nader and Donna were anxiously waiting. Donna spoke first. She was slightly irritated by the disruption to her daily schedule and found the whole thing overly dramatic. She initially thought that it was a practical joke, but she knew that such would be out of character for both Addis and Sacha.

"Hi, guys. What is this whole cloak-and-dagger thing all about? Frankly, both Nader and I are very concerned. You made it sound ominous."

Addis spoke first, while Sacha approached Donna and held her hand. "I know that this sounds very strange, but you have to believe that what I'm about tell you is real. I believe that both of you are about to be arrested by a well-trained special police force that believes you're about to commit a heinous crime or a terrorist act."

Nader couldn't contain his shock. "Terrorist?! What the hell are we talking about here?"

"I don't know. All I can tell you is that I saw it as clear as day in a vision."

Donna quickly responded, "We dropped everything and we're standing here in the middle of the day in an abandoned warehouse because you had a vision?" She turned around to look at Nader, expecting the same look of indignation, but she was surprised to see a blank look, as if he were reexperiencing a distant memory.

"Addis's visions were legendary when we were growing up back in Palestine. He once saved my ass from a whooping by three jealous schoolmates. He came to my rescue just in the nick of time. He seems to have known what was going to happen before it happened."

Donna asked, "Are you guys for real?" She added, "I'm going back to my apartment to take a nice long, hot shower, make a nice hot cup of tea, and start studying for the exam I have on Monday."

Sacha said, "Donna, listen to me please. I believe Addis. You know I'm not into this parapsychology shit, and as you can see, Nader's gut feeling is telling him to listen to Addis.

"Let me suggest we all take a ride to my family's cabin in the Adirondacks for the weekend. If nothing happens, we would have all had a relaxing, quiet time enjoying each other's company for the weekend. I see you have your school bag and laptop with you. You will have plenty of time to study for your exam!"

Addis said, "Laptop?! Can I see that?" He was somewhat miffed that Donna had brought her laptop even though he had told both her and Nader not to bring any electronics of any type.

Donna handed Addis her laptop. He pulled a Swiss pocketknife from his jacket pocket and began to take off the back of the laptop, when Donna began to object. "What are you doing?" she asked.

"I'm disconnecting all the communication capabilities from your laptop. This thing is like a tracking device!"

Sacha said, "Nader, you and Donna take Addis's car and drive to the cabin. The address and a detailed map are on the dashboard. Follow the map exactly. It will take you longer than usual to get there, but we are purposefully trying to avoid all toll roads and street cameras. No stops and no calls of any kind. Addis and I will see you there in a few hours."

Addis handed them his keys as he assured them that everything would be okay.

A few minutes later Sacha and Addis were in her car driving to the cabin, when she received a call on her Bluetooth. The screen read "Dad."

Sacha asked, "Should I take this?"

Addis replied, "You should. Make up some story."

Sacha said into the phone, "Hi, Dad!"

Zack said, "Hi. How is Addis?"

Sacha replied, "Oh, he is fine. It must have been something I fed him. You know how wonderful my cooking is."

Zack asked, "Can I speak to him?"

"Oh, he is taking a nap right now. We decided to go to the cabin for the weekend. I will have him call you on Monday."

Zack said, "Okay. Enjoy yourself. I will see you Monday."

Zack hung up the phone, finding his daughter's tone a little suspicious, but he thought at least she and Addis would not be in town when the whole thing with Nader went down.

That night the four of them settled down for the evening at the cabin for a dinner of pizza that Sacha had picked up on the way down. Although the setting was cozy and otherwise the gathering would have been festive, the air was full of tension and anticipation. Addis unexpectedly asked his guests, "Can you guys think of anything that you might have done inadvertently to cast suspicion onto your allegiance or intentions?"

Nader said, "Of course not. I love this country and all it has afforded me since I came here."

Donna said, "Of course not."

Sacha asked, "Can you think of anything at all, even sites you might have visited on the internet, that could be misinterpreted as hostile to the United States?"

Donna replied, "When I was researching Islam before converting, I visited a lot of Islamic sites, but they were mainly about the Koran, Islamic ideology, and Islamic history. None of them espoused fanaticism or a terrorist ideology."

Addis asked, "Is the laptop you brought with you the one you used to research those sites?"

Donna replied, "Yes."

Addis asked, "May I see it again, please?"

Donna pulled her laptop from her pack and handed it to Addis.

"Wow, this is not your typical retail laptop. Where did you get this?" he asked.

Donna replied, "I'm not at liberty to say."

Sacha asked, "Can I look at it?"

Addis handed the laptop to Sacha. Her facial expression immediately turned into a frown. "This is not a retail laptop; this is a very sophisticated piece of machinery that was specifically designed by Leapp Technologies for their top programmers. Where did you get this?"

Donna hesitated for a few minutes; she had always wanted to tell Nader about her position with Leapp Technologies and hated keeping secrets from him, but she feared losing her lucrative position or, worse still, being sued in a court of law.

Donna replied, "I have been working for Leapp Technologies for a few months now, and as a condition of employment, I had to sign a nondisclosure agreement and agree not to divulge my position in fear of a security breach."

Sacha asked, "Who are you working for at Leapp Technologies? And who hired you? What project are you working on?"

Donna answered, "I only interviewed with one person, Tom Schafer, the head of HR. My job is to run some analytics on a massive database. Frankly, I find the position very boring."

Nader asked, "When were you going to tell me this?"

Donna replied, "Sorry, honey. It really bothered me not sharing this information with you, but they asked me not to divulge anything about my position as a condition of my employment."

Addis, beginning to dismantle the laptop, disconnected the hard drive. He took the hard drive and connected it to a highly sophisticated in-house desktop. After he'd run some analytical software on the contents of the disk drive, data began to pour onto the screen. However, there were several bytes of data that were encrypted. The encryption didn't present a challenge for Addis, Nader, or Sacha. Within a few seconds they were able to break the code. Their findings left them breathless. There was a drove of data showing communications with terrorist sites and searches about target locations, bomb building, and planning.

Donna, aghast at the highly incriminating content on her laptop, began to vehemently proclaim her innocence. "I've never been on any of these sites and never made any of these searches. How the hell did this stuff get on my computer?"

Addis said, "It seems like you were sharing all this information with another IP address. I would guess that would be Nader's computer."

Nader said, "We are fucked. Who would do this?"

Sacha responded, "You were set up by someone with a great deal of sophistication. I don't know who, but it has to do with the origin of Donna's computer. Her computer is a Trojan horse."

Nader said, "This all leads back to Leapp Technologies."

Addis said, "It might, but you also created a lot of enemies at the UN, and Donna was an easy conduit given her searches on Islamic sites."

Donna asked, "What are we going to do?"

Sacha responded, "We definitely can't do anything about it right now. Let's all get a good night's rest. We will figure it out in the morning."

They all retired to their respective rooms. In the morning, both Nader and Donna woke up to loud banging on their bedroom doors. They simultaneously opened their doors to see Sacha and Addis standing outside with a frightened look.

Nader said, "Good morning. What is going on?"

Sacha said, "You've both got to see this."

The television was on, and the news announcer was talking about a foiled terrorist attempt. In the background there were pictures of SWAT teams heavily armed, storming an apartment building before the break of dawn. Nader immediately recognized the building. He said, "That's my building!"

The announcer said, "The FBI has indicated that they received an anonymous tip about an imminent terrorist attack on an unidentified location in New York City. The suspects were not found at their respective apartments and were identified as Nader el-Shafique and Donna Kramer. Mr. el-Shafique is a professor of physics at MIT and is of Palestinian descent. He came to the States several years ago on a student visa. Ms. Kramer is also a PhD candidate at MIT and is a US citizen who has recently converted to Islam. So far this is the only information released by the FBI, but we anticipate more details will emerge during the scheduled FBI news conference at 11:00 a.m. In the meantime, the FBI has issued a nationwide manhunt for these individuals and is asking the public to consider them armed and dangerous and to immediately call 911 if they encounter them." On the screen, both Nader's and Donna's driver's license photos came into focus with the caption "Armed and dangerous."

Nader said, "What armed and dangerous? These hillbillies around here will shoot us at first sight if we stick our heads out of this door. We need to call an attorney right now."

Sacha asked, "That will do what, exactly?"

Nader answered, "That will negotiate our surrender and make sure that we leave here without getting shot."

Donna said, "We have been set up for some reason. Whoever did it has meticulously planned every step. How can we fight these allegations from within a high-security prison cell, most likely in Guantánamo?"

Addis said, "Donna is right. This is too well planned for the brain behind this scheme not to have thought of what they will do after you get caught, that is, if they were planning on catching you alive in the first place."

Nader said, "What?! We have done nothing wrong. Who would do this? This has your father's fingerprints all over it."

Sacha replied, "Zack might be a lot of things, but he is not malicious and would never put your life in danger knowing how important you are to me. We have no time to figure out the who, what, and why. We have to start thinking about how to get you both out of this shithole you're in and into safety. I don't want to speak on anyone's behalf, but I'm all in, and I will do whatever it takes to get you to safety."

Addis said, "I'm all in as well. We need to figure out how to get you both out of this country first. Then we can figure out how to exonerate you."

Sacha said, "I've got an idea. Let me make a few arrangements."

An hour later, both Sacha and Addis arrived at the company's private airplane hangar in a Range Rover that Zack usually kept at the cabin. The car windows were tinted with almost no visibility of any passengers occupying the back seats. Sacha positioned the car next to the airplane staircase, making sure that the security cameras had no direct view. Both Nader and Donna exited the car and snuck into the cargo storage area beneath the plane. A few minutes later, Sacha was taxiing to the runway as she was receiving her clearance from the tower. Immediately after takeoff, Addis left the cockpit, leaving Sacha to pilot the plane while he helped Nader and Donna from the luggage portal into the main cabin. It took eight hours before they landed at a private airport outside Geneva, Switzerland.

24 The Escape

Once they had landed, Nader used a landline to call his brother, Mustafa, in Germany. He disguised the call as a solicitation call and left a message on Mustafa's voice mail.

"Mr. el-Shafique, this is Shu Shu, calling to inform you that you have been selected to receive a prize as a result of your recent credit card purchases. It is urgent that you call us back as soon as possible at [number redacted] to claim your prize."

The nickname Shu Shu was what Nader's mother had called him growing up. He hated the nickname and always protested when his family called him by that name, but he knew that his brother would immediately recognize it.

Half an hour later, Mustafa retrieved his message and immediately recognized his brother's voice and nickname. The news of the raid on his brother's apartment was now being talked about on every news outlet, including CNN Europe. He was worried out of his mind about his younger brother and had made several attempts to call him, but he'd received the same message each time: "This phone number is no longer in service." He realized quickly that his brother must be on the run and that he needed to use absolute discretion before contacting him. He got in his car and drove for a while, making sure that he wasn't being followed. He parked the car and walked for a while, until he felt comfortable that there was nothing out of the ordinary. He stepped into an old café that he knew still had a public phone and called the number on his voice mail.

After the first ring, Nader answered the phone. "Hello!"

Mustafa immediately recognized the voice. "Hey, Bro, what the fuck is going on?"

Nader said, "I'm in deep trouble, and I didn't have anyone else to call. I'm sorry to get you involved in this, but I need help."

Mustafa said, "Of course. What do you need?"

Nader responded, "I need to go into exile for a while until I figure this whole thing out. I didn't do any of the things they're claiming I did on the news. You've got to believe me."

Mustafa said, "You don't have to convince me. No one else in the world knows you better than I do. You used to get angry with me when I yelled at the cat growing up. You don't have a malicious bone in your body, and you are not the type to indiscriminately hurt innocent people. Where are you right now? Don't give me the specific location, just the country and city."

Nader replied, "I'm in Geneva, Switzerland."

Mustafa said, "Okay. Sit tight. I will call you back."

After hanging up with Nader, Mustafa immediately dialed his deceased father's best friend in Palestine, the imam who had replaced his father at the mosque after Imam Mohdi's death. After a relatively short conversation, arrangements were made to get Nader and Donna out of Europe.

Mustafa called Nader back half an hour later. "I want you to leave the location you're at immediately. Find an inconspicuous location to lie low in for the next couple of hours. Two hours from now, call the number I'm about to give you, and someone will come and pick you up and help get you and your friend out of Europe."

Nader said, "I don't know how to thank you."

Mustafa replied, "You can thank me by staying alive. Good luck. I pray to Allah he will protect you and your friend."

In the meantime, Addis was able to secure a car rental by posing as a tourist looking to enjoy the local scenery and cuisine with his girlfriend for the weekend. The four of them drove around for the next few hours, until it was time for Nader to make the call. Nader called the number given to him by his brother. On the first ring, a very deep and stern voice with a heavy Middle Eastern accent answered and immediately asked in Arabic, "Where are you?"

Nader gave him his exact location. The man on the other end of the line replied, "I will be there in fifteen minutes."

Nader returned to the car and informed Addis, Sacha, and Donna that his and Donna's ride would be there in fifteen minutes. Both Donna and Sacha began to cry as Nader looked at Addis and Sacha with a look of deep gratitude. Nader said, "How can I ever repay you for this? You both came to my rescue again with total disregard for your own well-being. I'm so fortunate to have you both as my best friends. I will miss you both dearly, and I love you very much. I hope I will get to see you both soon and under different circumstances."

Donna looked at them with tears streaming down her cheeks. "I'm so sorry for all the trouble I have caused you. Frankly, I'm still very confused about what happened, but now I know why Nader loves you and trusts you both implicitly. I only wish I had had the time to get to know you better. Thank you for everything."

As promised, fifteen minutes later, a very indistinct, dark, fifteen-year-old Renault Mégane rolled into the designated rendez-vous location. Addis drove adjacent to the car, and Nader rolled down his window simultaneously as the driver of the Renault rolled down his. It was an older man with a taqiya (Muslim skullcap), a full gray beard, and a dark complexion. Without any formalities, he quickly asked, "Nader?" His pronunciation of the name clearly indicated that he spoke fluent Arabic.

Nader said, "Yes."

The driver, with urgency, commanded him in Arabic, "Yella!" asking him to join him in the Renault.

Sacha and Addis embraced Nader and Donna in an emotional farewell as the former couple bid the latter couple good luck.

Three days later, Nader and Donna were standing on a deserted beach in Southern Italy at 3:00 a.m. The only thing they had with them was a small plastic shopping bag with meager belongings and some food their smugglers had provided them for the sea trip across the Mediterranean. It was a cloudy night, and the visibility was almost zero. From nowhere, a large dinghy appeared and swiftly landed on the beach. The boat was full of humanity, men, women, and children occupying every inch of the boat. Every nationality from Africa seemed to be represented, including lighter-skinned occupants from Syria and Lebanon. Their handlers began to bark orders at them to disembark quickly as women and children were falling face-first into the choppy water and struggling to make it to shore. In less than twenty minutes, the boat was relieved of its contents except for the three armed smugglers in command. The immigrants began to scurry in the dark in every which direction, leaving only their footprints on the beach as evidence of their existence.

The man who appeared to be in command approached Nader and Donna. With a slightly politer tone than the one he had used with the immigrants, he asked, "Nader el-Shafique?"

Nader nodded, and the man directed him and Donna to board the dinghy. An hour later, the dinghy rendezvoused with a larger, sturdier boat for the trip back to the coast of Libya. The solitary voyage to what seemed to Donna to be another planet filled her with trepidation and fear of what the future would hold. Only a few days ago, her life had been orderly with the future full of new possibilities. She had a man in her life whom she loved dearly and a new spiritual awakening that seemed to have quitted her lifelong quest for answers to questions about her own existence. All of that was now gone, and a new chapter in her life was emerging with blank pages, to be written only by a fate that she had no control over. The only response she had was to hold on to Nader more tightly as if he were the flotation device that kept her head above water. He was the only thing that was real that still remained from her previous life, a life that was real only a week ago and that now seemed to be a distant memory.

Nader remained stoic, occasionally grasping Donna's hand more firmly to assure her that she was not alone. His thoughts, however, were focused on connecting the dots and solving this mystery that life had posed to him. To him it was a chess game against a formidable opponent where he always had to be three moves ahead if he were to have any hope of winning. Ironically, he found the experience liberating as if he always had been destined to be a Bedouin roaming the vast desert, unencumbered by borders, modern-day trappings, and his own ambition.

Donna turned around and looked at Nader. She asked, "What happened? Only a week ago we were upstanding citizens with a bright future and a very comfortable life. How did everything go to shit so quickly? This doesn't seem real to me. Are we going to be okay?"

Nader answered, "We're going to be fine. Everything is going to be okay. I have this very strong feeling that this is what you and I are destined to be, and strangely enough, I don't feel fear but adulation."

Donna said, *"Adulation?!"*

Nader answered, "Yes. Strangely enough, I feel euphoric, as if everything prior to this point was in preparation for this. My father would often say to me, 'Your destiny is a dance where you never get to lead but always have to follow. The trick is to follow with grace and poise.'"

Donna said, "Whatever journey we're on, as long it's with you, I'm happy and at peace. Life became a lot more interesting all of a sudden, as if there is no more comfort zone, no repetition, and no routine, just space and time."

The sun was coming up on the horizon, and the Libyan coast was now in sight. It had been a thirty-hour journey with very little food and sleep. They were both exhausted and anxious to see what the future would hold for them next. The smugglers were racing to land before the break of dawn under the cover of darkness. The last mile of the journey was by dinghy as the rubber raft struggled to land on the rocky shore against the onslaught of crashing waves that made both Nader and Donna seasick. On the shore, there were two Toyota pickup trucks with mounted guns and armed men awaiting their arrival. The smugglers assured Nader that the welcoming party were friends, not foes. As soon as they landed, a Hamas commander emerged from one of the trucks and quickly whisked them into the back of the lead truck.

"Assalamu alaikum, brother. Please help yourself to the food and water in the plastic bags next to you. It's my honor to be of service to the son of Imam el-Shafique. He was loved by all. Our journey is long, but by the will of God, inshallah, we will have you in a safe location soon."

Nader asked, "Where is that?"

The commander replied, "I can't tell you that, for your own safety and security. It's a safe house in a very secure location."

For the next five days, their trip followed a smuggling route between Libya and Egypt, using treacherous roads through the Egyptian desert. There was nothing to see except sand, dunes, and arid mountains, except for the occasional Bedouin tribe that appeared like a mirage every now and then, nestled next to an oasis. With every encounter, the Bedouin hospitality was always the same. They shared their limited resources and their sweet tea with their guests regardless of how poor or hungry they were. It was the desert code that had been in existence for thousands of years. At the end of the trip, Nader and Donna found themselves at a small village in northern Sinai. They were housed in different huts until the next day, when the village women adorned Donna with a colorful traditional wedding dress and some jewelry, and painted her hands and feet with henna in an intricate mosaic design. She was given the name Zahraa (Woman of Jannah) by the village women. She looked stunningly beautiful, a blonde-haired, blue-eyed desert goddess who was the perfect combination of East and West. The village chief and imam performed a Muslim marriage ceremony, followed by a tribal wedding feast in their honor. Donna sat next to Nader under the wedding tent while women bellowed the festive Zaghrouta sound with their mouths and while men danced with bamboo sticks to the rhythmic sound of the tabla and the Komenga, firing their guns in the air.

Nader looked at Donna with an adoring expression and uttered, "You look so beautiful."

Donna responded, "In spite of everything that has happened in the last two weeks, I'm happy, and this feels like home, where I always was meant to be. I love you very much."

Nader said, "You're so right. This does feel like home as if I was destined to be here with you for the rest of my living days. I love you more than words can describe." Then he kissed her.

The next day, Nader was asked to attend a tribal meeting after Fajr prayer with the imam and several Hamas operatives. Nader came to the meeting with Donna, which elicited several looks of disapproval from the all men who had gathered. Nader quickly dispelled any misgivings about Donna's role at the outset of the meeting.

"Salaam, brothers. You all know my wife, Zahraa. Please forgive my impertinence, but my wife is my partner and my equal in every sense. She is well educated and very smart, and I value her opinion and intellect very much. I believe she will be a great asset to you as she is to me. I hope in time you all will feel the same way."

The meeting was immediately dominated by the voices of extremists and religious zealots who were advocating for violent resistance against the West and Israel by any means necessary. They were under the impression that Nader and Zahraa would be enthusiastic allies in this fight, given their recent experience.

Nader politely interrupted the discussion. "Brothers, my father was a man of peace who was loved and hated by many for his beliefs. I'm the same man, and I believe in civil resistance by appealing to the best, not the worst, in humanity. I have to stay true to myself and to my understanding of my beloved religion of Islam and the Prophet Muhammad's true message. I will not be an instrument of violence, and I will not shed a single drop of human blood in the name of any cause. What I will do is shed light on the falsehood that is being perpetrated upon humanity by those who are serving their own interests over God's interests as I understand it. May Allah give us the wisdom to see his message clearly. In our beloved Koran, it says, 'If anyone kills a person, it will be as if he killed all mankind.' I will not be that person. My wife and I are here today to ask for your help and your assistance to unveil the evil that is permeating and infecting our moral conscience by turning its tool of choice against our conscience—technology and social media, not bullets, bombs, and countless innocent men, women, and children being harmed in the process. That is what my wife and I can do. I hope you will join us in this quest."

The imam stood up and spoke after Nader had assumed his seat next to his wife. "We have been fighting this battle against our oppressors for so long, using the power of the sword and not the pen, and look where it has gotten us: using weapons from the Dark Ages to wage a twenty-first-century battle. And the only thing we've got to show for it is our beautiful religion hijacked by cutthroats, despite an unempathetic world that sees us as terrorists rather than human beings with the same God-given right to be free. It is time for a change, a new approach that respects the tenets of our faith and brings truth instead of lies. I, for one, am willing to make that change and join Brother Nader and Sister Zahraa in that journey. Now, for the first time, we have someone who knows how the system operates from inside this shadowy and dark place, and all we have to do is get them the tools they need to turn the light on. Brother and sister, please let us know what you need, and we will find a way to get it for you. Assalamu alaikum, and may God's blessing be on all of us."

The meeting was immediately concluded after the imam's comments, leaving no doubt in Nader's and Zahraa's minds who was in charge.

On the Monday following the trip to Europe, Sacha confronted her father in his office. "Did you hear about Nader and his fiancée?"

Zack replied, "I sure did. And frankly, I'm not surprised. He always struck me as a radical."

Sacha said, "You never liked him. Did you have anything to do with this?"

Zack replied, "What? Of course not! How can you even suggest that? I didn't agree with the man's ideology or political persuasion, but not to the point of having anything to do with this despicable act. He did that all on his own. I find the question very disturbing, especially coming from you."

Sacha said, "Okay, Zack, I will take you at your word."

Sacha found Zack's moral indignation somewhat disingenuous, but she always wanted to give her father the benefit of the doubt.

It had been several weeks since Addis and Sacha had heard anything about Nader and Donna, and they were anxious to find out if they were okay. Addis put in a call to his sister, Sarah, and his brother-in-law, Mustafa, to see if there was any news about them. A week earlier he had sent two packages to his niece and nephew as a prelude to this call.

Sarah answered the phone on the third ring. "Hello?"

"Hi, Sis. It has been awhile."

"Hi, stranger. It *has* been awhile. The kids miss you. We're looking forward to seeing you and Sacha soon. I'm going to put you on speakerphone so Mustafa and the kids can say hi."

"Okay."

Mustafa spoke first. "Hi, Addis. I hope everything is going well for you back in the US. Thank you very much for your gifts."

Addis said, "Everything is fine over here. I'm glad to see that all three gifts arrived safely."

Mustafa said, "Yes, all three gifts arrived safely. Thank you again for your friendship and generosity. The kids want to thank you as well. I will put them on. Be well. Thank you again."

For the next few minutes, Addis, Sarah, and the kids talked about their respective lives and all the things that had happened since the last time they'd spoken. After hanging up the phone, the kids asked their dad, "What third package? We only got two."

Mustafa said, "Yeah, there was a third package for me."

One of the children replied, "I'm sure Mom is disappointed that she didn't get a present as well."

Immediately after the phone call ended, Addis sent a text to Sacha: "Good morning, darling. Our gifts to my sister and the kids arrived safely. Thank you very much for all your help. I love you and look forward to seeing you tonight."

25 The Tech Revolution

Zack emerged from the UN building with several of his assistants. They walked toward an awaiting black stretch limo with the engine already running. The chauffer was outside the car with the back door to the limo open and ready to receive Zack and his assistants. Between them stood a horde of reporters from every news outlet, vying to get some face time with Zack so they could ask the main question that was on everyone's mind: had the UN council granted approval for the worldwide distribution of the Grok technology?

Zack looked around the crowd of reporters and found the individual he was looking for, the reporter from the business network who had championed his cause and had been his greatest advocate. He made a beeline to the reporter of choice as every other reporter and cameraman advanced toward him like linebackers determined to stop the advance of a running back on the five-yard line. His security detail partitioned the crowd of reporters like Moses parting the Red Sea, and he proceeded directly to the reporter of choice. The reporter immediately took advantage of the opportunity. With a degree of familiarity as if he were addressing an old friend, he asked, "Zack, how did your meeting go?"

Zack said, "I'm confident that we made a compelling argument before the UN General Council Science Advisory Board. After all, the evidence of the benefits of this technology to the world is no longer hypothetical. The benefits that the small African nation of Zushaka has realized since deploying this technology are indisputable. We will patiently await the decision of the board, and if it's in the affirmative, Leapp Technologies is ready to ratchet up its production of the device and launch phase one."

The reporter asked, "And what is phase one?"

Zack replied, "Our goal is to distribute this technology to the least fortunate throughout the world first before we tackle the rest of the world. We believe that by doing things this way, we will make the greatest impact on world hunger, illiteracy, and mortality, not to mention income inequality."

The reporter said, "As you're well aware, Mr. el-Shafique was a fierce opponent of this project, and his objection to distributing the Grok technology worldwide is well-known. Did his absence pave the way for receiving the approval from the board? And do you believe that he was plotting a terrorist attack?"

Zack was taken aback by the question, having expected softball questions from this specific reporter. He maintained his composure and, in a sorrowful manner, replied, "I was, frankly, very surprised to hear the news about Mr. el-Shafique. Despite our difference of opinion, I respected him as scientist. I believe that in this country, you're innocent until proven guilty, so I for one will reserve all judgment until all the facts are proven in a court of law. As for his absence during our presentation to the board, I will let the facts speak for themselves. Although I disagree with the manner in which he evaded the authorities, I'm confident that he and his partner will surrender once they have the assurance that they will receive fair and impartial due process. Thank you very much." Zack proceeded to his limousine as every reporter was shouting questions at him. He parried their microphones as if he were in a fencing match.

A week later, the UN board unanimously approved the worldwide deployment of the Grok wearable and immediately afterward notified Zack of their decision. The news of the decision became the top headline news for every news outlet and the internet immediately following. Pundits on both sides of the issue incisively debated the issues on news programs and in editorial articles. The news also prompted a flood of calls from heads of state, advocating for their countries to be the first to receive the device.

Zack assembled all his department heads at 7:00 a.m. the day after for an all-hands-on-deck meeting to launch the Grok technology worldwide. There was great anticipation and trepidation among the participants, not knowing full well what to expect. With Zack, a meeting of this kind only meant more work, or else heads would be rolling. In attendance were Sacha and Addis, who had also been kept in the dark as to the purpose of the meeting.

"Ladies and gentlemen, I apologize for getting you here so early in the morning, but based on the news I'm about to announce, we will all need to get used to getting to our desks early and leaving late. And if anyone is planning on taking a vacation in the next six months, I suggest very strongly that they cancel their plans." Zack let that information sink in for a few seconds as he carefully studied every facial expression in the room. The attendees were all aware that any expression of disappointment or a disgruntled look would not go unnoticed by Zack and that, if they were to express such discontent, there would be consequences to pay. They all remained stoic, trying very hard to conceal any expression of disapproval. This was Zack's form of psychological intimidation, letting his managers know that he would not tolerate any dissent and that there was only one person in command—him. After a long pause, Zack proceeded:

"Yesterday, I was informed by the UN General Council Science Advisory Board that Leapp Technologies has received the approval to distribute the Grok technology worldwide. We will immediately execute on all plans formulated in anticipation of this decision. The tenth floor has been fully converted to be the brain center of this operation. Before you is the list of the countries and a timetable for completing phase one of the launch. Any questions?"

They all looked at the list, but no one dared to raise their hand, except for one person.

Sacha said, "This is a very ambitious timetable, and it seems that every country on this list is a Third World country with little or no familiarity with anything even close to this technology. Wouldn't it be easier to launch in countries with a greater degree of technological sophistication and a well-educated population?"

Zack said, "You're right, it would be easier and less burdensome to launch in developed countries, but I'm saving those for Grok 2.0."

Sacha asked, "Grok 2.0?"

Zack answered, "Yes. Hopefully by the time we are finished with phase one, we will have all the kinks figured out related to the inject-able version. Of course, with the help from Addis, I'm confident that we will get there by the end of phase one."

Immediately after making that statement, Zack directed his gaze toward Addis for a response. Addis lifted his head from his notes and responded with a polite smile.

Another hand went up. This time it was the chief financial officer.

Tom said, "Zack, my team has been working on multiple financial projections, and frankly, the cost–benefit analysis does not pan out. The cost is in the billions, and there is no revenue to offset that cost. This has the potential of bankrupting Leapp Technologies."

Zack said, "I appreciate your concern for the survivability of the company, but a very wise businessman once said, 'Sometimes you have to give the cow for free in order to be able to sell the milk and cheese.' You have to trust me on this one.

"As all of you are well aware, my campaign for the presidency of the United States is now in the last stretch. With nine months remain-ing until the election, I will be spending most of my time on the road campaigning. Sacha will be in charge in my absence, but I will be in frequent contact and will be monitoring our progress very closely. Are there any other questions?"

There was absolute silence in the room.

"Okay, folks, if there are no other questions, let's go to work and let's get this thing done. Good luck. Sacha and Addis, will you please stay behind? There are a few things I'd like to discuss with you."

Sacha and Addis remained seated as the rest of the participants began to stream out. Once the boardroom had been cleared of all others except the three of them, Zack began by addressing Sacha first. He said, "I know I'm asking a lot of you, but you're the only one I can trust with this task. Although the campaign will be consuming most of my time, I will be very much involved, just not with the day-to-day details. I will be relying on you for that. I will be available day and night if you have any questions. You know how important it is for us to get this first phase right. I'm very confident you're the person to get this done without a hitch. After all, you executed with absolute perfection the deployment of the device in Zushaka."

Sacha said, "Thank you for the flattery, but this is a very aggressive timetable you have laid down, and I don't know if we will be able to manage the manufacturing, distribution, and training, not to mention the monitoring of the device effectively. I think you're overtaxing this firm and its employees and putting the firm in financial jeopardy."

Zack said, "You've got to have faith. I'm confident that I have accounted for all contingencies. I'm not about to risk this firm on a whim. Today, the most valuable commodity is data, and with the worldwide distribution of the Grok technology, we stand to be the largest reservoir of data bar none. Every other company has a very small window into human behavior, whereas this company will have a three-hundred-sixty-degree view unrivaled by the others. That information will be very valuable to governments, industries, and research institutions, just to name a few. This is what I meant about giving the cow for free in order to be able to sell the milk and cheese."

Sacha said, "Okay, Zack, I hope you've got this all figured out. Don't worry, I will get my part done."

Zack said, "Thanks, honey. I know you will." Redirecting his attention, he asked, "Addis, how is it going with the nanodevice? Are you anywhere close to making the energy self-sufficient?"

Addis replied, "Our latest experiments have been showing a great deal of promise. We are able to capture the God particle for a longer and longer time with every try."

"The God particle?" asked Zack.

Addis answered, "Yes. That is the name my colleagues and I coined for the biochemical synthesis that occurs naturally in the human body to produce constant and sustainable energy to support every living organ. The challenge is to make the nanodevice, or Grok 2.0 as you call it, seamlessly integrated within the host, making it a part of the organism infrastructure."

Zack said, "That is wonderful to hear. Let me know what resources you need to get the device fully operational. I wish you both great success as we embark on this new tipping point in human evolution."

Both Addis and Sacha were struck by Zack's last statement, "new tipping point in human evolution." It sounded godlike.

That evening Sacha and Addis were having dinner at their favorite Japanese restaurant in Boston. The day had been a long one, and both were overwhelmed by the task before them. The Japanese sake began to have the desired effect as the stress of the day began to melt away. Addis finally broached the conversation that both of them desperately had wanted to avoid. Neither of them wanted to talk about business; they just wanted to enjoy each other's company and have a low-key meal without any drama. As hard as they both had tried not to think about it, their minds kept on replaying the events of the day and the overwhelming tasks before them.

Addis said, "I think your dad is asking a lot of you!"

Sacha said, "As he is of you. I feel a total loss of control. My life is no longer my own, and I feel that I have dragged you into this."

Addis said, "You shouldn't feel that way. I'm a big boy; nobody dragged me into anything. Although the idea of being close to you made his proposition a little more persuasive."

Sacha asked, "Just a little?"

Addis answered, "Well, a lot more persuasive."

Sacha said to him, "That is just what I mean, honey; if it weren't for me, I think you would have chosen a totally different path. I'm so sorry I dragged you into Zack's insane world. He is a human hand grenade."

Addis said, "Look, to be totally honest, I have a very bad feeling about this, and sometimes I think Nader's apprehension about the Grok technology mightn't be totally unfounded. If I figure out the nano version, it might be Grok on steroids. But in some ways I'm conflicted about all the benefits it will bring to humanity."

"I feel the same way. I have been thinking about this a lot. I also think that Zack's unbridled ambitions shouldn't go unchecked. Somehow, we need to figure out some stopgap measure in case things go wrong," Sacha replied.

"What do you think can go wrong?" Addis asked.

Sacha responded, "We're messing with some powerful shit. We're tapping into the human psyche, and there is a very delicate balance that we might be disrupting. I don't know, there are so many unintended consequences that we haven't even begun to consider. Nader was right when he spoke about the spike effect. This technology we're mass-distributing to the world might have so many unintended consequences that it will be impossible for us to innovate quickly enough to negate any of the possible side effects."

Addis said, "As you know, my father said once, 'The universe is balanced on the tip of a needle. Every action requires a simultaneous reaction of equal force to maintain the balance. Everything we do matters.' What if this technology is the tipping point, the thing that will disrupt this balance, the thing that humanity collectively will not be able to come back from, the thing that will undermine our innate ability to adopt a corrective course? You know, throughout our history, human beings at times have gone to polar extremes, but there has always been a catalyst that brings us back to the center. This time, I don't know!"

Sacha said, "Exactly. You are referring to free will. That is what I noticed from the data we mined in Zushaka. The artificial intelligence device began to morph in order to modify the host's natural tendencies in a manner that steered the host back in the direction of the embedded code in the program. Although the data wasn't con-clusive, it scared the bejesus out of me. It feels as if we're playing God here! Frankly, that is exactly what came to mind when Zack said 'new tipping point in human evolution.'"

Addis said, "You're right, there is a lot of scary shit we are tamper-ing with, but at this point it's all speculation. Until proven otherwise, the benefits still outweigh the costs, but that doesn't mean that we should be blinded by the headlights. You couldn't be more right; we ought to work at a stopgap measure in case this thing goes to shit."

Sacha said, "At least Zack will be consumed with his political campaign and won't be micromanaging every detail of this operation. You and I need to figure this out. There is a lot at stake. I wish we had Nader's input; he would have been of great help. I miss him a great deal."

Addis said, "Me too, but somehow I feel his presence as if we're connected through some spiritual intermediaries."

"Are you a spiritual medium now?" Sacha asked. "Because if you are, you need to let me know whom I'm making love to—because I'm not that kind of girl."

They both laughed.

26 The Launch

Three months later, Sacha was sitting in her glass office overlooking the command center on the tenth floor. She was reviewing the latest streaming data from the Grok device from all over the world on a large hologram display. At this time, the device had been distributed to over 90 percent of the countries on Zack's wish list. She'd run the operation flawlessly and with the precision of a well-conceived and well-executed military operation. In private, her colleagues began to refer to her as "the general." Although they feared her, they were also in awe of her leadership ability and intellect. She was meticulous and seemed to be able to anticipate the unexpected before it happened. Every minute detail was accounted for with contingency plans for the possibility of anything going wrong. Her sixteen-hour, seven-days-a-week work schedule was unsustainable, but she demanded no less from her staff. The stress of the job was beginning to affect the morale of her staff, and more and more were beginning to be absent or call in sick. At this rate, she feared that her top talents would begin to defect out of sheer exhaustion.

She announced an all-staff meeting for this evening in which she intended to announce a two-week, all-expenses-paid respite for her staff and their families at a high-end all-inclusive sea resort. She hoped the time off would revive morale and provide a much-needed rest for her weary crew. She knew that Zack would object, but she didn't care.

Addis's schedule was no different. He was on the verge of breaking the code of the God particle. His latest tests were more and more successful with every try. He was confident that his next test would yield the ultimate result of making the Grok nano version fully energy self-sufficient. So far, his experiments using animals had shown great promise. The nanodevice began to adopt the same cellular mechanism as the animals by using the slight imbalance between positive and negative ions inside and outside the cell. It was able to achieve this charge separation by allowing charged ions to flow in and out through a membrane. The flow of charges across its membrane allowed it to have an infinite amount of energy and guaranteed that it was fully integrated within the host's body. All that was left was to have human trials. The idea left Addis morally conflicted.

As he was sitting at his lab looking at the latest results, there was a knock on his door. Addis said, "Come in."

His assistant said, "Good morning, Doctor. I was wondering if I could have a few minutes of your time?"

David was one of his brightest research assistants whom Addis had brought over with him from the Geneva lab after accepting the position with Leapp Technologies.

David said, "Sir, do you remember, prior to coming to the States, that I presented you with a rather odd finding that I came across during my research on black holes?"

Addis replied, "Vaguely. Please refresh my memory. And please call me Addis."

David said, "Well, sir—I mean Addis—I presented you with data about a black hole in our Milky Way, MS13, showing that the black hole's gravitational pull and size seems to be growing at a faster rate than in any of my previous observations. At the time, sir—sorry, I mean Addis—you dismissed the finding as a computational error. After arriving at Leapp Technologies, I took the liberty of using their satellite network to monitor the same black hole, MS13, and to my surprise, not only were my original findings confirmed, but also the rate is even getting faster."

Addis said, "Let me look at the data." After a few minutes of reviewing the data, he answered, "You're right. This seems to be irrefutable. How can this be possible? It doesn't make any sense. I want you stay on top of this and give me an update daily. I want you to also contact NASA to see if they're able to confirm this finding. If this is true, it could have a profound effect on our ecosystem."

The cell phone on his desk began to vibrate. Addis looked down at the phone to find Sacha's picture looking back at him. He immediately dismissed David. "Okay, David, keep me updated." As soon as David had departed, Addis picked up the phone. "Hi, honey!"

Sacha said, "I miss you. I'm leaving work early today. Can I pick you up on the way home? I need to hug you, kiss you, and smother you for the rest of this evening."

Addis replied, "You don't know how wonderful that sounds. I'm all in."

"I can't wait," Sacha said. "I will order out so we don't have to see another human being for the rest of this evening."

Addis said, "Hurry up. I feel all giddy."

"See you in a few." Sacha hung up the phone.

That evening Sacha was setting the table in anticipation of the takeout order's arrival from one of their favorite local pizzerias. Addis was opening a five-thousand-dollar bottle of Château Lafite Rothschild, a cabernet blend that they had received from Zack as a gift and were saving for a special occasion. The idea of consuming this wine with a slice of pizza would have appalled any respectable wine aficionado, but this was Addis and Sacha's way of giving the proverbial middle finger to Zack.

The pizza was delivered. As they sat down, each took a bite from a slice and a sip of wine. They looked at each other and laughed. This was, finally, the first night in a long time when they would get to relax and enjoy each other's company. They both wanted to avoid talking about business, but Sacha desperately needed Addis's opinion.

Sacha said, "I hate to bring business up, but I'm very worried about some trends I have been noticing in the latest data stream I received from the Grok device."

Addis asked, "What is it you're seeing?"

"You know I created a dashboard based on my PhD dissertation, which I titled *The Tip of a Needle*, a phrase that I borrowed from Nader when he was telling me of one of your father's more memorable lines," Sacha replied.

Addis said, "Yes, we discussed that, but I didn't know that's where the name of your algorithm came from. My father would be flattered."

Sacha said, "Well, anyway, the algorithm is intended to measure several behavioral markers, the same way a blood test utilizes a metabolic panel to see if a patient's blood count is right and the different organs are functioning correctly. Like with a metabolic panel, these markers ought to be within a certain range in order to reflect that the individual in question has a healthy emotional response to his environment. One of these markers is empathy, and by all measures, it seems like the patient is getting sicker!"

"What do you mean?" Addis asked.

Sacha answered, "The dashboard is showing a direct correlation between the length of time people have had the device and how much time they spend on it and a diminishing empathetic response to the environment around them. They seem to be less and less affected by the pain and suffering of others. They also seem to be becoming more and more reclusive and less and less interested in social interaction. They are more interested in living in a world of their own creation through the device's unencumbered connectivity to the Web. They are going on the dark web to places that cater to their most perverse tendencies. Some, however, are going in the absolute opposite direction and are becoming obsessed with religion. What is also becoming very clear is that their creativity, productivity, and learning trajectory is going off the charts. It is as if their brains are on speed."

Addis said, "I also have been noticing a lot of things that are out of the ordinary. My assistant David came into my office today with a very strange finding. The black hole he has been tracking seems to be growing larger. Not only that, but also it's growing at rate that is unprecedented. Frankly, everything seems to be operating differently, as if the laws of physics have suddenly changed. To add to the confusion, our latest test of the Grok 2.0 on animals was a total success."

Sacha said, "I don't know if I should say congratulations or be remorseful."

Addis said, "I think it's time to try it on a human being, but the only one I would dare to try it on is me."

"What? That's crazy!" Sacha said. "That thing is still in the experimental stages. Why would you take that risk?"

Addis replied, "If there is any risk to be taken, it ought to be done by me, not a random individual."

Sacha said, "There must be another way. Can't you find someone who is terminally ill and has nothing to lose to volunteer for the right amount of money?"

"The problem is that their health status and any pharma they are taking might interfere with the performance of the device," Addis answered. "It's has to be a young healthy individual in their prime. Plus, I can act as the stopgap we discussed, in case things go wrong. There is no better way to do it than from inside the system."

Sacha said, "If there is anyone who should do it, it should be me."

Addis said, "What? Absolutely not!"

"Look, you're the physicist, the one who invented this very complex monstrosity," Sacha said. "I need you to be on the outside in case things go wrong. Plus, I will be able to experience firsthand what the hosts are experiencing. On top of that, there are some very subtle psychological nuances you might miss."

"We're getting totally over our heads with things," Addis said. "I don't like it, and I have a very bad feeling about it. I wish you and I could escape somewhere and live a simpler life, maybe become desert nomads like Nader and Donna."

"Wouldn't that be wonderful, a life where we could shut the rest of the world out, just the two of us? Speaking of Nader and Donna,

I miss them awfully. I wish they were here. His advice and counsel would have been invaluable."

Addis suggested, "Let's call them. His brother sent me an encrypted message after their escape that contains his contact number. We can use your secure satellite phone. It will be around two in the morning where they are. Hopefully he will answer."

Sacha took the phone number from Addis and dialed it. After the third ring, Nader answered: "Hi, sunshine! What took you so long?"

Sacha said, "Nader, how did you know it was me?"

"I recognized the number," he replied. "Plus, all calls are scrambled and screened prior to being patched through."

Sacha said, "Wow. That sounds very sophisticated for someone in hiding."

Nader asked, "Very impressive for a tent dweller, don't you think?"

"Addis and I were talking about you and Donna. We miss you guys very much and just wanted to hear your voice. What are you doing being up so late at night?"

"Here in the desert," Nader said, "we have different working hours. Donna is sitting next to me; I will put you on speakerphone."

Donna came on the line. "I have been thinking a lot about you guys, and we miss you something awful."

Addis said, "The feeling is mutual. How are you guys adapting to your new environment?"

Donna replied, "We love it. It's free of all the worldly trappings, and we feel free. It's hard to describe, but it feels like we're meant to be here. Nader and I have found our calling!"

Sacha asked, "What do you mean?"

Nader responded, "We have started a grassroots resistance against corporate greed, geopolitical manipulation of the voiceless, and technological changes gone unencumbered and unchecked."

Sacha said, "It sounds like you're targeting Leapp Technologies and Zack."

Nader replied, "Among others! The resistance is growing faster than I ever expected. We have built a network of very sophisticated tech wizzes who are of the same mindset and who believe in our mission."

"What mission?" Sacha asked.

Donna said, "We believe we have to be the immune response to this technological virus that, if left unchecked, will infect all of us in ways that we can't imagine. There are a lot of people who believe in the same thing, and the recent blitz of the Grok wearable is pushing a lot of people to join the resistance."

Addis said, "Frankly, that is what we have been noticing, as well. There are a lot of oddities that seem to be directly correlated to the spread of the Grok technology."

"Like what?" Nader asked.

Addis responded, "Well, Sacha has been noticing several behavioral trends that by all measures appear unhealthy. Also, oddly enough, one of my assistants has noticed that a black hole in our galaxy has been growing at a rate that we have not seen before."

Nader said, "I don't know if Sacha remembers this, but when we first met, we had a philosophical discussion about God and religion, and I stated that I believed that the whole universe is our celestial body and we are its body. Everything in the universe is there to support our existence just like every atom, cell, and molecule in our body. So, to me, it's not inconceivable that when the head becomes sick, the whole body gets sick. I think that is what your father meant, Addis, when he said, 'The universe is balanced on the tip of a needle. Every action requires a simultaneous reaction of equal force to maintain the balance. Everything we do matters.'"

Addis said, "It pains me to say this, but just to add insult to injury, my latest experiments with the injectable version of the Grok device have been extremely successful. We're ready to test it on a human being!"

Donna said, "Guys, you can't do this. This new version will be the tipping point that humanity will not be able to come back from."

Sacha said, "We have considered that, and we believe we have devised an effective stopgap measure in case things go wrong. The benefits of this technology to the world and humanity are too great for us to play judge and jury on a whim."

"You guys are taking a big bite of this proverbial apple. Just be careful," Nader cautioned.

Addis said, "You and Donna as well. And keep on fighting the good fight. I think it's very healthy to have a counterbalance to all the new changes."

Sacha and Addis said in unison, "Good luck."

Donna, with Nader nearby, said, "Best of luck to you as well. Hopefully we will get to see each other soon—and under better circumstances. Bye."

27 The Campaign

The side of the campaign bus featured a US flag that ran from front to back. In the middle of the flag, the caption "Leaders lead by example" was emblazoned in bold blue letters for all to see. Zack was on the bus, putting the final touches on his speech for this evening's event. He had been on the road for the last three months, traveling from coast to coast, holding campaign rallies in states that he needed to win if he wished to have any chance of winning the general election. Today's rally was especially important; it was a state that leaned to the left and was fiercely independent with a natural animus toward the establishment and billionaires. Tonight would be the ultimate test of whether his campaign message was resonating with a wide swath of electorates and whether his appeal crossed demographic divides. This state, after all, was the state of California, and his chance of winning the electoral vote of such a liberal state had been calculated at the beginning of his campaign to be almost zero. Tonight's campaign rally would be held in one of the largest venues in Los Angeles, the Banc of California Stadium, which had a capacity of accommodating over twenty thousand people. If his organizers were able to fill all those seats, it would be a feat unrivaled by any other candidate in the race. The optics would send shock waves and would devastate his opponents, who were barely able to garner enough enthusiasm to attract more than a few thousand participants to their rallies. The media would have no choice but to make Zack Zimmerman the centerpiece of every political news story.

Zack had just completed the last minor adjustment to the speech and was ready to take a quick nap, when he received a call from one of his executives at Leapp Technologies. Zack regretted having to answer the phone, but when he looked at the caller ID, he knew that this was a call he must take. This was his inside man at the company whom he had tasked with keeping him informed of everything going on in the company in his absence. It wasn't that he didn't trust Sacha; it was that he didn't have 100 percent confidence in anyone else's capabilities except his own.

The executive said, "Good afternoon, sir. Sorry to bother, but I wanted to give you a very important update. The Grok 2.0 is fully operational, and the latest tests have been a resounding success."

Zack answered, "Great news! Who else knows of this?"

The executive said, "Of course Dr. Ackerman, your daughter, and a select few of Dr. Ackerman's staff. They were all told to keep the information confidential."

"Have any human trials been conducted?" Zack asked.

The executive replied, "No, sir. I believe there has been a great reluctance to do so from Dr. Ackerman and your daughter."

Zack said, "Okay, understood. Keep me informed!" He hung up the phone.

He immediately called Addis's private number. Addis was with Sacha, enjoying a quiet evening at home, when his cell phone chimed. His facial expression instantaneously changed, and Sacha took notice. She asked, "Who is it?"

Addis replied, "It's your father. I really don't want to take his call right now. I know the reason he is calling."

Sacha said, "He is relentless. He will not stop until he gets whatever he is fishing for."

The phone stopped ringing after the fifth ring.

Sacha said, "He will call back, and he is going to ask for a status update on the device. What are you going to say?"

Addis replied, "I have to tell him the truth; I'm convinced he already has spies in the lab, and I'm sure he already knows. This is one of his tests."

"Just don't tell him that we decided to test the device on me. He will never allow it."

Addis said, "I'm not convinced either, but as a condition, I must be able to closely monitor you. So, what do you think of moving in with me? Or perhaps I can move in with you."

Sacha said, "Wow, going out on a limb comes with fringe benefits. I like it. I thought you would never ask! How about my apartment, since it's twice the size of yours?"

Addis's phone rang again. He picked up on the second ring. "Hello!"

Zack said, "Addis, it's Zack. How are you?"

"I'm fine, thank you for asking," Addis replied. "I have been following your campaign very closely, and it appears things are going very well."

Zack said, "Yes. We're cautiously optimistic. More importantly, I wanted to ask you where we are with Grok 2.0. Have we made any progress?"

"Our latest experiments with chimpanzees were 100 percent effective, but we haven't had any human trials at this juncture," Addis answered.

Zack said, "Well, that is great news indeed. I think your unit has gone as far as it can with the initial developmental phase of Grok 2.0. You and your team have done a wonderful job; we wouldn't have been able to reach this milestone without you. I'm going to direct our Life Science unit to take over from this point and initiate the second phase."

Addis asked, "And what is that, exactly?"

Zack answered, "Grok 2.0 should no longer be positioned as a tech device but as a medical device."

"That is a little bit of a reach. I don't see how you can possibly market it as medical device" was Addis's response.

Zack said, "All the recent reports I have been seeing from your latest experiments show that the device is able to monitor the host's vital signs at a molecular level. That means that it can detect DNA mutations, cancer, and the onset of every disease known to human-kind. If my assessment is correct, then this will be the most effective health-monitoring device ever. Just imagine the impact it will make on the delivery of health services and the cost savings, not to mention longevity of life."

Addis said, "Zack, I appreciate your enthusiasm and long-term vision, but we haven't begun to consider all the unintended consequences. I think we need to pull the reins back a little bit, until we have a better understanding of what can go wrong."

"Unintended consequences?!" Zack said. "Now you're beginning to sound like your friend Nader. If the world spent endless time deliberating the so-called unintended consequences of every innovation, we would still be in the Stone Age. Leave it to me, my boy. I will have the Life Science unit do the necessary due diligence before they fast-track the application to the Food and Drug Administration. After all, there are specific mandates that have to be met before they're able to submit the application. Thanks again. You and your team have done a wonderful job. But now I have to prepare for tonight's rally—it will be a big one. Tell Sacha I said hi and that I will call her after the rally."

He hung up, knowing that Sacha had been listening to their conversation.

Addis looked at Sacha and asked, "What do you think?"

"He knows about our reluctance, and he is trying to box us out. We need to figure out the stopgap mechanism ASAP and have the device injected in me before he wrests this whole thing out of your control."

Addis said, "I know we agreed to move forward with the injection, but I still have a very bad feeling about this."

Zack had the slightest smirk on his face; he knew his plan was falling into place as he had envisioned. He was always three steps ahead of his adversaries and knew their plans before they did. He turned to his speech to put the final touches on it before taking his ten-minute power nap. His energy was boundless; he operated on less than four hours of sleep a day.

The venue for tonight's event had already been changed several times by Zack's staff. His appeal had been growing by leaps and bounds as his message began to resonate with more and more people across the demographic spectrum. His success as an entrepreneur, a philanthropist, and a new and independent political voice had made him one of the most admired men in the country and, for that matter, the world. Tonight's rally was already a success. The Banc of California Stadium, with a capacity of over twenty-two thousand people, was fully sold out. Outside the stadium, there were still long lines of people hoping to score a ticket to the event. The mood was festive; his supporters were energized by his message and felt as if they were a part of a new movement, a movement that would redefine politics and wrest control from those entrenched politicians of old who still put the interests of their party over the interests of the people they had been elected to serve.

Zack walked into the stadium to a standing ovation. The jubilation of the crowd was palpable; it was akin to a rock concert with Zack being their most coveted rock star. Zack walked onto the circular stage in the middle of the stadium. He climbed the stairs two steps at the time, skipping the last step and leaping onto the stage like a graceful animal. There were no teleprompters and no podium, just him with an almost invisible headset. His wardrobe displayed wealth: a $5,000 Italian pinstriped black cashmere suit, a light gray silk turtleneck, and an expensive Italian leather loafer. There was a clear message for all to see: *There is no shame in being wealthy.* In the background, the Beatles song "Taxman" was blasting through the stadium's surround-sound speakers.

> Let me tell you how it will be:
> There's one for you, nineteen for me.

'Cause I'm the taxman, yeah, I'm the taxman.
Should 5 percent appear too small,
Be thankful I don't take it all.
'Cause I'm the taxman, yeah, I'm the taxman.

The crowd was singing along in unison as Zack stood there for a few minutes to let the lyrics sink in. He did a 360, looking at his adoring fans, and soaked in the energy of the moment. The music slowly began to fade as he started to speak.

"Good evening, ladies and gentlemen. Please remain standing. Take a look at your neighbor to the left of you and your neighbor to the right. Tonight, and at this momentous point in time, united we stand and divided we fall. Please hold your neighbors' hands and together declare to the world that regardless of our differences, creed, religion, gender, color, or financial status, today and forever we stand here as one unbreakable link, unwavering in our desire to change the world for the betterment of all humanity. United we stand, divided we fall." He raised his clenched fist in the air and declared again, "United we stand, divided we fall."

The crowd began to chant "United we stand, divided we fall" in unison, as Zack did a 360 again, taking in the power of the moment and the optics that were being televised all over the world. After a few minutes, the crowd began to settle down as they assumed their seats. Zack began to speak again.

"There are some snake oil salesmen out there who are trying to sell you on the idea that the person whose hand you just held is your foe, that it's a zero-sum game, and that, because of their success, color, religion, or gender, you are not receiving your fair share. These people argue that this world is inherently unfair and you need them to bring balance. They ask you to empower them as your advocates to take from whom they wish and give to whom they wish. They say, 'Let me take the pain away that is being inflicted on you by your neighbor. Give me the power to punish whom I wish and reward whom I wish. Let me feed you, educate you, medicate you, and nurse you when you're old, because you're not smart enough, creative enough, or energetic enough to do it on your own.' I say to those people, 'Bullshit.'"

The crowd broke into laughter and began to chant, "Bullshit. Bullshit. Bullshit."

"I say to these people, go peddle your bullshit somewhere else. I'm born free, and I will die free. I will not give my freedom to you or anyone else for the few crumbs you promise. I will not appoint you as my caretaker or my brother's keeper. I will not give up my power of self-determination so you can have the power of self-enrichment. Don't give me a fish and make me a dependent; teach me how to fish so I can be independent. Don't give me a fish; teach me how to fish."

The crowd again stood up on their feet and began to chant, "Don't give me a fish; teach me how to fish."

"I tell you now and without equivocation, social engineering doesn't work, socialism doesn't work, and communism doesn't work. They're the failed policies of an elitist class who believes that you're not wise enough to manage your own affairs and that capitalism is inherently evil. They want you to believe that you need them as your protectors, and for that you need to give them more and more of your freedom, your independence, and your God-given right to self-determination. They peddle the narrative that those who have created wealth for themselves and their families through a free and capitalistic system are rigging the system against you, the working-man and workingwoman. Those bureaucrats who never started a business, never created a single job, and never created anything of value are the ones who are asking you to appoint them as your caretakers, babysitters, and lifelong pacifiers. They engage in class warfare by telling you that those successful entrepreneurs who accumulated wealth by taking risks and working hard, along with being creative, don't deserve to reap the fruits of their labor. They say that we as a society should confiscate that wealth and give it to a corrupt and dysfunctional bureaucratic elite so they can redistribute it to whomever they think is worthy of their generosity. They say that being a millionaire or a billionaire is too much wealth for one individual to have.

Let us look at the statement for a second and ask, What does that millionaire or billionaire do with all that money? There are only four possible things that they can do with that money: (1) spend it, (2) give it away, (3) put it in a bank, or (4) invest it. Well, if they spend it, they are spending in your stores, construction businesses, hospitality businesses, and so on, creating wealth for small and medium businesses and creating jobs. If they are giving it away, they're giving it away to religious, medical, or philanthropic organizations and to other good causes for the benefit of the least fortunate among us. If they save it, that means that your local bank has money to lend you for a home, a business, or your kid's college education. If they invest it, they are investing in their companies and other companies, which creates jobs, provides medical benefits, and generates wealth in the form of 401(k) s, saving plans, and retirement security.

"Their argument is, 'No, no, no. Let's take a big chunk of that so they're not able to spend as much in my store or small business, or give away as much to the poor and needy, or have enough capital in the bank so I can buy a home or start a business, or grow their business so they can hire more and more people. No, give us that money so we can manage it for you, so you're beholden to us, so you're dependent on us and our handouts.' This from the same people who have the worst track record of managing anything but what to order for lunch and dinner.

"Tell them bullshit."

The crowd again stood up and began to chant, "Bullshit, bullshit ..."

"Those bleeding-heart liberals want to play God. They sit at the top of a tree in the African savanna and look at a herd of beautiful gazelles and a pride of lions and say, 'Look at those beautiful gazelles being eaten by those mean lions. I will make these gazelles a little faster so those mean lions cannot eat them.' Well, their misguided intentions result in the lions dying of starvation. Then the herd of gazelles grows uncontrollably, devastating their food supply. And with no means of pruning the sick, disease spreads throughout the herd. Your good intentions just killed the lions and gazelles. Social engineering does not work. What does work is natural law created by God. And in that law exists the profound element of pain, which creates balance, which causes us and every living species to evolve, grow stronger and faster, and create a defense mechanism in order to survive. I submit to you, ladies and gentlemen, that capitalism is the closest thing to natural law, God's law. It is exactly what we need to survive as a society and grow stronger and more prosperous. My opponents are promising you utopia by taking all the trials and tribulations of life that make us grow stronger and faster and that help us survive as a republic of free and independent people. These are the ingredients that made this country the best and most prosperous nation on the face of this earth. It's capitalism that made us who we are. It is capitalism and free enterprise that has raised so many throughout our history from poverty to middle class or upper class. It is the USA that everyone around the world wants to come to and flee from communism, socialism, and totalitarian dictatorships. It is the USA that everyone wants to emulate. Don't let those tax-and-spenders destroy this wonderful union for the few crumbs they promise you. They're the party of pain and suffering. Their own survival depends on your being in either a real or conceived state of suffering, and they are the only path to curing that ill; otherwise, they can't sell you their socialist agenda. How can we trust a party whose only path to power is possible to reach if you're in pain? Send them a loud and clear message during this election: 'Not in the USA.'"

The crowd stood up again and began to chant, "USA, USA, USA!"

"Now, ladies and gentlemen, let me tell you how we are going to do this together without a bloated government that has control over every aspect of our lives. Let me also tell you how we are going to pay for it without putting our kids and grandkids under a mountain of debt."

Zack began to go through his proposed plan to a very enthusiastic and receptive audience, detailing how a smaller and more efficient government bureaucracy, in concert with the private sector, would bring about these profound changes.

28 The Messiah

Nader looked at the clock next to his bed; it was 4:00 a.m. and still dark outside. He sat at the edge of the bed and looked at his beautiful wife, still asleep next to him. He couldn't help the urge that had arisen in him to lean over and kiss her angelic face, but he refrained in fear of disturbing her peaceful state. He stood up and felt his way around the dark room until he found the doorknob. Then he quietly exited the room and proceeded to their makeshift office. Although they lived in one of the remotest areas of the Sinai Peninsula, Nader's benefactors had been very generous and had made sure that all his needs were met. Their office was equipped with the most sophisticated tech-ware and communications equipment, including the latest in satellite technology. The small brick compound was nestled at the foot of the mountain and was well camouflaged from any prying eyes lurking in the sky above. He and Zahraa had everything they needed to do their research and to spread their message of rebellion to the world and to a growing community of like-minded individuals.

Nader had washed for the Fajr prayer before sunrise, but he had decided this morning to pray at one of his favorite spots. It was a cave that he had discovered while hiking one day, near one of the mountain peaks. He grabbed his notebook that contained his manifesto and the Koran; tucked his traditional Bedouin dress in his undergarment; and quietly exited the house. He pushed his dirt bike out of range from the house, until he was at the beginning of the dirt road leading to the mountain, before he turned the ignition on. The half-hour ride up the narrow mountain pass was treacherous, but he knew every inch of this road. This was his secret spot where he went to pray, meditate, or just think while looking at the most panoramic view of the Sinai mountain range. He felt close to God and his beloved father and mother at this height and in this beautiful spot with its view of God's creation.

Nader spread his prayer rug at the entrance of the cave at the cliff edge, facing east. After he had completed his prayer, he sat in the lotus position facing the east mountain range, staring at the starry sky with its billions of stars looking back at him. It was like a canopy made of a black velvet canvas with millions of small pinprick holes projecting streams of light from a powerful energy emanating from behind. It always reminded him of his childhood, when he used to hide under a makeshift tent made of an old blanket and a stick. Every afternoon after school, he would take his mom's sweet tea and cake and sit inside the tent, daydreaming of all the great things he would do when he grew up. Next to him, at the edge of the cliff, was the Koran and his notebook. He sat quietly, waiting for the break of daylight to illuminate the contents of his two favorite books.

A slight orange glow began to appear from behind the mountain range in the east; this was a sight that, as many times as he had seen it, he couldn't help but feel as if God himself were emerging from behind the mountain to speak to him. The warmth of the sun was like an invisible hand wrapping his exposed body with a warm blanket. It was a feeling of warmth, contentment, and peace that always left him in total awe of God's creation, along with the sensation of being directly connected to his Creator. This experience always made him feel that this was what heaven must be like.

The sun began to emerge from behind the mountain, first as a faint orange glow, and within minutes it grew into a large fireball that immersed the whole landscape and transformed it from black into a multidimensional kaleidoscope of colors and shadows of gray, highlighting the sharp edges and contours of the mountain range. Nader opened the notebook and flipped to the section that had all his father's text messages sent when he was in college. Every time he read these messages, his father came back to life; he could visualize his face more clearly, could hear his gentle but firm voice, and could see his distinct mannerisms. His heart still ached for his beloved father. He always harbored profound regrets for how they had parted company, for his foolish ways as a teenager, and for the missed opportunity of spending more time with his father and showing him how much he loved him. The words in his father's texts spoke to him as if they were a flashlight illuminating a dark and unfamiliar path.

Nader began to read the messages. With every message, he could visualize his state of mind and his struggles at the time the messages were sent to him:

"Life is a journey of self-discovery. What you learn about yourself will enlighten you more than what you learn about others."

"Both angels and demons walk side by side with us. Their proximity depends on whom you offend and whom you please with your action."

"No man can serve two masters. Let the voice inside your heart and mind be your master, not the voice outside."

"Adversity is the ultimate test of one's mettle. For some, it reveals their vulnerability; for others, it shows their resolve."

Tip of the Needle

"The only antidote to man's insatiable appetite for worldly pleasures is the quest for spiritual relevance."

"Spirituality is a perch with a view of the universe, while self-indulgence is a hole from which your view is limited to your addictions."

"Your destiny is a dance where you never get to lead but always have to follow. The trick is not to resist and to follow with grace and poise."

"Normal is consistency, even when it is abnormal. Beware of consistent abnormality for it might alter your perception of what is normal."

"Moderation is when less is more, and when contentment is the prevailing state of mind, and when your vessel is so full that you'd rather give than receive."

"Liberalism's greatest agent is chaos. In the absence of morality, laws and an all-supreme bureaucracy become a necessity."

"Religion is not the word of man; it's the Word of God, which is encoded in every person's soul. Never confuse the two."

"Self-esteem is a house that is a lot sturdier built with you own hands than one built by the hands of others."

The two men Nader most admired were his father and Addis's father, Rabbi Ackerman. They were the wisest men he'd ever had the good fortune of knowing. The words they spoke and the way they led their lives was like a beacon that brought light to all the dark places in which Nader often found himself trapped because of his or others' actions. His manifesto that he had been promoting through the dark internet to anyone who was willing to listen was deeply grounded in his childhood experiences with his father and Rabbi Ackerman. The underground movement that he and Zahraa cultivated had been gaining a lot of traction, especially with young tech-savvy individuals around the world. They were becoming more and more convinced that technology was the tipping point in human history and that, if left unchecked, it would cause human extinction. Nader's message was based on his long-held belief that human beings are created in God's image and are the only intelligent beings in the universe. He also believed that the whole universe was created to support human existence, along with the idea that the universe is our celestial body and we're the head. If the head gets sick, then the rest of the body will also get sick. He would often quote Rabbi Ackerman, saying, "The universe is balanced on the tip of a needle. Every action requires a simultaneous reaction of equal force to maintain the balance. Everything we do matters."

Nader had come to be known as "the Messiah" among his followers. Although he was very flattered by his new handle, he didn't want be perceived as a religious figure, but only as a very concerned scientist.

Nader was in deep thought, when he realized that the sun was getting higher in the sky and it was getting late in the morning. He feared that Zahraa would begin to get worried, so he packed his belongings, fired up the bike, and headed down the mountain path, riding back to their compound. Once he reached their dwelling, he opened the door to find Zahraa comely standing behind the stove, preparing breakfast.

Nader said, "Sorry, honey, I lost track of time."

Zahraa answered, "No worries. I knew where you were. You always come back from these excursions with a beautiful glow all around you. I hope one day you will invite me to come with you. That place seems magical. Sit down. I made you your favorite breakfast."

"Thanks, honey," Nader said. "I would love to bring you with me. I can't think of anyone else I would love to share this place with but you."

Zahraa said, "By the way, you should look at the latest correspondence we have been getting on the dark web; we're getting inundated with messages from all over the world. It appears that the resistance is taking root and growing faster than we ever thought. There was one particular message from an individual in India that I think you should look at."

Nader asked, "What is it about?"

Zahraa replied, "Well, it's a picture with the caption 'He will lead you to the source of all your troubles.'"

They grabbed their breakfast and went into the office. Nader fired up his server, and the screens of the multiple monitors came alive. Zahraa did a quick search for the message of interest, and once she'd located it, it immediately came up on one of the screens. Nader gazed at the picture for a few seconds with a look of wonderment and said, "I recognize this face, but I can't remember from where." It was the face of a Middle Eastern man with a thick head of dark hair with a slight touch of gray. Recently, with the help of one of their devout followers and a renowned name in the world of hackers, Nader and Zahraa had been able to hack into the facial recognition software of Interpol. They applied the picture to the database, and in a few minutes a drove of pictures of the same individual at different stages of his life came up, along with dates and sources.

Nader began to go through the individual pictures, until he reached one particular picture that shocked him to his core. It was part of a news article from an Israeli newspaper published when he was a boy in Palestine. The article was about a peaceful protest that was organized by a rabbi, an imam, and a priest advocating for peaceful coexistence between Palestinians and Jews that had turned deadly. The article spoke of the assassination of Rabbi Ackerman by a Hamas operative and the escape of the assassin into the crowd, never to be found. There was a grainy picture of the perpetrator but no other details of his identity or his whereabouts. Other pictures showed vaguely similar-looking individuals with different identities in South Africa, Europe, and the United States. When Nader and Zahraa searched the US database, their search yielded very sparse details as if the information on this man had been intentionally scrubbed. It became immediately obvious to Nader and Zahraa that this individual was some kind of intelligence operative who wanted his identity to be kept secret and who maintained a very low profile. Intelligence agencies commonly scrubbed the World Wide Web of information about their agents, which clearly indicated in this case that this individual had top security clearance. Nader and Zahraa used the software to search for news articles mentioning anyone who resembled the mystery man in the photo, and to their surprise they found what they were looking for. It was an article featured in a science and technology magazine that talked about the introduction of the Grok technology in the African country of Zushaka. There was a picture in the article of Sacha in a small village, distributing the device to its inhabitants, while the village chief was standing next to her with a look of approval. In the background stood her security detail, and among them stood the mystery man dressed in military fatigues. Nader looked at Zahraa and asked, "How can this be? Is the same man who shot Rabbi Ackerman also an employee of Leapp Technologies? And how is this man the source of all my troubles?"

Sanja was sitting in his home office in his New Delhi apartment when the email message flashed on his computer screen. "Thank you for your recent message, but I'm not sure what your interest is in all of this?"

Sanja replied, "I'm a fan of your work and a big believer in your cause. I also have information that will expose your true enemies, known and unknown. I'm a friend, not a foe. To prove my true intention, search for *Jeopardy!* game show episode no. 5019 and the recent US presidential debates, and tell me what you see."

Sanja sat back in his chair, looking at his empty apartment, which still was adorned with all the pictures and furniture that his ex-wife had brought with them from the United States. He thought that life was perfect back then with a beautiful wife and a great career as a rising star at Leapp Technologies. All of it was now gone because of an impulsive decision. He regretted having made a deal with the devil and uprooting his life based on promises made that were never fulfilled. After making the deal with Zack to take the fall for the *Jeopardy!* scheme, Sanja had hoped his exile to India would last for only a few years, but such was not the case. There was a concerted campaign to trash his reputation on the internet after his sudden departure to India. His newfound wealth and the two-million-dollar payment he had received was theorized as a payment from competitors of Leapp Technologies looking to derail the development of the Grok technology. He was painted as a traitor and a corporate spy. All his attempts to reach Zack went unanswered, with no hope of ever returning to the States. After a year in exile in India, his young wife had left him, taking with her a large portion of the two-million-dollar payment. Sanja knew who the collaborator behind the false information was and how he himself had been set up by Zack. Now it was his life's mission to get retribution and to repair his reputation.

Sanja's position as one of the top engineers at Leapp Technologies had given him a great deal of knowledge of the inner workings of the company and its systems. He used his knowledge to hack into the company database in a stealth manner and without being detected. His skills as one of the top computer science engineers allowed him to hack into files that had the highest security classifications. What he had found left him breathless and had caused him to become more committed than ever to sharing that information with the world.

Knowing that he couldn't be the source of this damning information, he needed Nader and his movement to be his conduit.

Nader and Zahraa had the *Jeopardy!* episode and the presidential debate in question playing on a continuous loop. They noticed that both Sanja and Zack had similar intonations and seemed to constantly take a split-second pause before answering the questions posed to them. Their heads seemed to lean to one side frequently as if they were attempting to hear a specific sound. It was akin to news reporters listening to information being fed to them by their producers through their earpieces. Nader enlarged the pictures of Zack and Sanja on the screen and saw the slightest hint of something in one of their ears. He had to enlarge the image several hundred times before he saw the small device embedded in their ears.

Nader typed his message on the screen and hit send. "Are you Sanja? And is this the Grok device implanted in both your and Zack's ears?"

Sanja typed back, "Bingo."

Nader said, "What are you asking of me?"

Sanja said to him, "Help me expose this fraud that is being perpetrated on the world and expose the collaborators' true intentions. I will send you information; use it as you may see fit! I will be in touch soon. Also, the bullet that killed the rabbi was intended for your father. And the assassin is not a Hamas operative. He is an Israeli intelligence officer. All trails lead to one man!"

A few hours later, Nader and Zahraa's server flashed an alert message on the screen: "File is too large to download." Nader quickly attended to the problem, and within a few minutes the zip files began to download. It took the server thirty minutes to download them all.

For the next week, Nader and Zahraa meticulously went through all the files and chronicled all the information. There was clear evidence that Zack, with the help of the ex–Israeli intelligence officer, was the one who had planted the terrorist information on their laptops and orchestrated the leaking of the information through an Israeli intelligence agency. The trail of information was very damning, everything from the *Jeopardy!* hoax to bribery of government officials in Zushaka. If leaked to the world, these revelations would certainly derail Zack's hopes of becoming the president of the United States and the worldwide distribution of Grok 2.0.

For the next two days, Nader and Zahraa debated how best to release this information to the world. They discussed whether to let Sacha and Addis know first, or whether to use this information as leverage to stop Zack's presidential ambitions and the distribution of the Grok 2.0 device. But first they had to get Zack's attention.

29 The Pandemic

It was an all-hands-on-deck, hastily arranged meeting in the Oval Office. The world had been hit with another fast-spreading virus that had originated in Africa and spread across every continent in a matter of weeks. The sitting president, a conservative Republican with only a few months left to his second term, was very concerned about his legacy. This was not the first time the world had faced a highly contagious virus that had the potential of tipping the global economy into a recession or, worse still, a depression. These pandemics were now coming at a fast and furious rate with each variation more deadly than the one before. All major cities were on lockdown, and all domestic and international travel had been virtually shut down. People were confined to their homes, fearful of any human contact. Their only interaction with the outside world was through social media and the internet. Restaurants were shut down, and all social gatherings, except for immediate family, were prohibited. People's food and everyday necessities were delivered via drones and self-driving vehicles. The streets were empty and quiet except for the buzz of drones flying overhead and the silent hum of driverless delivery trucks and cars. The mood was surreal and eerie, akin to a scene from an apocalyptic sci-fi movie.

The previous administration's playbook had as a first step the enlistment and mobilization of the private sector in this fight. This meeting was intended to do just that. Among the corporate chieftains in the meeting who represented different industries was Zack. The vice president opened the meeting by asking each attendee to present their ideas on how to contain the virus and combat its spread throughout the US population. Several pharmaceutical heads spoke of developing and ramping up the development of a test kit. Others spoke of pharmaceutical therapies and vaccines that needed to be developed and fast-tracked through the Food and Drug Administration's approval process. At the same time, other, nonpharma leaders assured the administration that they stood ready to provide the necessary financial, manufacturing, and technological support.

It was Zack's turn to speak. "Ladies and gentlemen, as you all know, I'm running for the presidency of the United States, and any assets or support that my company lends to this fight might be perceived as self-serving. So, frankly, I'm torn between serving the country that I cherish and love and being perceived as furthering my own political ambitions. Frankly, I believe that at Leapp Technologies we have developed—and we currently have—the technology that will address all the concerns raised in this meeting. My concern is that if this technology is deployed and I become the president, then it will be perceived as a conflict of interest and the media and my political enemies will use it against me."

The president quickly interrupted. "Look, Zack, we have known each other for a long time, and I know you are not that thin-skinned. Your political enemies will always find a reason—real or fabricated, it doesn't matter—to attack you. As for the media, we can't help you with that. From what I see, it seems that you have a very cozy relationship with them. What I can do is to issue a presidential directive exempting you and your company from any conflict-of-interest laws because of national interest. Plus, from what I understand, you have been very philanthropically minded with regard to giving some of your technology away for free to some Third World countries. We would love to see some of that generosity being extended to us here at home."

Zack said, "Mr. President, fair enough. The technology I'm speaking about is Grok 2.0. Our scientists at Leapp Technologies have developed a second-generation wearable device that is injectable and resides in the host indefinitely without the need for an external source of power. The device was originally designed as a communications and connectivity apparatus, but as an added advantage, the device can be used as a health monitor."

The president asked, "What does that mean, exactly?"

Zack replied, "Well, sir, the device can detect the first onset of a bacterial or viral attack, mobilize the host's immune system with the help of existing therapeutic drugs, and induce the host's immune system to produce antibodies to recognize the virus and fight it in the future. The device is programmable, so it can be made to recognize the DNA of a new strain of viral infection and induce the body to generate the specific antibodies to kill the virus. It's three things in one: a monitor (in the form of a test kit), a therapeutic solution, and a vaccine."

The president asked, "Where are you with the approval process for this magical device?"

Zack answered, "We have concluded phase one and phase two. Both animal and human trials of the testing have been completed, and the results have been a resounding success with no to very minor side effects."

"What do you need from my administration?"

"Well, first, sir, we need to fast-track the approval process so we can bring the device to market," Zack answered. "Second, I believe we will need a national immunization decree; otherwise, if some in our population have been vaccinated and some haven't, we will be faced with the same situation again when the next virus hits our population—and I assure you, it will happen. And finally, we'll need some governmental assistance with regard to gearing up our production. As for me and my company, we will be giving this technology to the world at no cost."

The president said, "Well, Zack, that is very generous. Anyone have any objections to what Zack is proposing?"

Zack had already made his sales pitch to each of the attendees prior to the meeting. Like a good salesman, he had persuaded each of the corporate heads that this device would be a windfall for their bottom line. A number of them were already allies and members of his election committee.

No hands went up.

The president said, "Well, if there are no objections, I'm directing the vice president and the secretary of Health and Human Services to validate your finding and expedite the approval process by the FDA. Gentlemen, I'm expecting that report to be on my desk in a few weeks, not months. We can't afford to have the same economic devastation we experienced during the last pandemic. Thank you all for your support. I appreciate the response our private sector is able to bring to bear during these difficult and unprecedented times. God bless you, and bless this country."

Two weeks later the report from the FDA granting full approval for the device was on the president's desk. That evening the president went on national TV to address the nation.

"My fellow Americans, we have been faced with an invisible enemy that has the potential to take many of our most vulnerable citizens' lives and to render many others sick. It also has the potential of devastating our economy and, for that matter, the global economy. My administration has been working diligently with our public and private sectors to mitigate the scourge of this new virus on our population. We are a country that doesn't cower when we are faced with adversity. We rise up to meet adversity and defeat it, as we have done so many times in the past. It is because of our free and democratic system that we are able rise to the challenge by working together with our private sector to find solutions to very complex problems. Today, I'm happy to announce that such a solution has been found that has proven effective in fighting this invisible enemy. Our free enterprise, along with our innovative and entrepreneurial nature that has no equal, has again risen to the challenge. One of our technology companies, Leapp Technologies, in cooperation with other business leaders, has brought to market a new device that will help us detect this and any new viruses and speed up the recovery of those who contract it. I'm ordering today a national immunization drive that will be facilitated by our health community in cooperation with the federal government. Multiple factories around the country have begun production of this device, and we anticipate within weeks that every man, woman, and child in the United States will be receiving this device at no cost. Once we have fully immunized our population, we will be gifting this life-saving device to the rest of the world. In the next few days, we will be mobilizing our National Guard, and in conjunction with health-care providers and life science companies, we will be providing the immunization through mobile injection sites in your individual neighborhoods. Please refer to www.mobileimmuization.gov for the time and the date the mobile unit will be in your neighborhood. Godspeed, and God bless America." The television shot panned to the presidential seal and the US flag.

That evening, the world financial futures predicting the next day's global stock markets' opening were up 20 percent.

Within the next few weeks, 80 percent of the population had been immunized using the Grok 2.0 device. However, there was a growing resistance of people who saw the device as intrusive and an affront to God's will. Others saw it as a conspiracy perpetrated by the government in order to exercise mind and body control over the population. Among the loudest voices on social media and the internet was Nader's, whose resistance movement was growing all across the world. Their rallies in major cities were getting larger by the day, and their message of resistance was growing in popularity. Their hand-held banners had the words "It's not that humans will be replaced by robots; it's that we will become robots. Don't let them take your free will away."

Zack was sitting in his office looking at the latest national polls; even the most adversarial and biased news outlets' polls had his popularity at over 70 percent. The polls predicted that he would win the presidential election, in less than thirty days, in a landslide. His opponents' campaigns had been devastated; they'd more or less given up the fight as their contributions dwindled to a trickle. After all, Zack singlehandedly had saved the world from the scourge of an invisible and deadly virus, and the world loved him for it. Everything was falling into place as he had planned. He was feeling as if he were on top of the world with no one and nothing able to stop him from fulfilling his vision.

All his department heads were already assembled in the boardroom for their meeting with Zack in five minutes, but he wanted to spend a few minutes with Sacha and Addis before the meeting. They were already waiting patiently outside his office when his assistant announced, "Your dad will see you now." Zack was sitting behind his desk, looking at the poll numbers, when Sacha and Addis waked into the office.

Zack said, "Good morning. Please sit down on the couch. I will be with you in a second."

He put the papers he was reading on the desk, grabbed his coffee, and proceeded to where they were sitting. His gait was steady and confident like that of a man in control. He sat in his favorite leather chair that was only reserved for him and crossed his legs. He looked at Sacha and Addis for a few seconds, building the anticipation for what he was about to say, then began to speak.

"As you're well aware, the election is in less than thirty days, and it seems, based on all the polls, that my chances of winning are very good. Going forward, my schedule will be very full with selecting my cabinet, organizing the inauguration committee, and formulating my first ninety days' legislative agenda. By law, I have to recuse myself from any and all private business dealings, and I have to put my private business interests in a trust. That trust will be headed by you, Sacha. And I hope that you, Addis, will be taking an active role in assisting her in the day-to-day management of Leapp Technologies and its various subsidiaries. It's a herculean task I'm asking of you, but

I'm very confident that you're both up to the task and more than capable of executing the firm's long-term strategic goals. These goals have been clearly delineated in the two folders before you. I have gotten the approval of the board for the appointment of Sacha as the chairman of the board and chief operating officer, and of you, Addis, as vice chairman and chief technology officer. With your approval, I would like to announce these appointments to the executive committee and the department heads who are assembled in the conference room as we speak."

Sacha said, "I'm honored and flattered by your vote of confidence, but don't you think this would be looked at as cronyism? And wouldn't it have been considerate of you to have given Addis and me some time to think about taking on this awesome responsibility?"

Zack asked, "What do you think, Addis?"

Addis replied, "I'm flattered as well. I will do anything to support Sacha and this company. After all, this company has morphed into something that has profoundly changed lives for the better and has elevated the interests of humanity over its self-interest. However, I would have liked some time to think about your generous offer as well."

Zack said, "Right! Unfortunately, we don't have the luxury of time. I'm going to need an answer from both of you before we head into this meeting in a few minutes."

Sacha looked at Addis as he nodded his head in agreement. After all, they had anticipated this move from Zack and had discussed it at great length before deciding that this was the only way they could control the company's runaway technology.

Sacha said, "We accept."

"Great," Zack replied. "Let's not keep these people waiting."

Zack stood up, grabbed his portfolio, opened the door, and proceeded to the conference room. Sacha and Addis lagged behind. Sacha whispered to Addis, "You really laid it on thick in there."

Addis said, "Yeah, I felt a little theatrical."

They smiled at each other.

Zack, standing before the assembly of directors and department heads in the large conference room, announced the appointment of Sacha and Addis as chairman and CEO and as cochair and CTO, respectively, in his absence. He took a seat at the head of the table as Sacha and Addis came around to the front of the table to address the attentive gathering. Sacha began by thanking Zack for his vote of confidence, followed by her long-term goals and strategic vision for the firm. Zack looked on with an expression of admiration and a slight smile as his mobile phone began to vibrate, indicating an email had been received in his private email account. This was a highly secure email account with only a handful of trusted individuals having access to it. Usually communications using this account required his immediate attention.

Zack opened the encrypted email, and upon seeing the subject matter, he immediately interrupted Sacha in midsentence and excused himself. "Sorry, I have an urgent matter that I have to attend to. Please excuse me." Zack went to his office and opened the email on his wall monitor. The email was from an unknown sender. It had as its subject line, "Read this. Your future depends on it." The body of the email contained a picture of Zack on the debate stage with an arrow pointing to his left ear; a picture of Sanja on the *Jeopardy!* game show set with another arrow pointing at his ear; a news article of the raid on Nader's apartment; a picture of Zack having a conversation with a Middle Eastern man with a thick head of black hair; and finally a picture of Rabbi Ackerman in the arms of Nader's father after the rabbi had been shot. The text read, "I know what you have done. Thousands of documents in my possession will be released to the world if you don't comply with the following requests. You have twenty-four hours to quit your presidential run and cease all distribution of the Grok 2.0 device."

Zack felt his heart palpitate. Beads of sweet began to form on his forehead. He looked at the pictures again and again and read the message several times, hoping that somehow, with every read, his interpretation of how ominous this message was would change. Seeing images of himself making a public announcement dropping out of the presidential race and suddenly denying the world the benefit of the Grok 2.0 technology, he determined that such a scenario was unfathomable. He would be a disgraced man, never again to be perceived as a captain of industry, a revered figure, and potentially the leader of the free world. He thought, *I would rather end my life than take the public humiliation.* He began to formulate the plan to do exactly that, by driving to the cabin in the Adirondacks under the pretense of taking a few days' sabbatical, then shooting himself in the woods. Then it dawned on him the connection between the pictures and the message. He instantaneously knew the collaborators behind the threat. He immediately picked up his phone and called one of his brightest programmers and computer engineers. On the first ring, the engineer picked up the phone, noticing that it was a call from the boss.

Zack said, "Jack, this is Mr. Zimmerman. I want you to drop everything you're working on and find out if our systems have been hacked in the last three years. I also want you to find out if there is any Trojan horse embedded in any of our servers, especially on my private server. Use every diagnostic tool you need. No one is to know about this. If anyone asks, tell them you're working on a special project for me."

Jack asked, "Sir, how much time do I have?"

Zack replied, "Hours!" He hung up the phone.

Zack made his next call, to the private phone of the prime minister of Israel.

"Hank, this is Zack. I have an urgent matter to discuss with you."

The prime minster said, "Zack, I was about to call you. Thank you for expediting the shipment of the Grok technology. What is this urgent matter that you want to discuss?"

"I'm being blackmailed, and I believe I know the individuals behind it," Zack replied. "This can put the presidential election at risk. And you know what that means for both of us."

The prime minister asked, "How can I help?"

Zack responded, "I need you to eliminate that risk within the next forty-eight hours and wipe the scene clean of any incriminating evidence."

"Why are you not using your connections in the US?" asked the prime minister.

Zack answered, "This can't be seen as coming from me or as utilizing US assets of any kind, for obvious reasons."

"Understood," said the prime minister. "Send me whatever you have ASAP, and I will take care of it. You owe me one."

Zack said, "I owe you bigtime. Good luck." He hung up the phone.

Within the next two hours, Zack had all the information he needed and then some. A short time after that, the information was being disseminated to an elite Israeli commando unit. The operation was a go, after a detailed plan had been drawn up and approved by the prime minister. The whole process had taken less than sixteen hours.

It was 4:30 a.m. Nader was rolling over in bed to wake up Zahraa for the Fajr prayer. There was a subtle humming noise outside their compound that Zahraa had noticed. She asked, "Do you hear that?"

Nader said, "I think it's the generator. It has been acting up lately."

Before he finished his sentence, there were two bursts of fire that found their mark were the laser beam was pointing. The shots to the head came with finality; both Nader and Zahraa were killed instantaneously. Explosive charges were then placed all over the compound. But before the assassins retreated to their stealth helicopters, they made sure that they collected all the files and hard drives they could extract from the location. This was contrary to Zack's instructions to destroy everything. When the helicopter climbed to a safe height, the commander in charge pushed the handheld detonator, causing a fireball that could be seen for miles in the distant Sinai desert.

Two thousand miles away, Sanja was in his apartment in New Delhi, seated in his office with a bullet hole in his forehead. No news of the incident was ever disseminated to the news media, by either the Israeli or US authorities. The Egyptian government took credit for the mission as an attack on a terrorist cell operated by the Muslim Brotherhood.

30 Hail to the Chief

It had been ninety days since Zack was elected as the president in a landslide victory. His ninety-day legislative accomplishments and presidential decrees were incomparable. He had

managed to accomplish in ninety days what the most popular presidents throughout the history of the United States had taken two terms to accomplish. His popularity rating was around 90 percent, and his political adversaries dared not challenge him in public for fear of losing their seats. For all intents and purposes, he governed as a supreme leader. With the legislative branch rendered impotent and unable to create any checks and balances over his powers, he was free to run the country as he saw fit. He had unleashed the entrepreneurial spirit by reducing regulation and incentivizing companies to grow and innovate through very accommodating tax legislation, and he had begun public and private partnerships in health, technology, and manufacturing. There was an unprecedented economic boom, with the US economy and gross domestic product predicted to grow at 7 percent annually for the next couple of years. Trillions of dollars in wealth had been created in the financial markets, and unemployment was running at below 2 percent annually. The Grok 2.0 was also fueling that growth through the continuous connectivity of people on the internet and with each other. The cross-pollination of ideas across the world were on hyperdrive, and these ideas were being transformed from concepts to products and services in record speeds.

Zack was sitting alone in the Oval Office at 6:00 a.m., looking at the economic and intelligence briefing, when again he was struck by how many natural disasters were taking place all over the world, including in the United States. There were superhurricane cells form-ing off the coast of Africa in early April that were predicted to hit the Caribbean and the East Coast of the United States in early summer. Wild, uncontrollable fires were engulfing most of Australia and South America and were quickly encroaching on major cities. Earthquakes and tsunamis in Southeast Asia and Asia Minor, and previously dor-mant volcanoes erupting in Europe and North America, were also observed. There had been a locust infestation in the Middle East and Africa, devastating crops and the local food supply. The economic models were forecasting worldwide recession or, worse yet, depression as a result of all these natural disasters all over the world. The conflicts and political unrest had the potential to derail his economic agenda, but Zack didn't see these events as an obstacle. Instead he saw them as an opportunity. Fear had always been a motive for change, and he was the one to orchestrate that change. He immediately called his chief of staff and ordered a meeting with his national security team and his economic advisors at 9:00 a.m. in the Oval Office.

Sacha was sitting with Addis in Zack's old office at 7:00 a.m. They were having their daily strategy meeting and looking at the latest data feed from the Grok 2.0 from all over the world. The information was very disturbing, with clear indications that human behavior was dramatically changing. Their conversation was interrupted by a call from the president of the United States.

Zack said, "Good morning, honey."

Sacha replied, "Good morning, Mr. President. I have you on speakerphone. I have Addis with me."

Zack said, "Don't call me that. I'm still your dad. And I'm glad you have Addis with you. I need to speak to you both. Good morning, Addis."

Addis said, "Good morning, sir."

Zack went on, "I need you to send my chief of staff the latest Grok 2.0 data feed and psychological algorithm from the TIP program you developed."

"What do you need that for?" Sacha asked.

"Well, it's top-security type of stuff that I don't want to bore you with," Zack said. "But what I can say is that there is a lot of bad stuff happening around the world in the form of natural disasters, and we need to tailor our message in order to have the world act in unison."

Sacha said, "It sounds to me like tailor-made propaganda. Plus, this will give you a lot of information about your adversaries. There are privacy laws here that the company will be in clear violation of if we share this information with any government agency, domestic or foreign."

Zack said, "I understand your reluctance, but this is becoming a national security issue that has the potential of driving the global economy into a depression. There is only one country that can take the lead and mobilize the world in order to prevent this from happening, and that is us."

"I'm sorry, Zack, but this is a legal matter that I have to refer to legal counsel. I will have them work on it immediately and contact the attorney general with their decision," Sacha said.

"You clearly don't understand," Zack said. "This is a top security matter that is not open for public debate. I clearly came to the wrong person. Have a nice day."

Zack hung up the phone, visibly fuming about how the call had gone. His next call was to his inside man at Leapp Technologies.

Sacha looked at Addis. "That went well."

Addis said, "It's obvious that Zack wants to use the Grok technology and the data feed to drive world opinion. He is bypassing the media and going directly to the source. They won't even know they're being manipulated; it will all be very subliminal. There will be no stopping him. He will become emperor and chief of not just the United States, but also of the globe."

"But how does he get access without our help?" Sacha asked.

Addis replied, "I don't know. But I guarantee you, he is figuring it out right now as we speak. If he or a surrogate gets inside the matrix, he can shut us out. And then we're fucked!"

Sacha said, "The only option for me is to get in before he does and lock him out. With you on the outside and me on the inside, we can create the necessary firewalls."

Addis told her, "I really don't like this. It seems like the whole universe is getting sick, and I'm convinced that Zack had something to do with Nader's and Zahraa's deaths."

"That is why I'm the only one who can stop him," Sacha said. "To him, everyone is dispensable except for me. I have to do it."

Addis said, "My assistant has confirmed with NASA that the black hole we have been tracking is growing exponentially and that its gravitational pull is growing stronger by the day. I'm convinced that all these natural disasters are not a coincidence. The universe is out of balance. I'm becoming more and more convinced that Nader's theory is true."

Sacha asked, "What theory are we talking about?"

Addis answered, "That the universe is our celestial body and that as the head gets sick, so does the body."

Sacha said, "The TIP algorithm is in fact confirming that the head is getting sick. Collectively, the people who have been immunized with Grok 2.0 are losing their willpower. The artificial program embedded in the device is mutating and seems to be stimulating the pleasure centers of the brain in order to enforce certain behavior. The people's empathetic response is waning. They seem to be creating a virtual reality that entertains their most perverted tendencies without any consequences. They're becoming extremely polarized and are gravitating to places on the dark web that reinforce and confirm these extreme views. They seem to have no compassion or tolerance for people of differing points of view. But more than that, they're perceiving those with a different point of view as their enemies and are engaging in virtual war games to exterminate those who don't espouse their ideology. They're becoming isolated and less social, preferring to spend time in the virtual world and not in the real world. There is a plethora of new pornographic and violent virtual reality sites that feel more real and intense than actual physical experiences. Then there are other people who are becoming religious fanatics who are convinced that this is the end of days. It seems that there is an epic battle going on between good and evil, and I don't know who is going to win and what will happen to the balance that has sustained us since the beginning of time. I'm very scared."

Addis asked, "What happens if we shut the device down?"

Sacha answered, "There are several examples of medical professionals who were a part of Nader's resistance movement who tried to extract the device from a host. The outcome was not good."

"What do you mean?" Addis questioned.

Sacha responded, "The device is more addictive than any drug ever invented by humankind. The withdrawal symptoms are so intense, they leave the host in a catatonic state or, worse yet, kill the host."

Addis said, "We've got to figure out a way to shut down the program without turning all these people into zombies or, worse, killing them. We have to come up with an antidote!"

"The AI has developed its own autoimmune response to any interference or invasion from the outside," Sacha informed Addis. "It has to be done from inside the matrix. There is no other way!"

The streets of major cities were empty, and those few who were out seemed to be walking in a dream state, totally unaware of the presence of others. Entertainment venues were empty; restaurants were empty; and more and more people were spending time in the isolation of their homes. All the economic activity that was the hallmark of this new technology was beginning to have the opposite of the intended effect. The impact on younger people was more profound; their impulsive tendencies and lack of personal experience or an established moral compass made them more susceptible to manipulation. They were becoming more and more reclusive and had isolated themselves from family and friends. They were engaging in virtual sex, which felt more real and intense than actual physical contact—and without the emotional attachment. There were no boundaries and no consequences; they went where their impulses took them.

The people on the opposite side of the spectrum were becoming militarized. The antivaxxers and the religious Far Right were mounting a religious crusade against the mutants, which was the label they had assigned to anyone vaccinated with the Grok device. In turn, "the carriers" were mounting their own war by hacking into government and military complexes and taking over nuclear stockpiles in Pakistan, India, and North Korea. Ethnic cleansing was on the rise all over the world, and antivaxxers were abducting the carriers and physically operating on them to extract the Grok device. It was brother against brother, and fathers against sons. Family ties were no longer of any value.

Sacha said, "The animus is so profoundly strong that it is not who you are, but whether you are an antivaxxer or a carrier. The world is in total chaos, and ethnic and ideological wars are raging in the Middle East, Africa, Latin America, and Asia. The developed countries are having their own internal problems as well. The world is on the brink of a nuclear holocaust! This is a problem that we can't defer on. I have to go in now!"

Addis said, "Give me a week to develop the antidote. Hopefully, your father is not able to figure out how to access the system before then."

31 The Matrix

It was time to enter the matrix. Addis has developed the antidote as promised, but he had had no time to test it. It was intended to shut down the AI program but to have the Grok device gradually reduce the stimuli to the pleasure centers in the host's brain. The difficult part was for Sacha to enter the matrix undetected and override the AI program before she was recognized as a threat.

It was 3:00 a.m. Sacha was already strapped to an operating table at Addis's lab at the far end of the Leapp Technologies campus. The lab, currently empty except for the two of them, had several large monitors that were connected to the lab's supercomputer. These monitors showed multiple dashboards that monitored traffic on the Web, the Grok operational data feed, and the AI program's response. There were heat maps sensing every human response and the intensity of each. Humanity was at war with itself, and these epic battles were being fought in cyberspace, a place of illusions and collective fantasies that knew no bounds, the only limits being in the imaginations of the creators.

Addis turned toward the intravenous line in in Sacha's left arm, delivering a light sedative into her veins. Within a few seconds, the sedative began to have the intended effect; she went into a dream state. Next, Addis activated the Grok device that was already injected but that lay dormant in her body. The monitors before him showed her vital signs, including blood pressure, pulse, heart rate, and brain waves. There was an instantaneous spike in all her vital signs as soon as the device was turned on.

Sacha found herself in a strange world of images and voices as if she were connected to the collective unconsciousness of everyone who was connected to the matrix. It was a dark and evil place with realistic images of horrific acts of violence and rape and with unspeakable acts of cruelty. There were others who were engaged in prayer and in worship of different deities, Allah, Jesus, Brahma, Vishnu, and many other gods.

Her vital signs were going into the red zone, and her brain activity was indicating sensory overload. Her body had begun to convulse violently. Addis increased the sedative, hoping to reduce her heart rate and slow down the convulsions. Worried that he might lose her, he was contemplating shutting off the device, but he feared that the sudden change might have a worse effect. He kept on calling her name, using the communication link they had created through the Grok device.

Sacha was hearing Addis's voice in the distance calling to her. She consciously forced herself to focus on Addis's voice rather than on the chaos that was streaming all around her. Slowly beginning to gain control, she charted her course toward the place in the matrix where the AI program resided. She had to be stealth and move undetected through the matrix. Addis had already devised a Trojan horse that mimicked a benign data point, thus gaining access to the AI program undetected.

Sacha reached the relevant piece of code in the program and was ready to encode the fix, when she was stopped cold in her tracks. It was Zack looking back at her. He was all aglow, and his aura was intoxicating. Its lure was magnetic. As hard as she tried, she couldn't resist its force. She was attracted to it like a moth to a flame. She moved closer to his force and saw a world of his creation. There was no chaos. It was an orderly environment where inhabitants acted more like robots with no free will. They were like a hive of bees acting in unison to build their home and protect the queen bee. No individual bee acted independently. Collectively, they displayed swarm intelligence by acting as one unit. It was a beautifully manicured world with modern efficient cities, no pollution, no congestion, no crimes, no jails, no laws, and no governments—just tranquility. It was a world with a population of people who only reproduced based on the need to support the social infrastructure. Every resource was efficiently utilized, and everything was there to augment the hierarchy and the queen bee. And that queen bee was none other than Zack. He was now the AI, the only one with free will in a world inhabited by robots, soldier bees, executing his master plan.

Addis kept on yelling and urging Sacha to put the fix in, but she could no longer hear him. She was enchanted by the world created by her father, a world free of pain and suffering where she got to be second-in-command and immortal. Together, she and her father installed Zack's code into the program.

The gravitational pull of the black hole grew instantaneously, and with every planet and star it consumed, it grew even stronger, until the universe was no more.

The last words Addis heard in his mind were from his father's quote: "The universe is balanced on the tip of a needle. Every action requires a simultaneous reaction of equal force to maintain the balance. Everything we do matters."

32 Rebirth

There was absolute darkness—no stars, no planets, and no galaxies, just darkness. The darkness was the result of single black hole with an accretion disc that covered the known universe. It omitted no light and no energy, just a gravitational pull that consumed everything in the universe. Inside it, time was on a continuous loop where the past and future were indistinguishable from one another. Traveling through the wormhole, as you approached the core, objects were stretched by the gravitational pull, until they disintegrated into particles, ultimately incinerated to become a fireball. At the core there was singularity, a one-dimensional point that contained all the known universe in an infinitely small space. The gravity and density were infinite; space-time was infinite; and the laws of physics no longer applied.

It was a calm beautiful place where there was no more chaos, just peace and tranquility. It was a place where time had been suspended and there was no beginning and no end, just is-ness. However, inside there were two bright stars omitting positive energy that were gravitating toward and being pulled by a third star with a more powerful gravitational pull and the emission of negative energy. The merger had released the energy encapsulated in this infinitely dense, small space, causing an explosion that had brought light back to the infinite darkness.

The universe was born again, and in it there was a distant galaxy of planets and stars. One galaxy in particular had a blue planet that was orbiting a bright star. It was a planet with an atmosphere that was covered with beautiful white clouds and with a surface of vast oceans, mountains, and a lush green landscape. Next to one of its bodies of fresh water stood two apes, drinking peacefully from the brook. When they looked up, they saw a third large ape approach them, growling and shaking a stick in the air. The snake lay watching in the tall grass in the distance, as the words were uttered: "The balance is restored."

"Life is a teaching moment. You either learn the lesson or get to go to summer school."

- Impressive ... what inspired you?
- Did you write during pandemic ...
  inspired
- What character are you most like
- Did you make up "tip of the needle" and all the fathers sayings?
- One great novel in you or more?

CPSIA information can be obtained
at www.ICGtesting.com
Printed in the USA
LVHW050213130121
676353LV00017B/443/J

9 781480 898295